Summer at the Cape

Also available from RaeAnne Thayne

Sleigh Bells Ring
The Path to Sunshine Cove
Christmas at Holiday House
The Sea Glass Cottage
Coming Home for Christmas
The Cliff House
Season of Wonder

Haven Point

Snow Angel Cove
Redemption Bay
Evergreen Springs
Riverbend Road
Snowfall on Haven Point
Serenity Harbor
Sugar Pine Trail
The Cottages on Silver Beach
Summer at Lake Haven

Hope's Crossing

Blackberry Summer
Woodrose Mountain
Sweet Laurel Falls
Currant Creek Valley
Willowleaf Lane
Christmas in Snowflake Canyon
Wild Iris Ridge

For a complete list of books by RaeAnne Thayne,
please visit www.raeannethayne.com.

RaeAnne Thayne

Summer at the Cape

HQN

Recycling programs for this product may not exist in your area.

ISBN-13: 978-1-335-93635-6

Summer at the Cape

This is a work of fiction. Names, characters, places and incidents are either the product of the author's imagination or are used fictitiously. Any resemblance to actual persons, living or dead, businesses, companies, events or locales is entirely coincidental.

For questions and comments about the quality of this book, please contact us at CustomerService@Harlequin.com.

HQN
22 Adelaide St. West, 41st Floor
Toronto, Ontario M5H 4E3, Canada
www.Harlequin.com

Printed in U.S.A.

After writing nearly seventy books,
I'm running out of new people in my life to thank, so this book is dedicated to Millie, my canine cowriter, who watched from her spot on the sofa in my office as I wrestled nearly every single word. She has brought untold joy, laughter and warm cuddles into our life.

As always, thank you to my family, especially my hero of a husband, Jared (who really didn't want another dog but loves her almost as much as I do!).

Summer at the Cape

1

CAMI

CAMI PORTER WALKED INTO THE LOBBY OF THE glass-walled building that housed the law offices of Porter, Garcia & Sheen, wishing she could curl up with her head down on her desk and take a power nap.

Insomnia sucked.

The past four months had been rough, worse even than those dark days after the implosion of her engagement.

She spent all day wishing she could stretch out on the nearest available flat surface and all night wondering why she couldn't shut off the wild monkey brain and find the sleep she so desperately needed.

For some people, struggling through occasional bouts of insomnia was inconvenient but not debilitating. But Cami needed to be mentally sharp to keep up as a junior associate in her father's firm, specializing in contract and intellectual property law.

She yawned, shifting her laptop case over one shoulder as she pushed the button of the elevator to take her to the top floor.

"Cut that out. Now you're going to make me yawn." Tiffany Tsu, a paralegal who worked for one of the junior partners, made a face at Cami as the elevator rose.

"Sorry."

"Don't apologize. I really hope that yawn means you had a wild night. Considering I was dealing with a teething baby all night long, I need to live vicariously through someone."

Cami made a face. "You know me better than that. I just stayed up too late reading through law journals."

And grieving.

She knew that was the reason for her insomnia. Every time she tried to settle into sleep, she saw her sister's face. After four months, she might have thought the shock and sadness would ease a little. No. If anything, she seemed to be struggling more now emotionally than she had when she first heard the news.

When she reached her floor, she waved to Tiffany and headed for her small, cramped office. If only she could slip off her shoes and lie down on the carpet for a moment...

"How did everything go?" a chipper voice asked from the copy machine.

Cami pushed away the exhaustion and mustered a smile for her assistant and paralegal, Joe Lopez, who had been with her for three years—almost as long as her ex-fiancé—and knew Cami's brain better than she did.

"Not bad. I think we're close to an agreement. Pete made it clear today—he's willing to walk away if they don't agree to our amended clauses in the contract. I'm going to let them stew over the next few days and see if they'll come back to the table with a counteroffer."

She was representing a video game developer in talks with one of the big players who wanted to take one of his ideas and adapt it for their system. It was Cami's job to make sure her client, a naive little fish in a big pond, didn't end up ripped to a bloody stump by sharks.

"Oh, that's good news. Pete is such a nice guy. I'm glad he has you on his team."

Joe gave her the look he did when he wanted to prepare her that something unpleasant was coming. "Now for some news that's maybe not so good. Your mother has called three times. She sounded increasingly urgent with each call. She seems to think you're ghosting her. That's exactly the word she used. I wouldn't have thought Rosemary knew what ghosting meant."

Cami had learned not to be surprised at anything when it came to her mother.

"She said she has called you four times and texted you as many," Joe went on.

Cami sighed. "My phone ran out of juice and my car charger isn't working, for some reason. And I forgot the battery backup."

"When it rains."

"I know. I was planning to plug it in the minute I got back to the office. What's so urgent?"

"She didn't tell me. The most recent time she called, I apologized that you hadn't reached out yet but told her you were in the middle of negotiations critical to a multimillion-dollar deal and promised her I would make sure you phoned her as soon as you could break away."

Her mother had been married to an attorney for more than fifteen years. She certainly understood that sometimes work had to come first.

"Thank you," Cami said now to Joe. "Remind me to give you a raise."

He grinned at her. "You just did that last month, but if you want to give me another one, I certainly won't complain. It all goes in the wedding fund."

Joe and his partner were planning a gorgeous Maui ceremony at Christmastime, and his lunch hour and breaks were filled with phone calls to their wedding planner.

Cami really needed to think about getting in shape, if she was going to attend a tropical wedding in December.

Inside her office, Cami fished her dead phone out of her laptop case and plugged it into her desk charger. As soon as it had enough juice to come on again, the phone immediately pinged with about a half dozen messages from her mother.

She was about to dial Rosemary's number when the phone rang again and, no surprise, she saw her mother's name on the caller ID.

She had only a few seconds to slip off her shoes under her desk and shove in her earbuds so she could take the call hands-free.

"Hi, Mom."

After a beat, her mother's voice came through with a frantic edge. "Darling! There you are! Oh, I'm so glad. I desperately need to talk to you."

Yes. That was fairly obvious by the deluge of phone calls. "I've been in meetings all afternoon. Sorry about that. I'm here now. What's up?"

Silence met her question. It only lasted about five seconds but long enough for her to begin worrying. What could be so dire? Her family had been hit with enough bad news lately, hadn't they?

Rosemary's sigh was long and heartfelt. "Oh, Camellia. Everything is a mess. I don't know where to start."

When Rosemary used her full name, things had to be bad. The thought barely registered before her mother burst into tears and muffled sobs came through the line.

"What's going on?" She fought to stay calm.

Rosemary launched into a fumbling explanation, something about leases and rights of way and unused property.

Through the sobs, she could only pick up about one word in three.

"Slow down, Mom. I can't understand you. Take a breath. Do some circular breathing."

She could hear her mother take an audible breath and then another.

"Okay. What's going on?" Cami asked again, when Rosemary seemed to calm.

"You know my neighbor Franklin Rafferty? The one who owns the land on the headlands that we're leasing for Wild Hearts?"

She didn't really, considering she had never lived in Cape Sanctuary. After Cami's parents divorced, Rosemary and the twins had moved into a rambling old farmhouse her mother had inherited from a great-aunt in the Northern California seaside town. Cami, fourteen at the time, had stayed behind in Los Angeles with her father.

"I know you've mentioned him," she said cautiously.

"Well, his son called me this morning, angry as a wet hornet. He's been out of the country, I guess. Apparently, he just learned about Wild Hearts and he's not happy about it."

Rosemary gave another hysterical-sounding laugh that turned into a sob. "He's so unhappy that he's threatening to s-sue," she sobbed. "He wants an eviction order right now. He didn't come out and say it, but he implied that he thinks Lily took advantage of Franklin and manipulated him into agreeing to the lease."

Rosemary sniffled loudly, though Cami couldn't tell if it was at the reference to Lily or at this threat to her sister's latest passion project.

"It's a horrid thing to say about your sister," Rosemary went on, "especially after she's...she's gone and can't defend herself.

Tell me this is all a terrible mistake. He can't just shut us down, can he? We're completely booked all summer long!"

Cami closed her eyes. She hated situations like this, thrown headfirst into something she knew nothing about. Rosemary obviously expected Cami to sort it all out instantly, when she didn't even know the particulars.

"I'm shaking, I'm so upset," her mother went on. "I feel like I'm having a heart attack."

"Do you need me to call 911?"

Rosemary made a sound halfway between a sigh and a sob. "Not yet. I'm sure it's anxiety over this whole thing. He can't put us out of business like that, can he? This was your sister's dream. Our dream together. It's…it's all I have left of Lily."

Her mother didn't sob again, but her voice hitched enough that Cami knew she was fighting back her emotions.

For the past four months, while Cami had been staring at the ceiling, desperately willing herself to sleep, Rosemary had poured all her energy into Wild Hearts, a ten-tent campground near her property offering glamping to discerning travelers.

The project had really been the brainchild of Lily, Cami's beautiful younger sister, who had drowned four months earlier.

All the members of Cami's nuclear family—Rosemary, Cami's father and Violet, Lily's identical twin—were trying to figure out how to go on without her.

Cami had a feeling a vital, unforgettable piece would always be missing from their lives.

"Jon Rafferty can't close us down. He *can't.* Your sister poured her life savings into this and I took out a second mortgage on the farm. I'll lose everything."

Oh damn. Cami sat up straighter in her chair. She'd had no idea Rosemary was so financially invested in the project.

"A second mortgage, Mom? Why?"

Rosemary turned defensive. "Because she couldn't get a small-business loan in time to open this summer. This seemed the fastest route. Oh, this is such a disaster! What should I do?"

Cami squeezed the bridge of her nose as the tension headache that had been building all day reached out with vicious tentacles to wrap around her brain.

"You have a legal lease agreement, though, don't you?"

Her mother didn't answer for a long moment. An eternity—certainly long enough for Cami's stomach to drop to the bare toes currently digging into the lush carpet of her office.

"Don't you?" she pressed.

"We definitely have a verbal agreement and he did sign a paper that is kind of a lease agreement."

"Kind of," she repeated, feeling that headache clamp more viciously.

"We never had anything notarized," Rosemary admitted in a rush. "Franklin Rafferty is the sweetest man but a little absent-minded lately. Lily made a couple of appointments with a notary and he didn't show up. She planned to take someone out to his house, but then I think she got so busy ordering the tents and the furnishings and… I guess it slipped her mind. And then she died, and in all the chaos, a formal lease agreement was the *last* thing on my mind."

Cami wanted to yank out her hair and utter a few well-chosen curse words but managed to swallow down both impulses. Still. Her mother knew better. Rosemary had an ex-husband and a daughter who were both attorneys. True, Ted was a criminal defense attorney, but Cami specialized in contract law. Exactly this sort of thing.

Rosemary herself had been a secretary to a lawyer, once upon a time, when she was putting her husband through law school.

Her mother certainly knew how vital it was to follow procedure and make sure all the details had been ironed out.

"I think I need an attorney." Rosemary's voice sounded a little stronger.

You needed one four months ago when you started setting up infrastructure for a glampground without the legal right to be there.

"Sounds like it," she said, trying to keep her tone mild and nonaccusatory.

"Can you please come up and sort this out?"

Ah. There was the crux of her mother's phone call. "Right now?"

Her mother lived in Cape Sanctuary, at least an eight-hour drive north from Los Angeles. Cami could catch a flight, she supposed, into Redding or Eureka, then rent a car.

Even as one part of her mind started sifting through possibilities, another more strident part was urging her to slow down. She had responsibilities in LA. Clients who needed her. Consultations. Contracts to read. Depositions to take. She couldn't drop everything to rescue Rosemary.

"Can you come? I hate to admit it, but I need help. Jon Rafferty was calling from Guatemala, but he said he would be catching a flight back to California as soon as possible. He expects to be here in the next few days and I don't have the first idea how to handle the situation. The man sounded absolutely livid on the phone."

Her mother's voice faltered. "If he shuts us down, I'll lose Moongate Farm. The gardens. The yoga retreats. Everything I've worked for here."

Cami felt a low thrum of resentment, an emotion she didn't want to acknowledge. Everything her mother had built there had been created after Rosemary walked away from her marriage, from her eldest daughter, from their comfortable life in Los Angeles.

Cami had never been part of that Cape Sanctuary life Rosemary had created for herself, except on the periphery. Yet her mother was turning to her now, expecting her to help salvage that life from the brink of disaster.

"I'm sure it won't come to that," she said, though she wasn't completely convinced of anything.

"I hope you're right. Will you come? You're the only one who can fix this. I need you, Cami."

Those words would have been a healing balm when she was a lonely teenager, living with a father she rarely saw in the big echoing house in Brentwood Park.

Before she could come up with an answer, Joe poked his head through the door she had left ajar.

"You've got a conference call with the attorneys for Cherrywood Properties in ten minutes," he reminded her in a low voice. "And Paulette Herriman wants a few moments to talk about the non-compete clause she wants to write into her new-hire contracts. I penciled her in for three."

The vise around her temples squeezed harder. "Thank you," she mouthed.

He slipped back out and she turned her attention back to her mother and the crisis playing out in Cape Sanctuary.

"It's a busy time here but I'll see what I can do. I should be able to swing a few days off."

She wasn't sure how yet, especially because she had planned to fly up later in the month anyway, but she would figure that out.

"Thank you, darling. Oh, thank you." The relief in Rosemary's voice was palpable and, Cami had to admit, gratifying.

"I'm not sleeping in one of your tents, though."

"You wouldn't say that if you saw them," Rosemary retorted. "They're absolutely gorgeous."

"I'll have to take your word for that."

"Anyway, you couldn't stay in one, even if you wanted to." Her mother's voice rang with pride. "They've been booked for months, almost from the moment Lily started taking reservations. But don't worry. I'll make sure you have somewhere to sleep. You and Violet can always share the bunkhouse."

"Vi's there?" She hadn't seen her younger sister, Lily's twin, since those first horrible days after Lily drowned. They had texted several times and Cami had tried to phone, but her sister was either extraordinarily busy or avoiding her calls.

"She's coming this weekend. Tomorrow is her last day of school. She has to clear out her classroom and finish final grades, then will be driving up to stay and help me with Wild Hearts."

"All summer?"

"She hasn't decided that yet. I'm giving her space to make up her mind." Rosemary paused. "I'm worried about her. Worried about both of you, if you want the truth."

"Don't worry about me," Cami said. "You have enough to stress about right now."

"I can't help it. Worry is part of the job description as your mother."

Cami ended the call a few moments later and looked down at the neat order of her desk: the pencils with their perfectly sharpened points in a holder, the inbox she worked long hours to keep empty, the briefs she had asked Joe to research for one of her cases, stacked in folders.

She had a wild impulse to take the neat stack of paper, the edges precisely lined up, and throw them all into the air.

She needed a break.

Other than the two days she had taken off to fly north for Lily's funeral, Cami had been working without a vacation or sick day for years.

Even when her fiancé cheated on her and then had the gall to break the engagement before she could throw his ring in his too-perfect face, Cami had worked.

She was so very tired. Maybe a few days in Cape Sanctuary would help her recharge a little.

She had plenty of vacation time coming to her, and her father would surely understand. Rosemary needed her, a rare enough circumstance.

Cami wasn't sure how she could solve her mother's dilemma, but she wanted to try.

For Lily.

She pulled out her laptop and started making a list for Joe of meetings that would have to be rearranged or changed to video conferencing.

As she made another list of files and briefs to take with her, Cami was surprised to realize the malaise that had been haunting her for months seemed to have lifted like sea fog receding in the sunshine.

2

VIOLET

WILD, FRENZIED BARKING RANG OUT WHEN Violet Porter let herself into the back door of her mother's comfortable kitchen at Moongate Farm.

Rosemary was nowhere in sight. Instead, a cranky-faced schnauzer–toy poodle mix planted himself in front of the door, telling her in no uncertain terms that she was an intruder who wasn't welcome here.

"Hi, Baxter," she said, mouth stretched thin in what she knew was an insincere smile. "How are you, buddy?"

Lily's dog only growled at her, baring his teeth with his hackles raised as if he wanted to rip her throat out.

The dog hated her. Violet wasn't exactly sure why.

She might have thought he would look more fondly toward her, considering she was the identical twin to his late owner. But maybe that was the problem. Maybe the fact that she looked so much like Lily but clearly *wasn't* her sister confused the dog and made him view her as a threat.

He had never really warmed to her, even when he lived in her condo with Lily. Since Lily's death, he had become downright hostile.

"Stop that. What's gotten into you? I could hear you clear back in my bedroom."

Her mother's voice trailed out from down the hall, becoming louder as she approached the kitchen, still fastening an earring.

She stopped dead when she spotted Violet.

"Oh! Violet! You scared me! What are you doing here?"

"You invited me. Remember? You've known for months I was coming to help you out during my summer break."

"You were coming *tomorrow*. Not today!"

Okay. That wasn't exactly the warm welcome she might have expected, Violet thought wryly. Instead, her mother was staring at her with an expression that seemed a curious mix of chagrin and dismay.

She shrugged as Baxter continued to growl. Wasn't *anybody* happy to see her?

"I finished cleaning out my classroom and calculating final grades this morning. Since all my things were already packed and loaded into my car, I couldn't see any reason to wait until the morning to drive up. Is there a problem?"

Rosemary, usually so even-tempered, looked at her, then at the giant wrought iron clock on the wall of the Moongate Farm kitchen with a hint of panic in her eyes.

"No. It's only…this is, er, a bit of a complication. I'm expecting dinner guests any moment."

"That must be why it smells so good in here."

It smelled like roasting vegetables mixed with garlic and cheese. Violet's stomach rumbled loud enough she was certain her mother had to hear, but Rosemary didn't seem to notice, looking at the clock again.

Why was she so nervous? Who was coming? If she didn't know better, Violet might have suspected her mother was expecting a date.

Not impossible, she supposed. Her mother was still a beautiful woman, with high cheekbones, a wide smile and the deep blue eyes she had handed down to Violet and her identical twin.

Rosemary didn't date much, though she'd had a few relationships since her divorce from Violet's father.

As far as Violet knew, she had broken up with the most recent man she had dated more than a year earlier and Rosemary hadn't mentioned anyone else.

Then again, just as Violet didn't tell her mother everything that went on in her life in Sacramento, Rosemary likely had secrets of her own here in Cape Sanctuary.

"No problem," she said, trying for a cheerful tone. "You don't have to worry about feeding me. If I get hungry later, I'll make a sandwich or something. I'll get out of your way."

"You're not in the way," Rosemary protested. "It's just, well..."

She didn't have time to finish before a knock sounded at the back door. Baxter, annoying little beast, gave one sharp bark, sniffed at the door, then plopped down expectantly.

Violet thought she heard a man's deep voice say something on the other side of the door and then a child's laughter in response.

Something about that voice rang a chord. She frowned, suddenly unsettled. "Mom. Who are you expecting?"

"Just some...some friends from town," Rosemary said vaguely.

She heard the man's voice again and her disquiet turned into full-fledged dismay.

No. Rosemary wouldn't have. Would she?

"Mom. Who's here?" Her voice sounded shrill and she was quite sure Rosemary could pick up on it.

"I didn't know you were coming tonight," her mom said defensively. "You told me you were coming tomorrow, so I…I invited Alexandro and his daughter for dinner. He's been such a help to me with Wild Hearts. I could never have set up all those tents or moved in the furniture without him. I've been meaning to have him and his daughter over for dinner but the time got away from me, until here we are. I'm sorry. You weren't supposed to be here until tomorrow and I didn't think it would be a problem."

The news hit her like a hatchet to the chest. Alex was here, on the other side of the door. Alex, who had once been her best friend, the man she thought would be her forever.

Alex, who had betrayed her.

She had seen him exactly twice since they broke up a decade ago.

One previous encounter had been a few years after he married Claudia Crane, when she had bumped into him at the grocery store while home from college for a brief visit.

The second time had been four months earlier at Lily's memorial service.

That was two times too many, really. Three encounters was asking far too much of her.

She wanted to jump back into her car and head back to Sacramento.

No. This was silly. She had known she would see him this summer. How could she avoid it? Cape Sanctuary was a small town. Not only that, but his house and boat charter business were both just down the road from Moongate Farm.

The concept had seemed fine in the abstract. Like algebra and the periodic table.

It had been nearly a decade, after all. She was a completely different person from that besotted girl she had once been.

He meant nothing to her anymore. She should be able to blithely chat with him about what he had been up to the past decade.

Yeah. Not happening.

Maybe she could turn around, climb back into her car and go hang out at The Sea Shanty until he was gone.

No. That was just kicking the can down the road. She had to face him eventually. Why not now?

She could come up with a dozen reasons, but none of them seemed compelling enough for her to flee without at least saying hello.

"I'm sorry," Rosemary said again, her hand on the doorknob.

"It's fine, Mom. Don't worry about it. Don't leave them standing outside. I'll just say hello and then head over to the bunkhouse to settle in. You won't even know I'm here. It will be fine."

She didn't believe that for a minute, but she forced herself to put on a pleasant smile as her mother opened the door.

And there he was.

As gorgeous as ever, with those thick dark eyelashes, strong features, full mouth that could kiss like no one else she had ever met…

Her toes curled at the unwelcome memories and she forced her attention away from Alex to the young girl standing beside him. She had dark hair that swung to her shoulders, bright brown eyes and dimples like her father.

Right now she was staring at Violet like she had just grown a second head.

"Miss Lily?" she whispered, big brown eyes wide and mouth ajar.

Of course. Ariana thought Violet was her sister. It was a natural mistake, as they were identical twins, though as an adult, Vi had mostly seen the differences between them.

She approached the girl with the same patient, reassuring

smile she used in her classroom when one of her students was upset about something.

"Hi there," she said calmly, doing her best to ignore Alex's intense gaze for now. "You must be Ariana. I'm Violet. Lily was my twin sister."

"You look just like her," the girl said breathlessly. Her gaze narrowed. "Except I think maybe your hair is a little shorter than hers was. And she had a tattoo of flowers on her wrist and you don't."

When they were in college, Lily had insisted on getting a tiny bouquet of flowers, intertwined lilies and violets and camellias to represent the three Porter sisters.

She had begged Violet and Cami to both get one, too. Cami, older by two years and always far more mature than either Vi or Lily, had politely explained that she didn't want any tattoos because of the serious nature of the law career she was pursuing. Violet had promised she would but then kept putting it off.

She still could go get a tattoo. After Lily's death, she had thought more seriously about it, but the loss of her sister was always with her. She didn't need a mark on her skin to remind her Lily wasn't here.

She forced a smile for the girl. "Right. No tattoo. That's one sure way of telling us apart."

Plus, she was alive and Lily wasn't. But she wasn't cruel enough to say that out loud, especially not to this child.

Lily had drowned after rescuing Ariana and a visiting friend when a rogue wave from an offshore winter storm dragged the girls out to sea. Lily had somehow managed to get both girls back to safety, but the Pacific had been relentless that day, and before Lily could climb out herself, another wave had pulled her under.

Violet certainly couldn't blame this child for a cruel act of nature.

Or for her parentage.

Alex stepped forward and she finally had to face the man she had once loved with all her heart.

"Violet."

That was all he said, only her name. His voice was the same as she remembered, deep, fluid, with a timbre that always seemed to shiver down her spine like a caress.

She ignored her reaction. She'd had nearly a decade to get over the man, for heaven's sake.

Once, she had known him well enough to guess what he was thinking most of the time. Either she was out of practice or he had become much harder to read over the years, because she had no idea what was going through his head.

"I didn't know you would be here tonight," he went on. "I thought you weren't coming back to town until tomorrow."

"Surprise." She gave him a cool smile, determined not to show by even a hitch in her breathing how he could still leave her flustered.

A timer rang out, and Rosemary, who had said nothing at this awkward reunion, hurried to the oven and pulled out a tray of what looked like her famous veggie lasagna, bubbling with cheese.

"Here we are," she announced. "Zucchini lasagna and salad with baby lettuce and early tomatoes from my greenhouse."

"Yum. It looks delicious." Alex gave Violet's mother a genuine smile. It was so familiar, once so beloved, that it made her heart hurt.

Rosemary looked at him with a fondness that baffled Violet. Had her mother completely forgotten that this man had once shattered her daughter's heart?

"Thank you," Violet's mother said, sliding the pan onto a trivet. "I hope it's as good as it looks."

She turned to Violet. "There's plenty for you. I just need to set out another plate and some silverware for you."

"Not necessary," she assured her quickly. "I'm not hungry."

It was a lie, but she wasn't about to sit down for a meal with Alex as if their shared past meant nothing.

Not to mention with his daughter.

"I'll just unload my things from the car and start settling into the bunkhouse."

"You don't have to leave on our account," Alex protested.

Oh, she absolutely did, but she wasn't about to tell him that. Instead, she forced another polite smile.

She waved at them all. "I'll talk to you later, Mom. Nice to meet you, Ariana. Enjoy the lasagna."

The girl still looked at her as if she expected Violet to start floating around the room any minute and disappear through the wall.

"Welcome back," Alex said, that beautiful voice low.

She couldn't think of an answer, so she hurried out of the kitchen, down the back porch steps and to her car.

She didn't realize Baxter, the cranky schnoodle, had followed her until he planted his haunches beside her car and gave her a baleful look.

She suddenly feared she had made a terrible mistake coming home.

Since Lily died, all she could think about was being here at Moongate Farm with her mother and the chickens and the quiet peace of the garden.

The notion had been the only thing keeping her going through the hectic end of the school year, when she was burned out from lesson planning and grading assignments and Individualized Education Plans with parents while her students were all wild with anticipation for the summer break.

Here beside the ocean, perhaps she could finally breathe past the ache in her chest and come to terms with the grief and the guilt that both seemed to prowl restlessly through her subconscious.

She hadn't lived in Cape Sanctuary for any length of time

since the summer after her freshman year of college, when she had come home for a few months to wait tables and to be with Alex, who was living at home and taking business classes at the nearby community college while he helped his dad at the marina.

That had been their last glorious summer as a couple. They had spent every possible moment together.

By the next summer, their relationship had shattered.

She had been back to visit, of course. Holidays. A week here or there. She had always carefully managed to avoid seeing him and the new family he had started with someone else.

She grabbed her suitcase out of her car.

She could do this. Alex meant nothing to her anymore. She was here to help her mother, not to spend even another moment thinking about a past she could never recapture.

3

CAMI

SHE COULDN'T DENY THAT CAPE SANCTUARY was a picturesque town.

The houses here were mostly built of honey stone from the nearby quarries. While a few older houses were simple, utilitarian affairs, the creative types who had moved here for the temperate climate and the stunning coastal scenery had added whimsical touches to their houses. Weather vanes, cupolas, turrets, widow's walks.

All the yards seemed to have bright flower gardens, and more colorful flowers overflowed baskets hanging on streetlights and in window boxes of well-kept downtown businesses. The town managed to look charmingly touristy yet authentic at the same time.

Beyond Cape Sanctuary, the Pacific Ocean gleamed in the afternoon sunlight. Depending on the day and conditions, it could be placid and blue or a wild, stormy green.

After Cami's parents' marriage had broken down, Rosemary had escaped here to the town of her youth to open a yoga retreat on property left to her by a beloved great-aunt.

Cami had hated Cape Sanctuary for a long time, blaming the area for providing a refuge to her mother that gave her a ready excuse to leave her marriage.

It had seemed pretty simple to her adolescent brain. If Rosemary hadn't inherited Moongate Farm, Cami's parents might have stayed married. The farm had been the catalyst.

As an adult whose own engagement had disintegrated when she wasn't paying attention, Cami had become much better at seeing subtle nuances. Her mother hadn't been happy in LA for a long time. She had spent years trying to be the perfect corporate wife to a high-powered attorney, but the country-club set, the ladies who lunch, had never been Rosemary's scene.

Running a yoga retreat and guesthouse in a small Northern California seaside town fit her mother's personality much better.

Cami was approaching the city limits when she spotted a small SUV on the side of the road and someone pulling a spare tire from the back with one arm, the other one in a sling.

She had a quick impression of a tall man with a dark beard. Lean, hard, gorgeous.

None of her business, Cami told herself. Though she might be the designated fixer in her family, she wasn't responsible for saving the world.

Not even a sexy wounded motorist.

Someone else would probably stop. Cape Sanctuary was a friendly place, where people went out of their way to help their neighbors.

The way her week was going, he was probably a serial killer laying a trap for his next unsuspecting victim. Wasn't that what Ted Bundy had done? Pretend to be hurt so women would stop and help him?

Just drive on by, she told herself, hands tight on the steering wheel of her rental car.

As she passed him, she made the mistake of glancing over just as he dropped the jack, which slid under the vehicle.

She drove another hundred yards before her conscience made her drive into a pullout and turn around. She couldn't let anybody struggle to change a tire with the use of only one arm. She could at least call road service for him.

She flipped a U-turn on the empty road and pulled up behind him. After slipping her can of pepper spray into her pocket along with her cell phone—she was helpful but she wasn't stupid—Cami climbed out of her car.

Crouched beside his car, he turned at the sound of her door closing and watched her walk toward him with an expression she couldn't read.

"Need some help?"

He looked even more dangerous as she approached, his hair a little shaggy and shadows under his eyes. "You know anything about changing a tire?"

"Actually, yes. My father wouldn't let me get a driver's license when I was sixteen until I could prove to him I knew how to perform basic maintenance on a vehicle."

"Smart dad."

"About some things. Put him in a kitchen and he can't boil pasta."

Dangerous yet gorgeous, she had to admit. She didn't want to notice his deep blue eyes or the little lines that radiated out from them.

Did serial killers have laugh lines?

She had no idea. The criminal justice arena was her father's, not hers.

"You really don't have to help me. Changing a tire is a little more challenging with one arm but not completely impossible."

"Says a man who has probably never tried to change a tire before with one arm."

"True enough." He smiled a little, making those lines even more pronounced.

Something tugged deep in her belly, something she'd had no idea lurked inside of her until this moment.

She pushed it away. What was wrong with her? She was here to help her mother with a legal dispute and then go back to Los Angeles as soon as she could manage it.

She wasn't the kind of woman to engage in a flirtation with a stranger, no matter how gorgeous.

"If you can manage to swallow your manly pride, I can finish the job in five minutes and you can be on your way."

He studied her for a moment and Cami could feel her face heat. Not for the first time, she wished she had inherited the same genes as the twins—that she could be tall and leggy and blonde instead of short, dark, average, with more curves than she wanted and a mouth too wide for her face.

Finally, he handed her the lug wrench.

In moments, she had the tire off and was replacing it with the spare he had set beside the car.

"So, how did you hurt your arm?" she asked conversationally.

"Do I get extra points if I tell you some dramatic, thrilling story about an accident with a machete at a lost jungle temple?"

That tracked for her, better than it probably should. He looked the part of an adventurer. Fit, sexy, athletic. Basically everything Sterling had aspired to but couldn't quite pull off.

In reality, the man had probably injured his arm in some mundane way, like shooting a basketball or tripping over a step, but it was fun to imagine the alternative.

She smiled. "I would probably give you points for creativity, if nothing else."

"I guess I'll have to take what I can get."

He gave her a full-on smile in return, and the sheer impact of it left her feeling like she was the one who had tripped over a step.

"Seriously. What did you do?"

He gave her a sideways look. "Now you're probably not going to believe me when I tell you I actually got in the way of my friend's machete as we were clearing the jungle away from a lost temple."

She had to laugh as she twisted the lug nut. "Okay. I guess you're going for it."

"Only because it's the truth. Thoughtless mistake on my part. It happened a couple of weeks ago. We tried to stitch it up at camp, but it got infected and apparently the original injury damaged some ligaments and tendons. I ended up having surgery a few days ago to repair it."

"Does it feel better?"

"I'm not having hallucinations from the high fevers anymore, at least. I've got some heavy-duty antibiotics and I'm supposed to keep the sling on for a week."

He lifted his arm. "I'll be lucky to make it through the day. My patience has just about run out. If you hadn't come along, I would have pulled it off already to change the tire. Thank you, by the way."

"You're welcome. Always happy to do my part to help my fellow humans."

She finished tightening the final lug nut and stood up. "There you go. That should keep you, as long as you're not going too far."

"I'm not. Only a mile or so. I probably would have ended up walking the rest of the way."

"I guess it was just your lucky day."

"I guess so," he answered with that smile again that left her feeling dazzled. "I would like to pay you back somehow."

"No need. When your arm's fixed, you can pay it forward by helping out someone else. And stay away from machetes next time."

"You can be sure I will. I'm Jon, by the way."

"Cami." Somehow her name came out sounding breathless.

"Well, Cami. Thank you. You've been a bright light in the midst of a couple of really lousy days."

"Glad I could help," she answered, aware of a slight pang that she wouldn't see him again.

Just as well, she told herself as she climbed into her rental and headed the short distance toward Moongate Farm.

As attractive as she found him, sexy wounded adventurers weren't really her type.

4

JON

HE SHOULD HAVE AT LEAST TRIED TO GET HER number.

Jon Rafferty watched his rescuer drive up the road, her taillights reflecting the setting sun.

She had been cute, curvy, sharp-witted. And kind. If she hadn't been kind, she would never have stopped to help a stranger change a tire.

Not that it mattered, as he didn't expect he would see her again.

Still, if he had managed to get her number, he could have bought her a drink or something at The Sea Shanty to thank her for stopping to help him.

He could have changed the flat himself, though it would have been tough and no doubt painful.

His arm throbbed enough without scrambling around in the dirt to change a flat tire. The ache was a constant reminder of his own inattention.

He had been doing fieldwork in Guatemala at the Tikal site for six months without even a scraped knuckle. Leave it to him to sustain a serious injury at the most inconvenient time possible.

Of course, he hadn't known his life would take such a rapid left turn. He had fully expected to be living his best life, working on the site and basically enjoying every new discovery.

Instead, right after that freak machete incident, everything seemed to have blown up at the same time, one of those weird chain reactions where one small incident unravels an entire life.

He hadn't expected to be back in Cape Sanctuary ever. After the last bitter fight with his father, he had vowed he would never return.

But once the fevers started, the director of the dig had insisted he head to Guatemala City for medical care.

Jon had been barely out of anesthesia and using the downtime and reliable internet to catch up on correspondence when he found in his spam folder a weeks-old email from Robert Layton, his father's law partner. The news had stunned him.

His father, the strongest man he knew, had apparently retired from their practice and Jon had had no idea. More shocking, Robert said Franklin was becoming increasingly erratic. His former partner was strongly recommending Jon step in to protect his father's extensive assets. In the email, he said Jon should begin legal proceedings to obtain medical and legal power of attorney or he would do it himself, as Franklin was making decisions that didn't make business or financial sense.

You are likely aware he has allowed the development of a campground atop the Rose Creek headlands, Robert had written. *Your father fre-*

quently told me after your mother died that the property would be placed in a conservation easement. It was with dismay at my last visit that I saw a series of tents, along with the infrastructure to support them.

I can't find a phone number for you and your university says you are out of the country until next year. I'm reaching out via email as a last-ditch effort to plead with you to come home, if only for a visit.

I believe your father could be dealing with a serious medical issue. He refuses to seek help and now will no longer let me into the house or take my calls. You are his only living relative, as far as I can find. I know your relationship with Franklin is complicated. If you have no wish to help him, please advise and I will begin the steps to seek legal and medical guardianship for him.

He should have come home before now.

Yes, he and his father had fought bitterly three years earlier. Hard, angry words had flown between them, words Jon couldn't unsay. In the end, his father had basically told him he was no longer welcome at Rose Creek.

Jon had tried to comply, telling himself he didn't want to come home to Cape Sanctuary anyway. Not when the house of his childhood seemed to echo with emptiness.

As he drove the short distance to his father's house on the edge of the sea, he knew he had been lying to himself all this time.

He had yearned for home.

Yes, he loved his work. He was passionate about researching Mayan civilizations, especially after the stunning discovery through advanced laser 3D imagery of hundreds, perhaps thousands, of ancient structures that had been hiding in plain sight under the dense forest canopy.

His work was important to him and, he believed, vital to the world's understanding of the civilizations that had come before.

Still, he yearned for home, as tense as things had become there after his mother died.

He passed the neighboring house, with its fanciful, flowery sign reading Moongate Farm.

He barely knew the residents there, but Robert Layton had told him when Jon finally reached him by phone that they were the squatters who were building the campground on Rafferty land.

What had his father been thinking?

The question wasn't a new one. Franklin Rafferty had his own way of looking at the world. Analytical, precise, emotionless.

He had a formidably sharp legal understanding and had been approached about a federal justice role more than once. He had refused, for reasons Jon still didn't understand.

So many of the things his father did baffled him.

If they weren't so different, perhaps Jon and his father would have been able to find common ground after Jon's mother died, at least through their shared grief.

Instead, they had fought more than ever. Jon had graduated high school early to take a scholarship in Austin, Texas, wanting to go as far as he could from this place of so much loss.

Now, as he pulled up in front of Rose Creek, an unexpected surge of emotion rose in his throat.

Home.

The house, a sprawling two-level structure covered in the pale honey-colored stone that made up so many of the houses in Cape Sanctuary, seemed more run-down than he remembered. A shutter was broken on one of the upstairs windows and it looked as if some of the roof tiles were missing.

He should have returned before now.

He had tried to call his father a few times over the past three years since that last blowup, but Franklin had stopped taking his calls, just as he had his law partner's.

Jon had finally stopped trying. What was the point? Their relationship hadn't been particularly strong in the first place.

After his father shut the door between them, Jon wasn't eager to continue kicking against it.

Now he had no choice. His father needed help, whether Franklin would admit it or not.

He reached across to open his car door, no easy feat with his left arm in a sling.

He was already tired of the limitations from being able to use only one hand. He would give the sling another day or two, and then the damn thing was coming off.

As he climbed out, he caught sight of the small spare tire that didn't match the other three on the rental and couldn't help thinking about the lovely woman who had helped him replace it.

He suspected her vehicle was a rental as well. He had spotted a suitcase on the back seat, and the midsize sedan had a rental's bland impersonality and distinct lack of flair.

He felt a pang at the idea that he probably would never see her again, but quickly dismissed it. Right now he had other things to face, including the inevitable strain of the next few moments.

He should have called ahead to let Franklin know he was coming. He hadn't been sure his father would even take his call, given their track record. And he also wasn't sure what he would say.

Hi, Dad. I hear you're losing your mind.

He would have to navigate his first encounter with his father more carefully than any overgrown jungle path.

What would he do if Franklin sent him on his way in no uncertain terms?

He wasn't going to think about that now.

He left his duffel in the rental and headed for the house. Before he could reach the small paved courtyard, where weeds poked through the bricks and leaves cluttered in the corners, his father opened the door.

Franklin blinked a few times but gave no other outward sign

of shock at finding the son he had basically thrown out a few years earlier.

"Jonny. What a nice surprise. Why didn't you tell me you were coming? I could have bought some steaks to grill when I was at the market this morning."

He spoke as if they had just met up for lunch a few days earlier, as if their last huge fight and the glaring silence of the past three years were nothing.

"Yes. I'm here. Hi, Dad."

His father met him halfway and gave him a brief hug. To Jon, Frank felt as hearty as ever, broad and solid as the headland beyond the house.

When he looked closer, though, he picked up signs that not all was well.

Franklin looked as if he hadn't shaved in a week and his hair could use a comb. He also smelled of body odor, stale coffee and clothes that needed washing.

Of course, after living in the jungle for the past six months, Jon needed a haircut and shave and probably smelled worse.

"There now. That's nice. It's good to see you," Franklin said, stepping away. "You're staying the night, aren't you? Can I help you carry your bags in?"

He was staying longer than that. At least long enough to get his father into some medical professionals to assess if something was truly going on with his faculties and then figure out how to organize care of his father so that Jon could return to his research.

Oh, and there was the small matter of figuring out how to boot out the squatters who had taken advantage of Franklin during a vulnerable time.

He was almost looking forward to that.

5

CAMI

WHEN SHE PULLED UP IN FRONT OF MOONGATE Farm, the place seemed deserted. She couldn't see anyone in sight, not even one of Rosemary's various cats who happily wandered the property, keeping it free of mice.

Someone had to be here. Hadn't her mother said Violet was coming in that day? Maybe they were up at the glampground or had gone to dinner or something.

Not sure what to do, Cami pulled her suitcase from the rental and walked to the house.

On the front porch, she hesitated, then rang the doorbell.

Cami always felt so awkward here. The ugly duckling daughter who didn't quite belong with the cool kids.

Cami didn't consider this home. She had stayed for random weekends throughout school and for a month or so every summer, but she still always felt like a visitor.

She listened for someone coming to answer the door but could only hear the sound of birds twittering at one of her mother's many feeders and the sound of barking coming from inside.

Did that mean someone was home?

A flash of wings caught her gaze and she spotted a hummingbird flitting toward the spun glass feeder while the ocean hummed in the distance.

Moongate Farm was separated from the Pacific by the Rose Creek headlands, a forested promontory that jutted out into the water, surrounded on three sides by ocean. The trees filtered some of the ocean sounds, but she could still hear the distant murmur over the dog's barking, which seemed to have gotten louder.

After another moment, Cami rang the bell again.

Still no one.

Finally, when the dog seemed on the verge of a complete mental breakdown, Cami pushed open the door.

"Hello? Mom? It's Cami. Are you home?"

Only a little tan-and-white schnauzer-poodle cross greeted her with enthusiasm.

"Hey, Baxter. How are you, sweetie?" Cami crooned, dropping her suitcase inside and scooping up the creature.

She loved Lily's little dog, who had been living with Rosemary for the past four months.

He was smart, funny and gave the best cuddles.

He licked at her face, his whole body wriggling with happiness. She couldn't help but laugh at his unbridled joy. He just might be the only creature on earth who was unreservedly happy to see her.

Why, again, didn't she have a dog?

She was still asking herself that and rubbing Baxter's ears when she heard the back door open, and a moment later, her mother poked her head out into the hallway from the kitchen, a wicker basket of produce over her arm.

"Oh! Cami. When did you get here?"

"A few minutes ago. I rang the doorbell, but nobody answered."

"I'm sorry. I didn't hear you. I was out in the back, picking some things for dinner. The doorbell is supposed to ring out there, but I don't always hear it. Hello, darling. Thank you so much for coming."

"You're welcome."

Rosemary frowned. "Is that dog being a nuisance again? I'm so sorry."

"He's not a nuisance. He's adorable. Aren't you, Baxie?"

The dog licked her chin again and Rosemary huffed out a breath. "That dog. He's such a crank to everyone else. I don't know how you got lucky enough for him to love you."

"I don't either," Cami admitted. She wasn't going to complain about it, though. It was nice to be someone's favorite, once in a while.

"I'm sorry your sister isn't here to greet you. I sent her to the grocery store when I realized I wasn't going to have enough blueberries to make syrup for tomorrow's breakfast."

"What time did Violet show up?"

"Last night, actually. I guess she decided to come a day early. It can't be easy for her, alone in her condo in the city."

Her poor sister. As much as Cami grieved for Lily, she couldn't imagine how tough it must be on Violet to lose her twin. The two had always been inseparable as children and the best of friends as adults.

"How is she?" Cami asked.

Rosemary sighed. "She says she's fine, but the circles under her eyes tell a different story. They're big enough to drive a truck through."

She gave Cami a pointed look. "I could say the same for you, darling. Haven't you been sleeping either?"

She thought of the insomnia she couldn't seem to shake. Maybe a few nights in Cape Sanctuary would help. She listened to the ocean sounds on her phone sound machine app. Maybe having the real thing outside the window would make all the difference.

"Not as well as I'd like," she admitted.

"Your father works you too hard," Rosemary said. "I've told him so."

Ted Porter might be a senior founding partner at Porter, Garcia & Sheen, but their paths rarely intersected on the job. Criminal attorneys and contract lawyers lived in completely different worlds. Her mother likely wouldn't see things that way and Cami decided there was no point in arguing with her about it.

"Should I take my suitcase to the bunkhouse?"

"Yes. Violet has already settled in there and is expecting you to join her."

"Great." While the name might sound primitive, the bunkhouse was a comfortably appointed guesthouse her mother sometimes rented out, with three separate bedrooms and a large communal area and kitchen.

When her mother hosted yoga retreats, she often used the common room for classes.

"In fact," Rosemary went on, "you could do me a favor and keep an eye on your sister to gauge how she's really doing. She won't talk to me."

Cami raised an eyebrow. "I thought you asked me here to sort out your lease dispute, not to tattle on my baby sister."

"Two birds," Rosemary said with a smile. "Come on. I'll help you with your bags."

"No need. I only have the one suitcase and my laptop. You don't have to help me."

"I know, but it feels wrong to just send you on your way. Helping you is the least I can do after you dropped everything to come help me."

With the dog following behind, Rosemary led the way back to Cami's rental car. She picked up the suitcase and carried it around the side of the old farmhouse along a gravel path that wound through vegetable and flower gardens.

Her mother had spent the first several years after the divorce renovating the house and the gardens, serving as her own contractor and doing some of the work herself.

The result was a large, comfortable house ideal for a coastal B and B.

Making money had never really been her mother's aim, at least as far as Cami could tell. Rosemary seemed to simply want to keep busy doing something she loved.

Cami understood that, but she still resented Moongate Farm. It was hard to remember that as she followed her mother through air thick with the scent of lavender and herbs. For a moment, she wanted to simply stand there surrounded by plants and inhale.

When they reached the bunkhouse, her mother unlocked the door and held it open for her.

Cami walked inside, admiring again the rustic beams and the large windows overlooking the abundant garden.

Rosemary loved creating relaxing spaces. Lily had been the same, she remembered. Not Cami. She suspected the decorating gene had completely skipped over her. After her engagement ended and Sterling moved both out and on, Cami had purchased a furnished condo with an easy commute to the office and hadn't bothered to change anything other than bedding and towels.

"I didn't ask about your trip," Rosemary said as she set down the suitcase. "How was it?"

"I couldn't get a flight into Redding today, so I ended up flying into Santa Rosa and renting a car."

"Oh dear. How was the traffic?"

"Not bad. I'm used to LA traffic, so anything is an improvement."

Oh, and I helped a wounded adventurer with a flat tire who left me all stirred up.

She didn't have the sort of relationship with Rosemary where she could admit that kind of thing.

"Looks like Violet set up in the Sequoia room. You could take the Maple or Spruce room. I'm afraid they're both a little small and you don't have an en suite bathroom like the Sequoia. I'm sorry."

"I'm only going to be here a few days. I could sleep on the couch, really. It doesn't matter."

For some reason, her mother didn't look happy about that.

"I would love to give you the grand tour of the tents. You haven't seen them since the memorial service, have you?"

"No. You only had a few up when I was here last and only one was partially decorated. But it's nearly dark. We could do it tomorrow."

"We still have an hour of daylight. I would love to show you. You're going to be so shocked. They're all decorated and so gorgeous, like a little luxurious neighborhood. I don't have your sister's flair, but I still think Lily would have l-loved the way they turned out."

Her mother's voice cracked a little and her eyes filled with tears. Cami didn't quite know how to respond. Rosemary was always so self-sufficient and composed. Seeing her give in to her emotions like this was disconcerting.

"I'm sure you're right," Cami said softly.

Rosemary gave a watery smile. "I truly would like to show you Wild Hearts."

Cami knew her sister had named the glampground Wild

Hearts Luxury Camping in an effort to appeal to those who loved the outdoors but also wanted a romantic retreat. All the glampground's social media worked to reinforce that brand.

She was tired from traveling all day and would have loved the chance to put her feet up for a moment and catch up on her emails, but she didn't want to disappoint her mother when Rosemary seemed so unusually fragile.

She smiled. "Sure. I would love to take a look."

They walked out of the bunkhouse just as a small silver SUV pulled up outside with Violet at the wheel, tall, blonde, gorgeous.

Violet waved and opened her door. When she stepped out, Cami was surprised when Baxter growled fiercely at Violet, earning a disgruntled look from her sister.

Cami picked up the dog, who immediately nestled into her neck.

"Oh, I'm so glad you're here," Rosemary said. "I was just about to give Cami a tour of the tents. Why don't you come with us?"

"I've seen the campground plenty of times when I've come up on the weekends."

"I know, but your sister hasn't. Come with us," Rosemary urged. "We can even look in one of the tents. That couple from Salinas who are checking in today haven't arrived yet."

Violet held up a flat of blueberries. "Where do you want these?"

"Thank you for grabbing those. Just set them in the kitchen while I go find some wheels."

After her day of sitting on a plane and then in a rental car, Cami wouldn't have minded walking up the hill to the glampground but didn't argue when her mother returned a moment later driving a four-seat golf cart.

"Nice wheels."

"Thanks," Rosemary said happily. "Lily got a good deal on them from a golf course that was closing. She bought one for each of the tents so the guests can park down by the barn and drive up to the campground in the carts. It's ecologically friendly and makes it easier for them to come back and forth for breakfast in the mornings."

She hopped in beside her mother with Baxter on her lap. Violet came out of the house a moment later and slid into the back seat.

The graveled trail to the campground wound through the trees and up to the bluff overlooking the ocean.

Cami had to agree with her mother. The tents did look like a little neighborhood, with each campsite separated from the others in the trees.

The beige tents were large, each about fourteen feet square, placed on a wooden deck that jutted out several feet in front to serve as a front porch, complete with sling camp chairs and a little side table.

She could see one couple sitting on their porch, both with books open on their laps. Two others were at a picnic table under a covered pavilion in a central area she assumed was the common space. They appeared to be playing cards. A man napped in a hammock strung between two trees.

Each tent, she saw, was positioned perfectly to take in the stunning view from the headlands of the Pacific, glinting in the afternoon sun.

"Wow," Cami exclaimed. "This is amazing."

She was bowled over, not only by the inviting tent village but also by the work and planning she knew must have gone into making the dream a reality.

She didn't know what she had expected, but it wasn't these charming accommodations.

It all seemed well planned yet organic at the same time, with the tents blending so perfectly into the landscape.

The depth of her astonishment made her slightly ashamed of herself.

When Lily had told her she was planning to open a glampground near Moongate Farm, it had seemed like only another of Lily's wild ideas.

Unlike Cami, who had always known she would go to law school, or Violet, who had talked about becoming a special education teacher since befriending a neighbor girl in Los Angeles who had cerebral palsy, Lily had struggled to find her way in life.

While she had graduated with a degree in business, she had moved from job to job, everything from sales to marketing to fundraising. Nothing ever seemed quite right, until Lily had come up with the idea for the luxury campground.

Over the holidays, the last time Cami had spent time with her mother and sisters, Lily and Rosemary had been bursting with excitement for the idea.

Cami obviously hadn't given their plans enough credence.

"So? What do you think?" Rosemary asked, with obvious pride in her voice.

"It's wonderful," she said sincerely. "You've done a great job."

"Lily always loved this spot," Violet said. While she spoke calmly enough, her eyes held deep pain.

Cami felt an answering tightness in her throat. Was it hard for Vi to return to Cape Sanctuary, or was she finding some kind of connection and peace to her twin here as they walked through the campground Lily had envisioned?

Cami couldn't tell. Violet seemed to keep her emotions tucked somewhere Cami couldn't see.

"This is the tent I was talking about," her mother said. "The cleaning crew has already been here, so we can take a quick look. I'll just ask you to look from the doorway so we don't get the floor dirty."

"I don't need to," Cami said. "I'm sure they're great inside."

"You have to take a look," Rosemary insisted. "The luxury comes from what's inside."

She led the way to a nearby tent and unlocked what seemed like a regular door, far from the typical tent flap.

"We call this one our Beach Daisy tent. Lily wanted to name each one after a different wildflower found along the coast. This is one of my favorites."

Cami stood on the porch and peered inside. A large bed covered in plush-looking linens took up most of the space. Two more leather camp chairs, along with a rattan pouf, created a cozy sitting area.

It even smelled expensive somehow, of leather and sage.

"The tents are totally eco-friendly, with solar power, composting toilets and low-flow showers. It can get windy up here on the bluff, so every tent is secured at multiple points for safety."

She smiled at her mother's sales pitch. "It's great. Comfortable, warm, welcoming, but still steeped in luxury."

"That's what we were going for," Rosemary exclaimed with delight.

"Well, you've nailed it. Don't you think, Vi?"

Her sister gave a smile that looked slightly forced. "It's fabulous. I can see Lily's style everywhere."

Cami reached out and gave Vi's arm a brief, sympathetic squeeze. Vi blinked at the gesture but Cami thought she looked grateful, too.

"Lily poured her life savings into this place," Rosemary said. "The entire nest egg she had been saving since graduating college for a down payment on a house. She worked day and night for months, ironing out all the details. And she was all over social media. She was determined to make Wild Hearts the hot spot destination in this part of California."

"I can tell you've both been working hard."

"Lily was the driving force. I was just along for the ride."

Cami didn't believe that for a second. Her mother had never been one to just sit on the sidelines and let other people plan her life. At least not since her divorce.

"Now that she's gone, I feel it's my mission to carry on her legacy," her mother went on. "She loved the idea of this campground so much and couldn't wait to see guests enjoying what she created. I can't let the dream die with her."

"Of course not."

Rosemary gave her an earnest look. "Thank you so much for coming all this way to help me save it."

"No pressure," Violet said under her breath, her voice dry.

Cami disguised her surprised laugh as a cough.

"I don't want you to get your hopes up. I'm not sure how much I can do," she admitted as they walked back to the golf cart.

"I can't believe Lily didn't have an ironclad lease before she built all this stuff," Vi said, shaking her head.

"We should have," Rosemary agreed. "But you know how Franklin Rafferty can be, don't you, Violet? He's a lovely man, don't get me wrong, but, well, a little irascible."

She sighed. "If you want the truth, I think he strung us along because he wanted Lily to keep visiting him. He insisted on having his old paralegal witness the agreement. He and Lily would set an appointment and she would show up, only to find no paralegal. She finally told him she would bring her own notary the next day, only to find him not home. She was so frustrated."

"It doesn't sound as if he was completely on board with things," Cami observed.

"He was, though. They had a verbal agreement and he cashed the check she gave him to cover the first year. Six thousand dollars."

To Cami, that seemed a ridiculously low amount for an annual lease of two acres of property with stunning ocean views. She didn't want to bring that up with Rosemary now, when her mother was already just about wringing her hands over the situation.

"Then I think she got busy with getting conditional use approvals through the planning commission and buying the tents and supplies, not to mention all the logistics involved in advertising and taking reservations. I honestly think she forgot it was still a loose end."

How could someone forget such a critical part of the business plan? And how on earth was she supposed to fix the situation if Franklin Rafferty's family members objected to his informal agreement with Lily?

Rosemary sighed. "She would be kicking herself now if she knew what was happening."

"Would she, though?"

Violet spoke so abruptly that both Cami and their mother looked at her in surprise.

"Of course!" Rosemary exclaimed.

Violet didn't look convinced. "Lily was great at big-picture stuff. She just didn't like dealing with nitty-gritty details."

"That's not a very nice thing to say about your sister."

"But true. You know it is. Why let hard reality get in the way? She wanted a glampground, so she moved ahead anyway, with or without Franklin Rafferty's signature on a legal and binding lease agreement."

The bitterness in Violet's voice took Cami by surprise. Rosemary looked stunned.

"And in true Lily fashion, she died the way she lived. She jumped in to save a couple of kids without any forethought. Was she a great swimmer? No. Did she have a life jacket? No. Did she have a plan for how to get herself and the kids out? I highly doubt it. In true Lily form, she just jumped in without thinking and left everybody else to deal with the consequences."

The last word came out as a sob. Rosemary pressed a hand to her mouth, her eyes devastated, and Violet looked horrified at herself.

Cami didn't know what to say into the sudden tense silence.

"I'm sorry," Violet said. "I shouldn't have said that. I think I'll walk back to the house. I need a minute."

She hurried away from them toward the path that Cami knew led down to the ocean.

"Oh, that poor girl." Rosemary's hands shook and her eyes filled with tears. "We should go after her."

Cami didn't know how to deal with all these huge emotions. Her own grief and sadness were hard enough to handle. How could she possibly help her mother and sister through theirs?

"I don't think we should. She said she needed a minute."

"Should we wait for her to come back?"

Why was her mother suddenly looking to Cami for all the answers? She was painfully aware that she didn't have any. She had heard once there were as many ways to handle grief as there were people who grieved.

"She knows the way home. It's not far."

"I'm sure you're right." Rosemary looked toward the beach. Violet was almost to the water's edge by now.

"I hope it wasn't a mistake to ask her to come back and help me this summer. Heaven knows, I do need the help, but I mostly thought staying busy would be good for her. Better than sticking around her condo by herself in Sacramento and brooding on her own."

That might be true, but Cami wasn't sure Violet would benefit from staying busy while being haunted by her twin sister's memory at every turn.

6

VIOLET

EYES BURNING, VI RUSHED DOWN THE PATH toward the water, hoping like hell she didn't bump into any of the glampground guests coming back to their tents.

She should not have lost it like that, especially not in front of her mother and sister.

She still wasn't sure what had set her off, but something about seeing those gorgeous tents, with their luxurious bedding and the poufs Lily had loved, had ignited a wild fury inside her.

Her sister should be here, enjoying the fruits of all her hard labor. This damn glampground had been the only thing Lily had talked about. Once the idea ignited, she had become obsessed.

Lily had finally found the one thing she loved but she never had the chance to see her dream realized. The unfairness of it made Violet want to scream.

She stopped several feet shy of the high water mark, not willing to go closer. She sank down onto a dried-out log that had washed up to the shore and gazed out to sea, where the waves glittered orange in the early evening light and gulls cried out overhead.

She wanted more than anything to turn around and find Lily walking down the path toward her, but she knew that wasn't going to happen. Her twin was gone. She'd had four months to get used to the gaping wound in her heart, but it still felt as raw as the day she had found out Lily had drowned.

She was still sitting there as the sun continued sinking below the horizon when she heard snuffling behind her. She turned around to find a large golden retriever bounding toward her across the sand, its tongue lolling and a leash trailing along behind it.

The dog barked and headed straight at her. Violet tensed instinctively, not used to big dogs, but relaxed when the dog stopped a few feet away, tail wagging with something that definitely looked like joy.

Finally. A dog that was actually happy to see her, unlike Baxter. Lily's dog had a definite aversion to Violet.

This dog, in contrast, gazed at her with instant affection, its eyes a warm, sympathetic brown that somehow made Violet's eyes burn again.

"Hi there," she said. "I'm Violet. Nice to meet you."

To her delight, the dog lifted a paw to shake her hand. She took his sand-covered paw in her hand, which seemed to be all the invitation the dog needed to come closer. It nudged its head against her leg, a clear sign it wanted to be petted.

"Aren't you a good dog? Did you run away from someone?"

Her question was answered an instant later when she saw a girl walking up the beach.

"Gus?" she called. "Gus? Where are you?"

"Over here," Violet called back. While petting the creature with one hand, she carefully snagged the trailing leash with the other so the dog wouldn't run off again as she watched the girl come closer along the beach.

A moment later, when her features came into focus, Violet felt herself tense all over again. She recognized the girl all too well. She had just met her the night before, at Moongate Farm.

Ariana Mendoza stopped short when she spotted her. "Oh. Hi. Sorry. Gus's leash slipped out of my hands. I guess he just wanted to say hi to you. He does that sometimes."

"It's fine. I love dogs." Except for cranky ones who treated her like she was an inferior carbon copy of their owner.

"You look so much like Lily."

"I've heard that."

Only a million times since the day she was born.

"It kind of freaks me out," the girl admitted, apology in her voice.

Violet didn't know what to say to that. She only knew it would soon get very old if everyone in town did a double take whenever they spotted her.

"Maybe I should dye my hair purple or something while I'm in Cape Sanctuary, so people don't think I'm Lily coming back to haunt them."

It was a lame thing to say but it still made Ariana giggle. "I would *love* to dye my hair. My friend has a green streak. I was thinking maybe pink. That's my favorite color. What do you think?"

"Pink would look good on you." Anything would, really. Ariana had sweet, pretty features and a wide engaging smile, along with those dimples.

"I like purple, too. That could be cool. I don't know. My

mom said *maybe* when I asked her if I could dye my hair, but my dad thinks I should wait until I'm in middle school, which won't be for two more years."

To Violet's surprise, the girl plopped into the sand and started petting Gus.

The whole situation felt surreal, sitting beside the water and talking to Alex's daughter—this girl she hadn't met until the day before but whose existence had impacted Violet's life so dramatically.

"Was it weird to be a twin?" she asked, but she went on without giving Violet time to answer.

"I always wanted to have a twin sister. I used to pretend I did, especially after my mom and dad got divorced. I used to pretend maybe I had a twin who lived somewhere else and we could reunite so we could bring our parents together, like that *Parent Trap* movie. Did you see that?"

"A few times."

She and Lily had loved that film, the original and the remake, and had watched it often. They used to wish for the same thing, that they could somehow figure out how to fix their fractured family and bring them all together again.

"My parents divorced when I was twelve," she told Ariana. "My twin sister and I moved here to Cape Sanctuary with our mom while our older sister, Cami, stayed in LA with our dad to go to school. It was a really tough time. Hard on all of us."

After the divorce, she and Lily hadn't had much of a relationship with their older sister. Their lives had diverged, with Cami going to college at only seventeen and then straight into law school.

There had always been a little distance between them. It couldn't have been easy on Cami to be the older sister of twins.

Lily and Violet always had each other. They shared everything. Books, toys, a bedroom. Cami had always been slightly on the outside of that.

The custodial arrangements after the divorce had only widened that divide. All these years later, Violet didn't know how to bridge it.

She wanted to try, though. She thought of that moment earlier when Cami had squeezed her arm with sympathy and a lump rose in her throat.

She really could use a sister and a friend right about now and she suspected Cami felt the same.

Cami would be there only a few days while she tried to sort out the lease debacle, but maybe they could still try to forge a new relationship.

Ariana was telling her about other movies she liked when Violet spotted a tall figure approaching them across the sand.

She did her best to ignore the sudden loud pulse in her ears as Alex made his way to them.

Alex. Her first love.

Okay, her only love, if she were honest.

"I thought we were going for a walk together, but you just took off when my back was turned. You can't do that, kid. I didn't know where you guys went."

Ariana pointed at the dog. "I wanted to wait but Gus tugged away from me when I was putting his leash on. I guess he wanted to come over to talk to Violet."

She finally had no choice but to lift her gaze to his. He gave her an apologetic look.

"Sorry. Gus is still young and doesn't always behave like he should. I hope he wasn't bothering you."

"Not at all. He's a good dog." She petted Gus again and was rewarded by a slobbery lick on her arm.

"Hey, do you want to walk with us?" Ariana asked. "We're just going down to the jetty and then back home. Dad said he's been cooped up in the office all day and needs to move."

She didn't want to spend more time with the two of them. The bruise he had left on her heart a decade ago still ached.

She didn't want to hurt Ariana, though. The girl seemed to have a sweet, generous soul.

"Sure," she answered before she could think better of it. "I'll walk a little way with you. Then I have to head back."

As soon as they started off, she knew it was a mistake. It felt so familiar, walking beside him like this. How many hours had they spent on the beach together? Surfing, having bonfires with friends, making out?

All those memories seemed to come rushing back.

She forced the past away and focused on living in the moment. The sea air, cool on her face, the sun continuing to set, the waves washing against the shore.

"It's beautiful," she said. "On evenings like this, it's hard to believe the ocean can be so vicious."

He was quiet for a long moment, his features dark in the fading light. "I can never tell you enough how sorry I am about what happened."

The sincerity of his words somehow reached inside her like a warm blanket around all the cold places.

"Lily was a hero, Vi. Straight up. I don't know what I would have done if she hadn't been there that day. Because of Lily, my daughter has a future, and I will be forever grateful for that, but I hate that Lily had to pay the ultimate price."

Tears burned her eyes but she refused to let them fall. Not now. Not in front of him. "Thank you for that," she managed.

He sighed. "Look. I know you hate me. You have every reason to."

She wanted to protest that she didn't hate him. Their history was long and complicated, but it was just that. History.

"I'm sorry about last night. I wouldn't have gone over to Moongate Farm if I had known you were coming home early."

"You couldn't have known."

"Spending time with Ari seems to comfort your mom somehow, and my daughter enjoys being with Rosemary, too. But I don't want to make things more uncomfortable for you while you're home this summer. If you would prefer we didn't come around Moongate Farm, I'll try to respect that."

What was she supposed to say to that? *No. My fragile feelings can't handle you being anywhere near me.*

After a decade, she should be over the man, right?

"You don't have to stay away on my account." Her voice sounded stiff, awkward. "Mom told me last night what a big help you've been setting up the campground and how you've been working with her to take her guests out on whale watching charters. I don't see any reason that has to change, simply because I'm home."

He looked relieved. "Good. But if you decide otherwise, you'll let me know, right?"

"Sure," she said.

She would prefer not having to see him again while she was in Cape Sanctuary, but something told her that particular wish, like most of her others, had no chance of coming true.

7

CAMI

THE BEST DEFENSE WAS A GOOD OFFENSE.

Though certainly a cliché, it was also a lesson her father had reinforced over and over, one of his favorite legal strategies.

If that meant Cami had to face the threat to her sister's dream head-on, she would manage it. Even if she didn't want to.

She decided to walk to Franklin Rafferty's house the day after she arrived, instead of driving her rental car. Just a neighbor walking over the back fence to chat with a neighbor. She dressed casually but carefully, in a favorite feminine sundress with a floppy hat and sandals. No power suit or chunky jewelry here. She wanted to convey warm, nonthreatening friendliness.

On impulse, she grabbed a basket out of her mother's kitchen and filled it with extra scones from breakfast and a small jar of locally sourced wildflower honey her mother offered for sale to her guests.

Violet walked in just as she was hooking the harness and leash onto Baxter.

Her eyes had deeper shadows under them and her nose was suspiciously red, but Cami decided not to mention it. Violet had to grieve Lily's loss in her own way.

"You look nice. Where are you off to, Dorothy from Oz?"

She made a face, even as she realized she probably did look a little like Dorothy, with her sky blue sundress and gift basket. She even had the little dog.

She wasn't going to be traipsing down any Yellow Brick Road, though, picking up cowardly lions or tin men. She was only heading over the hill to chat with the neighbors on a lovely summer day.

"Taking a walk over to the Rafferty place to have a little chat about leases."

Violet tilted her head. "I'm sorry you had to come clean up Lily's mess. Thanks for coming to the rescue, though."

"I haven't done anything yet. I'm not sure if I can change anything. I don't have a lot of ammo here."

"Scones and honey are a good start."

"Let's hope so."

Baxter danced around on the end of his leash, eager to go. Cami tucked the picnic basket over her arm and her phone in the pocket of her sundress and walked outside the back door.

The day was truly glorious, with everything green and lush from a quick rainstorm during the night that had awakened her from the best sleep she'd had in months.

The air smelled of pine and sea and Rosemary's lavender plants lining the driveway.

Baxter sniffed at every plant and rock alongside the road as they walked the short distance to the neighboring house.

She wasn't looking forward to the upcoming interaction, mostly because she didn't know what to expect. Still, Cami could feel some of the tension seep away as she walked through the towering redwoods and lushly scented pine.

She always felt so conflicted when she visited Rosemary in Cape Sanctuary, as if two disparate parts of her psyche were warring ferociously. On the one hand, being back with her mother always seemed to dredge up all those old feelings of being an outsider.

On the other, the surroundings inevitably brought her peace. She found it difficult to hang on to stress and old grievances when surrounded by ocean and ancient trees.

She had never been to Franklin Rafferty's house, but it wasn't hard to find. A short distance from Moongate Farm, a long paved driveway led toward the sea. A mailbox beside it read simply Rafferty.

She walked several hundred yards up the driveway. Finally the trees opened up and the sight of the beautifully elegant house made her catch her breath.

The front door was through a small welcoming courtyard. It would have been lovely with a little maintenance.

After ringing the doorbell, she hitched her basket higher on her arm and waited for an answer.

An older man with vivid blue eyes and a shock of white hair opened the door a few moments later. He squinted with suspicion at her, then her basket. "What are you selling? I probably already have it. If I don't, I probably don't need it."

"I'm not selling anything, Mr. Rafferty. I'm Cami Porter. My mother is Rosemary Porter."

He frowned. "Cami? I don't remember a Cami. Rosemary has those twin girls. Tall, blonde. Pretty. You don't look anything like them."

Yes. She knew. She was the mutant baby changeling. Short, curvy, forgettable. The ugly duckling in a nest of leggy blondes.

"One of those girls died," he said suddenly before she could answer. "She drowned, I believe."

"Yes. That was my younger sister Lily. I'm Rosemary's oldest daughter."

"I don't remember seeing you around."

"I live in LA but I visit when I can."

"LA? Why would you want to live there with all the traffic and the people and the smog, when you could have this?"

He definitely had a point.

"May I come in, Mr. Rafferty? I brought you some of my mom's scones and some local honey."

His features brightened. "Oh. That sounds good. Come in."

"What about the dog?"

He looked down at Baxter. "Your dog looks just like your sister's."

"It's the same dog. This is Baxter."

"Hi, Baxter. You can come in, too, as long as you behave yourself and don't bother Cleo and Mark Antony. Those are my cats."

Franklin led her into the house. The entry had mail piled up on the console table and a pair of rubber boots haphazardly discarded. A curved staircase dominated the space, and several paintings that looked like original works of art hung on the walls.

He moved through a doorway that opened into a large bright kitchen with marble countertops and high-end appliances.

She again had the impression of luxurious neglect.

She had done some online research about Franklin Rafferty the night before so she might have some idea what she was up against. The few news articles that mentioned him usually referred to some court case or another, but she had found one feature article in a magazine focused on Northern California that talked about various generous donations to local arts organizations.

Her mother had told her the night before on their golf cart ride down to the house from the campground that Franklin came from wealth. The Rose Creek property, including the headland, the meadow and the beach down to the high water line, had been in his family for several generations. In fact, Rosemary had told her, Moongate Farm had once been part of the larger property but had been sold off by Franklin's father to Rosemary's great-aunt years ago.

She handed him the bag full of scones. He instantly shoved a hand in, pulled a blueberry one out and started chewing it.

"Your mother is a great cook. Reminds me of my wife. Elena makes the best lemon blueberry muffins. They melt in your mouth."

Cami frowned. During her internet search, she had found his wife's obituary and a news article about her death in the local paper. Elena Rafferty had died in a tragic car accident nearly twenty years earlier, when her car drove through a guardrail and plummeted into the ocean.

"I'll have to get the recipe." She tried to smile while disquiet pinched at her.

"I'm sure she's got it around here somewhere," he said with a wave around the cluttered kitchen. "I'll have to ask her. Sit down, why don't you?"

He pointed to a large rectangular kitchen table that looked French Provincial, then took a seat at the head of the table.

With Baxter following her, she perched on a nearby chair. The dog settled at her feet.

Meanwhile, Franklin finished off the scone in about four bites. "Thanks for that. Tell your mother it was delicious. I didn't realize I was so hungry."

"You're welcome."

He gave her a careful look. "Is that the only reason you dropped by? To bring me scones and say hello?"

The way he went straight to the heart of matters made her hope that lapse of memory, speaking about his wife as if she were still alive, was more the exception than the rule. It would make dealing with him so much easier.

She shook her head, deciding to be frank. "No, though I'm glad you enjoyed it. Mr. Rafferty, I need to speak with you about finalizing the lease agreement for the campground my sister and mother started on your property."

He picked out another scone from the bag. A raspberry one this time. "My son told me we need to talk to an attorney," he informed her, taking a big bite.

"Great. I'm an attorney!" she said cheerfully.

"Are you? I'm an attorney, too. Or at least I used to be."

His mouth drooped briefly but he took another bite of the scone.

"I know. I heard you were a good one, too."

"I tried to be. Wasn't always easy with some of the nonsense out there. People were always trying to take advantage of other folks. What kind of an attorney are you?"

"Contracts and intellectual property," she said. It might not be as sexy as clearing the name of an innocent person, but she was good at what she did.

"That's why I'm here," she went on. "I was hoping I could help you formally sign the lease agreement you verbally agreed to with my sister so we can make sure everything is in order."

"Tea sounds good," he said abruptly. "Wouldn't that be just right with these scones? Would you like some? I'll put the kettle on."

He didn't wait for an answer but rose abruptly and headed to the stove, where he retrieved a rather grimy kettle. He filled it from the sink, then returned it to the stovetop. For several seconds, he fiddled with the gas burner but couldn't seem to light it.

"This stupid thing," he muttered. "It never works."

She rose as well, leaving Baxter's leash looped over the finial of her chair. "May I see?"

He stepped aside, and she twisted the burner to ignite the flame, then reduced the heat so it wouldn't scorch the teapot.

"I guess you have the magic touch," he said as he sat back down.

"I guess so. Now, about the lease." She wasn't about to let herself be distracted. "I brought a copy of the original lease my sister prepared, which outlines the terms I assume you two talked about."

She set it down on the kitchen table in front of him. As he looked at it, a few flaky scone crumbs immediately sprinkled down on the paper. She didn't bother to wipe them away.

"I've contacted a notary who can be here in five minutes. It will only take a moment of your time and then I can get out of your way."

He picked up the pen, and for a moment, she thought things might be that easy.

After a pause, he set the pen down again, regret on his features.

"I would like to help you, but my son told me I shouldn't sign anything right now."

She frowned. The son again! Where was he, if he was so concerned about his father?

"Mr. Rafferty, have you given your son power of attorney for you?"

"No. Why would I do that?"

"If he doesn't have power of attorney, he can't stop you from signing something you verbally contracted to with my sister. Lily recorded your conversations on her phone. I have a recording of you agreeing to the land lease agreement for the Wild Hearts Luxury Camping LLC. I'm only asking you to please sign the legal documents you agreed to before my sister died so that Wild

Hearts legally can remain operational. You're an attorney. You understand about making sure everything is done properly."

"I don't know." He frowned. "Maybe I should ask Jonny first."

He looked up. "Oh, look. Here he is now. Jon, this is Rosemary Porter's older daughter. She's a lawyer. I'm sorry, dear. I forgot your name."

She turned around and felt the blood rush from her head.

Jon. Jonny. The same name as the sexy motorist with the flat tire she had helped the day before. Because his son Jon *was* the sexy motorist with the flat tire she had helped the day before.

He looked as hot as ever, though maybe a little less ragged at the edges. He had shaved off that dark beard and she thought he might have even trimmed his hair a little.

He still had one arm in the sling, though.

Had it really been a machete? She still wasn't sure if he had been truthful to her about that.

Wasn't it just her luck? The first gorgeous guy she had met in months was the very person she had been sent here to confront.

His eyes widened as he recognized her from the day before.

"Cami?" he said, his voice shocked.

"Yes. That's exactly her name," Franklin said triumphantly. "Cami Porter."

"You're the one who started this Moongate Farm glampground on the headland?"

He said the word with the same kind of distaste in his expression someone might have at finding a slug in their salad.

"I didn't start it. My sister Lily did."

"She drowned."

The blunt sentence from Franklin Rafferty drew her attention and his son's as well.

Baxter shifted at her feet, suddenly restless. Was it possible he knew they were talking about Lily? Impossible. He was smart but not that smart.

"Did she?"

"Yes. Four months ago. She was trying to rescue a couple of young girls hit by a superwave," Cami said.

The kettle started to whistle before he could answer.

"That's my tea." Franklin jumped up and hurried to the stove. Cami was a little worried he would hurt himself and was relieved when he grabbed a hot pad to pour water into a nearby mug.

"Anyone else want some?"

"None for me, thanks," Cami said.

Jon also shook his head.

Franklin set the kettle back on the stove, then, oddly, headed toward the door Jon had come through only moments before.

"I need to empty the tank before I drink more tea," he announced, then hurried out of the room, leaving an awkward silence between her and Jon Rafferty.

"I'm sorry about your sister," he said, his voice clipped. "That doesn't change the fact that the entire operation was illegally developed on private property."

She had hoped they could do this in a friendly way, without having to make things confrontational from the outset. Apparently Jon Rafferty wasn't going to play nice.

"Private property that your father agreed to lease to her."

"He says he doesn't remember signing any papers."

"He agreed to sign a lease but didn't have the chance before my sister died."

"That's very convenient for you and your family, isn't it?"

"Convenient that my sister is dead? No. Far from it. My mother has been left with the sole responsibility for running a glampground that is booked solid until October."

"Advance bookings can be canceled. All it takes is a phone call. You can even do it by email. Businesses cancel reservations all the time because of exigent circumstances."

"And what is my mother supposed to do with ten fully furnished luxury tents? Not to mention all the infrastructure they have paid for on the property."

"Maybe find somewhere else to put them. And next time, she should perhaps make sure she actually has a legal right to set up shop instead of trusting a verbal agreement made with a man in no mental state to sign any contracts."

"Has your father been formally diagnosed with dementia?"

A muscle worked in his jaw. "I'm trying to get him into specialists while we're here, but it's fairly obvious. You can't miss the signs. Your sister had to have noticed. I suspect she *did* know and used that knowledge to her advantage."

"What is that supposed to mean?" she asked sharply.

"Under normal circumstances, my father would never have agreed to allow strangers to traipse across my family's property. He always valued his privacy here at Rose Creek and believed the headland especially should be protected."

"People can change their minds."

"Or their minds can be changed for them, especially if they're in a vulnerable position to be manipulated."

Good thing Franklin hadn't given her tea or she might have tossed it straight into his son's face. How dare he imply Lily, her creative, funny, brave sister, somehow had taken advantage of his father!

She was beginning to wish she had left Jon Rafferty to rot on the side of the road with his flat tire and his injured arm.

"How can you presume to know what went on between my sister and your father? From what I hear, you haven't bothered to talk to him in years."

Even as she heard her words, Cami wanted to cringe. She was not going to win any wars by alienating Jon Rafferty. She needed him on her side. Her goal here was to persuade him that having a glampground on his property wouldn't cause any environmental harm and, indeed, was in his family's best interest.

She drew in a breath and tried to shove down her anger and annoyance. "Look," she said calmly. "Let's start over. My mother has asked me to approach you and see what we can do to work this out and come up with a formal lease agreement."

"Nothing," he snapped. "You're wasting your time."

She frowned. He wasn't leaving her much room to negotiate here. If he was going to take a hard-line position, Cami wasn't sure there was anything she could do to change his mind.

"I have a recording of a verbal agreement between your father and my sister. In addition, Wild Hearts Luxury Camping LLC has paid in full for this calendar year to lease two acres. Your father has deposited that check and spent it, for all I know."

She could see that surprised him. Pressing her advantage, she pulled the bank records out of her bag and presented them to him with a flourish, grateful she at least had those for verification purposes.

He looked at the amounts and sent her a disbelieving look. "Six thousand dollars. Five hundred dollars a month. That's ridiculous."

"For undeveloped acreage? I don't think so. My understanding is the property has a conservation easement so no permanent structures ever can be constructed on the bluff and it's not suitable for agriculture use. My mother acted in good faith when she moved forward erecting the tent sites on the property, knowing my sister had verbal confirmation from your father to the agreement and that money had changed hands. A formal lease agreement is only a technicality that would certainly have been in place if my sister hadn't died."

"My father has all the signs of mild to moderate dementia," he snapped. "Something like that doesn't come on overnight. He couldn't have been in his right mind when this so-called conversation took place, no matter what recording your sister may have made of it."

She tightened her hands into fists. "I only had a brief chat with your father, but he seems perfectly competent to me. Lovely, even."

Before she finished speaking, Franklin came walking back into the kitchen wearing only a pair of rather ragged boxer shorts along with the cardigan and blue oxford shirt he'd been wearing earlier.

His legs were thin, pale and hairy, and Cami couldn't help noticing he wore one black sock and one white one.

"Did either of you change your mind about tea?" he asked, walking toward the stove.

Jon made a strangled sound in his throat. "Dad. Your pants."

Franklin looked over his shoulder with a furrowed brow. "What about my pants?"

"Where are they?"

Franklin gazed around in confusion. "I'm not sure. Did I have them earlier?"

Cami stood frozen for a moment, torn between horror and compassion. Jon was right. As much as she wanted to believe Lily had pursued the lease agreement in good faith, it was obvious that Franklin Rafferty couldn't have been in any fit state to sign a contract.

Right now, the bigger issue was helping the man regain his dignity.

"Let's go find them," she said gently. "I'll help you."

"You don't have to do that," Jon protested. "Come on, Dad."

"She said she would help me." Franklin's voice had a definite stubborn note. "Anyway, you have a bad arm."

"I don't mind," Cami said.

He had left the water in the sink running as well, so it wasn't difficult to find the bathroom. His slacks were lying in a crumpled heap on the floor in front of the toilet.

"There they are," Franklin exclaimed. He didn't seem at all embarrassed to be caught in his underwear. He simply grabbed his slacks and pulled them on again and fastened the zipper.

"There you go. Did you wash your hands?"

"I'm not sure. I'll do it again."

He scrubbed his hands, humming a little song she didn't recognize, then turned off the faucet, dried them off and headed out of the bathroom.

"I'm ready for that tea now. Maybe even another scone. That really hit the spot. Be sure to tell Rosemary, won't you?"

"Of course."

Jon was waiting in the hallway, as if he didn't trust her not to convince his father to sign the lease agreement if they were out of his sight.

"Perfectly competent?" he said, his voice low, as Franklin returned to the kitchen ahead of them. "Weren't those the words you used?"

She really hated when people threw her own words back at her. "Okay. Maybe not perfectly. But you have no evidence my sister knew that."

She had to believe Lily wouldn't have deliberately taken advantage of the situation.

They stood in the hall outside the kitchen. Inside, they could hear Franklin humming again as he grabbed his tea and took a seat at the table.

Nothing good would come of antagonizing the son. With this tension between them, she would have no chance of keeping the glampground on Rose Creek land.

"I'm sorry," she said, nodding toward the kitchen and Franklin. "It must be terribly difficult to see him like this."

His mouth tightened. "My father and I have not been close for many years."

Yet he apparently had hurried home from Central America straight out of surgery so that he could take care of him. It was difficult to view a man willing to do that as the enemy.

"He's still your father. It's still not an easy situation."

"No. It's not. And to find out people whom he trusted might have taken advantage of his vulnerability only makes it harder."

She closed her eyes, trying to wrestle her temper down. "Look,

I wasn't here during their conversation and I haven't listened to the recording yet, but I have to believe my sister thought she was negotiating in good faith. I know my sister. Lily would not have taken advantage of your father's condition."

"I'll have to take your word for that. I didn't know your sister. All I know is how it looks from the outside."

What was her best strategy for coming out with a win here for her mother?

Ordinarily she would never show her hand to someone on the other side of a case. The person with the most to lose in any negotiation automatically came from a position of weakness.

She decided to go against her lawyerly instincts and tell him the truth.

"I know this isn't your biggest concern right now. That's completely understandable. But my mother is heavily invested in my sister's dream of this campground. She mortgaged Moongate Farm to help Lily buy the tents and the furnishings for them. If you shut them down and evict them from the property, my mother will be ruined. There's a good chance she might lose everything. Is there any way I can convince you to let the verbal lease agreement stand?"

8

JON

HE WAS RIDICULOUSLY WEAK WHEN IT CAME to soft, curvy women with big blue eyes and kind smiles.

Right now, as Cami Porter looked up at him in the hallway outside the kitchen, Jon wanted to give her anything she wanted.

He couldn't stop thinking of how gently she had led his father into the bathroom and helped him with his slacks, then reminded him to wash his hands.

Either she was playing a very deep game or Cami Porter was an inherently kind woman.

She had helped Jon the day before, simply because he had been a stranded motorist trying to change a flat with a bum arm. By the surprise she had tried to hide when he walked into the kitchen earlier, he was quite certain she hadn't known his identity then.

All evidence indicated she had stopped to help purely because she had seen a need, unless she was an exceptionally fine actress.

That didn't mean he was willing to let her family take advantage of his father.

"Not happening," he said firmly. He didn't want to be a jerk about things, but he was the only one left who could protect his father and his family's legacy.

She studied him with a frustrated expression. He could almost see the wheels spinning in her head as she tried to figure out where to go next.

"What if we doubled the lease amount? It will cut into the campground's slim profit margin, but we can figure out a way to make it work."

"This isn't about the money."

She looked skeptical. "If I've learned one thing since passing the bar, it's always about the money."

"Not in this case. My father does not need the stress of a bunch of strangers traipsing across his land."

"That's it? No room for discussion?"

"Do you mind if I eat this last scone?" Franklin called from the kitchen.

Jon's stomach rumbled. He had hardly eaten since his arrival the night before, too busy trying to make appointments for his father with the leading neurologists in the area.

He would grab something when she left.

"Go ahead. Enjoy it," he replied.

When he looked over, he found his father already eating the scone. Good thing he hadn't wanted it.

"Can I give the dog a bite?" he asked.

"Better not," Cami said. "I don't know what is safe to feed him and what's not."

Franklin apparently accepted that, though he didn't look happy about it.

Cami turned back to Jon. "I'm going to be honest with you. My mother doesn't have the emotional resources to fight this legal battle with you, but financially, she can't afford not to. If you try to evict her right now, we will countersue and I will play the recording of your father agreeing to the terms of the lease he and my sister discussed. I am one hundred percent certain we will win, even without a notarized lease agreement."

"You can't be a hundred percent certain of anything. A judge only has to have a five-minute conversation with my father to figure out he's not competent to agree to anything. Every judge in the region has to know him well from his years as an attorney before them. They will see the difference in him immediately."

"That might be true. But I'll be certain to bring up the inarguable fact that, as of today, your father has no medical diagnosis. He certainly didn't six months ago when he and my sister first negotiated the lease agreement in good faith."

So much for being inherently kind. Right now, Cami Porter was a shark going right for the throat.

His arm throbbed but he wasn't about to show any sign of weakness.

"Good faith? His condition couldn't have come on overnight. Your sister must have known something was up, especially when he didn't sign the lease agreement."

"You weren't even in the country. How can you possibly argue that he wasn't competent when you haven't spoken with him in years?"

That bite found his jugular.

She was right. He hadn't been home. He had been off pursuing his own dreams while his father was alone at Rose Creek with his ghosts.

He wanted the campground off his family's land by tomorrow and had no doubt that he would eventually win, no matter how persuasive she was.

He had enough to deal with right now and didn't really want to engage in a long and costly legal war with his father's neighbors.

He also wasn't completely unreasonable. He was willing to make concessions to clear this up quickly and definitely so he could focus on finding the best possible care for Franklin.

"From what I understand, your campground is only open from mid-May to early November. Is that right?"

"Yes."

"What if we give you until the end of this season to find another location and recoup the initial investment? After that, everything needs to go."

She didn't seem to appreciate the concession, which he considered a huge one, considering he wanted them out right now.

"It isn't that easy to simply pack up and move an entire tent village somewhere else."

"Isn't it? That's kind of the point of them, isn't it? They're not permanent structures, so they should be easy enough to move somewhere else."

Anywhere else.

She looked down at the papers in her hand and then at his father. He couldn't tell what was going on in her head, but after a long moment, she sighed.

"Giving my mother until November is better than serving her with an eviction notice right now, I suppose."

Her begrudging tone almost made him smile. He wasn't finding too many things humorous since he had driven back to Cape Sanctuary, the last place on earth he wanted to spend any time.

He was becoming increasingly aware of how much his father had needed him here. He should have come home long before now.

The house was falling into disrepair, bills hadn't been paid, his father had lost weight, probably because he forgot to eat.

Would he have been able to help earlier? Jon wasn't sure.

He had stayed away from Cape Sanctuary because his father *told* him to stay away. Whatever he thought about his father, Jon did not want this fate for him.

Did Franklin understand what was happening to him? Could he feel the memories slipping away like driftwood on the tide?

Jon hadn't been here long enough to figure that out.

"I will prepare an official lease agreement with the new terms and bring a notary back. It's nebulous who should sign it, as I'm assuming you have not attained guardianship or power of attorney for him yet."

"No," he admitted. "I'm not sure where to start. We're meeting with my father's law partner tomorrow."

She couldn't hide the sympathy in her expression. "It will be easier once you have an official diagnosis. At that point, you'll need to go through the court system to seek legal and medical guardianship. A guardian ad litem will be appointed to represent your father. The ad litem will go through the medical paperwork and interview your father as well, to assess his competence."

"Thanks for the information, though I have to admit I'm not sure why you're being so helpful."

She shrugged. "Because I like to think I'm an inherently nice person. The kind who stops to help wounded strangers fix their tires."

She gave him a pointed look, then walked into the kitchen. "I'm leaving now, Mr. Rafferty," she said to his father. "It was nice to meet you."

"Do you have to take the dog?" he asked. The curly-haired little dog she had brought along was now sitting on his father's lap, clearly enjoying the company.

Jon didn't quite know what to think about that, considering his father always claimed he didn't like dogs. Jon had one anyway when he was a kid, a large black Labrador his father had basically ignored.

"I'm afraid I do," she said.

"I hope you come visit again. You can bring the dog and more scones."

"I'll do that."

She smiled brightly at both of them, then walked to the door with a basket over her arm and the little dog trotting behind.

Jon watched her head back along the trail to Moongate Farm, telling himself he had absolutely no reason to feel forlorn.

9

VIOLET

HER MOTHER WAS NOT HAPPY. AND WHEN Rosemary was not happy, Violet knew everyone needed to watch out.

Her mother might seem like a go-with-the-flow nature girl, but her temper could make the air crackle and birds stop singing in the garden.

She was never cruel or vicious and rarely raised her voice in anger, but that was somehow worse, like tiptoeing around a seething hot volcano, bubbling with fiery lava on the inside but placid and calm on the outside.

She and Lily used to joke that they could always tell when

to leave their mother alone by the way her mouth would flatten into a thin line and her eyes would turn blue and stormy.

Lily.

She almost pressed a hand to her chest but stopped herself just in time. How was it possible that she missed her twin more every day?

The day had been a hard one. Violet had volunteered to work on the Wild Hearts social media properties, as Rosemary hadn't had a chance to even look at them.

Several of the guests had checked out that day, so she used the time before the new guests checked in to take photographs of different details in the individual tents so she could potentially post those.

She had felt her twin's presence all day, as strongly as if Lily walked beside her, chattering with excitement as she showed off the dream she had created.

She wasn't sure if she was strong enough to do this all summer long.

"How can you possibly say it's not bad news? It's a complete disaster," Rosemary said now to Cami.

While her mother's voice might be level, her expression matched the dangerous intensity of her words.

"Not completely," Cami said. "I was able to buy you several more months, to the end of the season. At least you don't have to vacate by the end of the week. That's better, isn't it?"

Rosemary gripped her napkin so hard, her knuckles turned white. "What's the difference? This week or November? We still have to close the campground eventually. All this work I've done. All the work your *sister* did. All for nothing."

"Not for nothing." Cami seemed contained, her emotions wrapped tightly away. Did she ever lose her composure? Violet wondered.

Though Violet loved her sister, she didn't understand her sometimes.

She had always seemed so mature for her age. Violet couldn't remember Cami ever really playing with her and Lily. She always seemed to be reading or doing homework or watching something boring and educational on TV.

Cami was an avid reader and always had a book with her. Even when they used to go to the playground when they were young, Cami would stretch out on a blanket with her book while Violet and Lily played on the slides, pumped on the swings to see who could go higher, chased each other through the grass.

Cami had been scary smart, one of those children who spoke like a small adult.

Their parents had always treated her differently. Ted had adored her. The two of them had a bond that Lily and Violet could never hope to match.

Violet and Lily had naturally shared a room while Cami had her own, so Cami wasn't in on the late-night talks or the occasional squabbles over personal space or scrunchies.

She and Lily had been their own little unit, with secrets and inside jokes. The Twins. That's what they were always called, by Rosemary and Ted and by family friends. Everyone referencing the children in their family would call them Cami and the Twins. If they had been at all musically inclined, that probably would have been their band name. Cami and the Twins.

Their lives since then had taken different tracks, but they were still sisters. They had both lost their other sister.

"Not for nothing," Cami repeated to Rosemary. "It was a big concession on his part, as he wants the campground gone tomorrow. With the profit gained through one season of paying guests, you should be able to recoup most of the capital expenses for the tents and furniture, right?"

Rosemary made a small scornful sound that Cami ignored.

"It's better than closing by the end of the week and having to repay all those people who gave deposits for their stay," she pointed out. "Plus, you now have the gift of time. While I'm not optimistic about it, there's always a chance you can change Jon's mind and he will allow the verbal agreement Lily made with his father to continue. If not, you have four and a half months to look for somewhere else for the glampground."

"Where? The Rose Creek headland was perfect! A gorgeous view, secluded sites in the pines, historic redwoods—not to mention easy access to Moongate Farm so I can provide breakfast to our guests. How am I going to find that all over again?"

"Maybe there's somewhere else even more perfect," Cami said with a determined smile.

She was wasting her time, Violet wanted to tell her. Rosemary wanted the glampground at the headland and nowhere else would do.

"I don't know what to tell you. I did my best," Cami said. She sounded tired. Was her sister having the same kind of trouble sleeping that had beset Violet since Lily's death?

"I'm sure you did, dear," Rosemary said. "What about legal action? We do have the verbal agreement, even if it wasn't notarized. Do we have any recourse there?"

Cami frowned. "I would like to say yes, but I don't think you can count on winning that argument. Franklin Rafferty is not of sound mind. I can't see any judge allowing any agreement within the past year to stand, especially when his son, acting as his legal representative, opposes it."

"Oh, come now. *Not of sound mind?* He's a little forgetful. That's all. Gracious. *I'm* a little forgetful."

"It's more than that, Mom. I was only around the man for a half hour and it was obvious something was amiss. He didn't seem to have any social filter and he bounced between the past and the present more than once."

Oh, how sad. While Violet hadn't interacted much with their neighbor, he had always seemed kind to her and Lily.

He had also been very generous in allowing her and Lily to use the path across his property to the ocean.

He had sent them congratulatory high school graduation cards, she remembered, including a nice little cash gift for each. They had thanked him by making homemade white chocolate macadamia nut cookies, which he had claimed were the best he'd ever tried.

"I see him at least once a week and he always seems perfectly sweet," Rosemary went on.

"Sometimes when you see someone regularly, it's not as easy to notice changes over time. His son seemed shocked at his behavior."

"He wouldn't have been, if he had bothered to come home. He hasn't been back in years. I wish he'd stayed away," Rosemary muttered. "Why did he have to return and muck everything up?"

"I can't answer that. Regardless of his reasons, I expect Jon Rafferty will be obtaining legal and medical power of attorney for his father soon, which ultimately gives him the right to make all the decisions regarding use of the property."

Rosemary looked hopeful. "Which means he doesn't have those things now, right?"

"Not yet. It's only a matter of days. Maybe a few weeks."

"Meanwhile, Franklin could still legally sign our lease agreement. What if we arrange for that before Jon is able to push for guardianship?"

Cami gave her a long look. "We can't. If I hadn't talked to him myself, we might have been able to pull it off, but knowingly encouraging a man with dementia to sign paperwork wouldn't be legal, ethical or moral. No judge would uphold the agreement."

Rosemary's sigh was forceful enough to flutter the petals of the wildflowers stuck into a Mason jar on the table.

"You're right. It was a dumb idea. I guess that's that, then. Your sister's dream, reduced to rubble."

"It's not rubble yet." Violet finally spoke. "You're booked out every weekend from now to Halloween. I've been going over the books. Lily at least kept good records. I have to admit, I'm surprised."

"Why would that surprise you?" Rosemary asked. "Your sister was passionate about the glampground. From the beginning, she was determined to make it a success."

Her eyes filled with tears. "I can't bear to see that dream die with her. I feel like I've failed her."

Cami reached for their mother's hand. "Her dream doesn't have to die. That's what I'm saying. I've done the math. Keep it going through the summer, pay back the second mortgage you took out for capital outlay. Then you'll be in a much better place to figure out what to do for next season."

Rosemary wiped at her eyes, looking completely defeated. "What other choice do I have?"

"You could close it today. Refund everyone's deposits and sell the tents and furnishings to someone else. Another glampground, maybe," Cami said. "You might lose some money, but you would probably get most of your investment back."

"I'm not doing that." Rosemary wiped at her eyes again, her look of defeat sliding into one of determination. "Your sister worked too hard to make Wild Hearts a success. I'm not closing it down before we even have the chance to see what we can do."

"Good for you," Violet said. "You know I'm here to do whatever I can to help."

"And who knows? Maybe Jon will see how much happiness Wild Hearts is bringing to those who stay there and he will change his mind."

"Maybe," Cami said, though Violet could tell by her expression that she didn't believe that for a second.

"Will you excuse me, girls?" Rosemary said, that determination still in her voice. "I'm going out to work in the garden while I still have daylight. It's an excellent way to work out aggression. Maybe if I spend an hour yanking weeds, I can be a little more calm before the evening social hour."

"I'm sorry I couldn't deliver a better outcome," Cami said.

"It's not your fault. I know you tried your best."

Rosemary smiled, though it looked slightly wobbly, then hurried away.

As soon as she left, Cami sighed deeply.

"Are you going to tell me I should have tried harder?" she asked Violet.

"Why would I do that? I'm sure you did what you could."

"What a mess. Why didn't Lily make sure she had a formal lease agreement? That should have been the very first step in her business plan."

Though she completely agreed, she couldn't fight the instinct to defend Lily. She supposed old habits died hard. She had been sticking up for her twin since they were old enough to talk.

"Not all of us are lucky enough to be perfect," Vi said flatly.

As soon as she said the words, she regretted them when Cami's cheeks turned pink. Was that a sore spot with her sister?

"I know that," Cami mumbled.

"If she hadn't died, things probably would have been different. She would have made sure the lease was legal and secure."

"If she hadn't died, we wouldn't be having this conversation. You would be in Sacramento and I would be in LA taking depositions and trying not to go out of my mind with boredom."

Now Cami was the one who looked like she regretted her words.

Violet raised an eyebrow. "I thought you loved your work."

"I do," Cami said quickly. "I'm just going through a little existential crisis right now. Lily's death has thrown me off balance. I'm sure it's nothing like what you're going through."

Despite their somewhat distant relationship, Cami had always been kind to her. After that disastrous summer when everything fell apart, she had escaped to LA for a change of scenery and to get away from Cape Sanctuary. She and Cami had a great time together, she remembered. They had taken sightseeing bus tours, had hung out at Venice Beach, had visited the Getty and the Broad museums.

When she returned to school after that summer, Violet had thrown herself into the social whirl, determined to prove to everyone that her heart wasn't completely broken. By then, Cami was a second-year law student. Their busy schedules had once more pushed them apart.

Violet should have tried harder. It saddened her that the two of them had this awkward, hesitant relationship.

"So what comes next for you?" Cami asked. "You're planning to spend your entire school break here?"

Vi thought of Alex living just down the hill with his daughter and wondered how she would be able to survive living in the same zip code again after all these years.

How stupid of her not to put more weight into how awkward things might become when she agreed to come back to Cape Sanctuary to help Rosemary. She wanted to think she had managed to forget Alex completely over the past decade. In truth, it was only her raw grief over Lily's death that seemed to have pushed everything else out of her head.

Again, she had the overwhelming urge to pack up her car and flee back to Sacramento.

She couldn't, of course. Rosemary was counting on her.

She forced a smile now for Cami. "Sure. Why not? Most people would jump at the chance to spend the summer in these beautiful surroundings."

"You and Mom surely can't do everything yourselves."

Vi shrugged. "We won't be. Mom has hired a couple of people for the housekeeping. She'll handle the cooking side of things and I'll focus on human resources, guest relations and social media."

"Is that all?" Cami gave a little laugh. "I don't know how you're going to do it, especially when you add in Mom's yoga retreats."

"She has backed off on those for now, which is how we were lucky enough to be able to stay at the bunkhouse. It will be a lot of work, but I'm sure we'll manage somehow."

A wild idea hit like her students swarming around her desk after Christmas vacation.

No. It was impossible.

But then she remembered that thread of discontent she had heard in Cami's voice when she talked about her work.

It was worth a try, wasn't it?

"Of course," she ventured, "you could always stay longer. The ceremony to honor Lily as Citizen of the Year during Summer Sanctuary is only a few weeks away. You could always stay until that's over. Like you said, Mom could definitely use more help around here."

Cami seemed stunned at the suggestion, as if Violet had asked her to parasail off the top of the headland. "Stay longer?"

"Sure. Why not? That way, you could make sure the temporary lease agreement is solid and Jon Rafferty doesn't try to pull a fast one on Mom."

Cami didn't look convinced. "I could always look over the documents from LA through a little thing called email."

"True. But it's not the same as you being here in person to monitor the situation. Anyway, Mom would never ask, but I know she would appreciate having you here, for emotional support, if nothing else."

"I…I can't just drop everything. I have clients. Hearings. Negotiations."

Violet had a feeling Cami was trying to convince herself, more than anyone.

She held her breath, astonished at how much she suddenly wanted Cami around for a few more weeks. Summer at the Cape would be much more bearable if she could have her sister at her side.

"How hard would it be to rearrange all those things? You said it yourself. Email is a thing. So are virtual meetings."

"True."

Cami gazed at her for several seconds, then looked out the window of the kitchen, where Rosemary was heading out to her vegetables wearing her floppy gardening hat and gloves.

Finally, Cami looked back at Violet. "I told the firm I needed a week to take care of the lease issues. I didn't know how long it would take."

"Great. So all you would have to do is add a few more days to that and you would almost be to the Summer Sanctuary event."

"I suppose I could try to rearrange a few things," Cami said slowly. "I slept better last night than I have in months. A change of scenery might be just what I need."

Violet almost couldn't believe what she was hearing. Had she really managed to convince Cami to stick around for a few more weeks? She gave herself an internal high five, thoroughly pleased with herself.

"Fantastic. Mom will be absolutely thrilled to have more time with you. So will I."

Cami blinked at that, then gave her a tentative smile.

Violet held out her hand. "As temporary human resources manager for Wild Hearts Luxury Camping, let me be the first to say *welcome aboard.*"

10

CAMI

SO MUCH FOR CURING HER INSOMNIA.

Cami overslept the next day, something she rarely did. She chalked it up to all the tossing and turning she did during the night while she tried to figure out why she had ever agreed to stay longer in Cape Sanctuary.

She still didn't have a good answer to that. She didn't even like it here.

All of Violet's arguments seemed logical enough. It made sense to stick around at least until the temporary lease agreement was in the books. And her mother clearly needed help with the glampground.

That still didn't explain why she had rashly agreed to stick around a little longer.

She had been up until the early hours of the morning going over her schedule for the next few weeks and emailing Joe about everything that would have to be rearranged.

When she did finally fall asleep, she slept hard and ended up dozing through her alarm.

By the time she quickly dressed, raced to the farmhouse and pushed open the door of the kitchen, the clock on the microwave read nearly 8:30.

In the dining room down the hall, she could hear the clink of glasses and muted conversation as guests enjoyed breakfast.

"Good morning," Rosemary said with a cheery smile. Apparently she had decided to forgive Cami for failing to persuade Jon Rafferty to change his mind.

Her mother looked beautiful, hair pulled back into a braid and her skin luminous.

"How was your night?" Rosemary asked.

Cami barely refrained from grunting as she headed straight for the coffee maker.

Only after the first glorious sip did she trust herself to speak. "Sorry I'm so late. I meant to be here an hour ago to help you with the breakfast rush, but I guess I overslept. I'm here now. What can I do?"

"About half of the guests have already had breakfast, which is quite early this morning. I think everyone is eager to go off on their adventures for the day. You can eat your own breakfast, if you want."

"I'm here to help."

"Thank you, then." Her mother gestured to the coffee maker. "Why don't you take the coffee out and see if anyone needs topping off? Then you can cut up a few more bananas and strawberries for the yogurt parfaits. Grab an apron in the pantry."

She found one with the colorful logo for Wild Hearts, two

entwined hearts under what was clearly a tent. She felt vaguely self-conscious as she headed for the dining room, coffeepot in hand.

Though she'd had full academic scholarships to undergrad and law school and her father had given her a healthy stipend for other expenses, Cami had worked as a waitress in a café when she was at school for extra spending money. It seemed a lifetime ago, yet it all came rolling back as she walked into the dining room to face her mother's guests.

The demographics in the breakfast room surprised her. She didn't know what she was expecting, but it wasn't the well-dressed couples at various stages of finishing the meal. They were older than she might have thought would be drawn to a camping trip. Then again, Wild Hearts didn't offer the usual run-of-the-mill drafty pup tent experience.

They all smiled at her with a friendliness she didn't expect.

She made her way around the tables, refilling coffee and making polite conversation. At the last table, a woman with short gray hair stopped Cami before she could move on.

"These croissants are fantastic. I think they're even better than the ones I had in Paris a few years ago."

"I'll be sure to tell Rosemary."

"Yes. Definitely. I would love to know what she puts in that jam to make it pop. It's not raspberry, but I can't put my finger on what it might be."

"Huckleberries, I believe." An educated guess, as huckleberry jam was one of Rosemary's specialties.

"Everything was so delicious," the man at the table said. He had a thick Spanish accent and a wide smile. "I had to have a second helping of all of it and would have gone back for a third if Barbara had not stopped me."

"I'm glad you're enjoying your stay."

"So much," a woman at a nearby table chimed in. "I slept

better last night than I can remember. The bed was so comfortable. Between that and the ocean sounds, it was heavenly."

"Agreed," one of the two men the next table over said. "Can you tell us if Cape Sanctuary has a farmers' market?"

She was the last person to give tourist advice around here. These people probably knew more about this area of Northern California than Cami did.

As she thought about it, she suddenly had a few memories of trips to the farmers' market, where Rosemary would come away with fresh flowers, goat milk soap and plump blackberries, when she and the twins would drink lemonade made from hand-squeezed lemons.

"They used to have one on Tuesday night and Saturday morning, but I'm not sure if that's still the case. I'll be honest—I am only visiting from LA to help out my family. Let me check with my mother and I'll get right back with you."

"Thank you," the man said.

She returned to the kitchen to find Rosemary pulling another tray of croissants from the oven. The smell made her mouth water.

"Everyone is raving about breakfast," she reported. "And some guests are wondering if Cape Sanctuary still has a farmers' market. You know I'm hopelessly ignorant about what goes on in town."

"Yes, to the market. It's still the same as always. Every Tuesday night and Saturday morning. I used to go on Tuesdays to sell my extra vegetables, but now that we have guests, I'm using up everything I can grow and then some."

"I'll let them know."

"Here. Take these fresh croissants. Let me transfer them to a plate for you."

"I can do that."

As she used tongs to carefully arrange the pastries on a cut glass platter, Cami ignored the grumble of her stomach. She would grab something later, after she had helped out with breakfast for the guests.

The pastries earned delighted exclamations. She reported what she had learned about the farmers' market and was about to head back to the kitchen when she spotted something out of place through the window of the dining room.

A person was standing in the middle of her mother's vegetable garden. At first, she thought it might be one of the guests stopping to admire the bounty there on the way from the glampground to the house for breakfast.

She squinted, then frowned with concern when she recognized the garden visitor.

It wasn't a guest. Franklin Rafferty was standing in the middle of her mother's garden, looking lost.

Oh dear.

She was almost certain he wasn't supposed to be there. She set down the plate of croissants for the guests and hurried outside.

She found him picking pea pods, splitting them open and popping the peas into his mouth.

He didn't notice her at first. She had to speak twice to get his attention. "Mr. Rafferty. Hello. Is everything okay?"

He gave her a blank stare for a moment, then looked down at the pea pod in his trembling hand. "Grandmother's garden is coming in nicely this year, don't you think?"

Oh. Right. She sometimes forgot that Moongate Farm had once belonged to the Rafferty family. They had sold the house and a few surrounding acres to Rosemary's great-aunt and -uncle years ago.

Should she correct him or simply go with it? She went on instinct and opted for the later. "It's lovely," she answered gently. "Look at all those bean vines."

"Looks like we'll have a good tomato crop, too."

He split open another pea pod with his thumb and raked out the raw peas inside.

"Mr. Rafferty, would you like some breakfast?" she asked impulsively. "There's quiche, I believe, and my mother made some delicious croissants."

His eyes lit up. "I *am* hungry."

"Come with me, then."

She slipped her hand through the crook of his elbow before he could wander off again.

"Does your son know where you are this morning?"

He gave her a confused look. "My son is in Central America. He's an archaeologist. He's exploring a lost city in the jungle."

By that, she inferred he had not bothered to tell Jon he was leaving. Unfortunately, she did not have the man's cell phone number.

"Did you bring a phone with you, by any chance?" Perhaps he might have his son's mobile number listed on his phone.

He felt in his pockets, then shook his head with a guilty sort of look. "I'm always forgetting the blasted thing. I'm sorry, dear."

"Don't worry about it," she told him as they walked inside. She would have to figure out another way to reach out. She didn't want to leave Jon worrying about where his father might have gone.

When they walked inside the farmhouse, Franklin stopped to take a dramatic inhalation. "Oh, it *does* smell good in here. I guess I was more hungry than I thought."

She smiled, charmed by him. "You're in luck. My mother is an excellent cook."

"My mother was a good cook, too. She made the best apple pie in the entire county. Won a blue ribbon at the county fair for it, too. I miss that apple pie. And my mother, of course. I miss her every day."

His voice held a note of sincerity that made Cami a little sad. She wanted that kind of loving relationship with her mother but feared some part of her would always remain a fourteen-year-old girl struggling to understand why she had been left behind.

She needed to let those feelings go and appreciate what she had right now.

The advice, like everything in life, was easier said than done.

At least Frank seemed to be once more in the present.

They walked together into the kitchen just as Rosemary pulled something out of the oven.

The kitchen smelled of onions and mushrooms and gooey cheese.

"We have one more for breakfast. Would you happen to have enough for Mr. Rafferty?"

Her mother looked up after lowering the casserole dish to a cooling rack. "Franklin! I wondered when you were going to stop by again. It's great to see you. Sit down, sit down. Cami, can you grab our friend some coffee? He takes it black with two sugars."

"I'd like the real stuff, but all you ever have is that organic crap."

"Which is much better for you," Rosemary retorted. "We have quiche and croissants today, or I can fix your usual scrambled eggs and toast."

"Quiche sounds good, if you've got any to spare, Rosie."

"Coming right up."

While Cami poured him coffee, her mother bustled away to cut a section from the dish she had just removed from the oven, chatting away to their neighbor.

The affection between them was unmistakable.

"Does he drop by often for breakfast?" she asked Rosemary in a low voice while Franklin inhaled the quiche.

Her mother shrugged. "Two or three times a week. I feed him and then take him home when breakfast is over. I think he's lonely up at that house by himself. Now that his son is home, I didn't really expect to see him much. I'm glad I was wrong."

That reminded her. Cami needed to figure out how to reach Jon, in case he was worrying about his father. "Is there a landline at Rose Creek? Franklin didn't bring a cell phone with him and I need to let Jon know where to find him."

"Good idea. Yes. The number is on the bulletin board next to the desk right there."

Rosemary pointed to a small organizational area of the kitchen, where a laptop rested among bills, correspondence and an earthenware jar containing pencils and pens of every size and color.

She found Franklin's name along with two phone numbers. She dialed the one listed under *home*, which rang six times before going to voice mail. She had worse luck with his cell number, which didn't even ring before going to voice mail, indicating his phone was likely switched off.

Cami sighed. She was going to have to go searching for Jon. She couldn't leave him to worry about his father.

"Mom, are you okay for a minute? I should go try to find Franklin's son, in case he's out looking for him."

"Good idea. Don't worry about me. I'm perfectly fine. I handle breakfast by myself most mornings. And Vi should be up soon. Both of you were sleepyheads today."

"That's because the beds are too damn comfortable."

Rosemary smiled, clearly delighted.

"Take the golf cart to find Jon. You can cover more ground. The key is over there."

If she could figure out a way to avoid it, she would. Right now, she couldn't see another choice. She grabbed the key off the rack and headed outside, where the golf carts were parked between the house and the barn. She found the one that said "Office" across the front. Soon, she was driving up the wide trail between the two properties.

When she crested the hill where the trail forked, with one side going to the campground and the other to the Rafferty land, she saw a man standing on a large rock that gave a better vantage point, sweeping the terrain with what appeared to be a pair of high-powered binoculars.

When he spotted her, he jumped down and hurried over, his eyes anxious. He smelled delicious, she couldn't help noticing, of cedar and pine and sexy male.

"Have you seen my father? He was still in bed, so I took the chance to jump in the shower. I was only in there ten minutes, but by the time I came out, he was gone."

Cami didn't want to think about Jon Rafferty in any kind of shower. She especially didn't want to think about wet hair or glossy, taut skin glistening with water droplets.

"He's fine. He's sitting in my mother's kitchen right now, eating breakfast."

His features softened with relief.

"He can't just wander off like that! I worried he might have fallen over the cliffs into the water."

"I found him in my mom's garden munching on peas. No harm done."

"Except to my nerves."

His worry over his father touched a chord deep inside her, especially given what she had heard about their tumultuous relationship.

She didn't want to think that Jon Rafferty might be softer than first impressions would indicate.

"Hop in. I'll give you a ride back to the house. If you haven't eaten, you can grab a bite. I'm sure my mom has fixed enough food to feed the entire coast guard."

He looked surprised at the offer but quickly hid it. "Thank you," he answered, walking around the golf cart and climbing in to sit beside her.

Immediately, the small space seemed to shrink. Even with the open sides, she suddenly felt surrounded by him.

She ignored the odd reaction and drove a little farther on the trail until it widened enough that she could turn the cart around.

"I should probably warn you this is my first time driving one of these," she said as one of the front tires went over a rock, jostling him toward her.

"Duly noted. Good thing there are no doors and windows. I can always jump clear if you run into trouble."

"Yes. By all means. Save yourself."

To her astonishment, he almost smiled, the first time she had seen any hint of levity on his features. The effect was as startling as if he had shoved her out of the golf cart and taken the wheel himself. His features lightened and he seemed younger and far more approachable.

She felt a quiver deep inside that she fiercely tried to pretend didn't exist.

"You know you can get alarms on the doors and windows of your house so you can be alerted if he leaves, right?"

She wasn't familiar personally with that sort of thing, though she had a close friend from law school whose mother suffered from early dementia. Cami saw Brynn a few times a year for lunch to catch up. The last time they met up, Brynn had told a rather bittersweet story about coming home from a date, only to end up lighting up the whole security system when she forgot to disable the alarms.

She regretted bringing it up now when John's lighthearted expression faded into one of worry.

"I guess I have to look into all of those protective measures. I really hate to take those drastic steps. He will feel like a prisoner in his own house."

"Better than a care center," she pointed out.

"You're right. I suppose I should focus on that and being grateful that we're not quite at that stage yet."

"It would be a stopgap measure, certainly. You have to think of his safety."

"You're right. I have to consider all of that. I guess some things might have to happen earlier than I expected."

"I'm sorry."

Despite the fact that they were technically adversaries now, at least when it came to Wild Hearts Luxury Camping, she couldn't help feeling sorry for Jon. She knew enough from Brynn to know what a heartrending experience it could be to lose a loved one through the slow torture of dementia.

"If he wanders off again, I would suggest you check my mother's kitchen first. She told me he stops there two or three times a week. She feeds him and then takes him home when breakfast is over."

His shoulders bumped against her when she drove over a rut in the road.

"I had no idea," Jon said slowly. "He hasn't mentioned it. That's…very kind of her."

"My mother likes to feed weary wanderers. She considers it her mission in life to heal Mother Earth and all her children."

She could sense his gaze on her as she navigated the trail. What did he see?

"I take it you don't share her philosophy."

"I'm an attorney. A little too prosaic to think healing crystals and chamomile tea will cure whatever is going wrong in my life."

Again, she had the impression he wanted to smile.

"What's going wrong in your life, Ms. Porter?"

Besides this completely inappropriate attraction to a man who seemed to hit all her buttons? Wasn't that enough?

"Absolutely nothing," she lied. "Aren't we all living the dream here in Cape Sanctuary?"

"Is that what we're doing?" he answered wryly.

She wanted to dislike him, but he wasn't making that easy.

Their arrival at the house spared her from having to come up with a response.

11

JON

BY THE TIME CAMI PORTER PULLED THE GOLF cart up to her mother's farmhouse, Jon's heart had almost stopped racing with anxiety over his father.

He had been certain Franklin had met some dire fate, that he had either fallen to his death or had gone for a swim and been pulled out to sea.

Which, sadly, had been the fate of Cami's sister, he remembered.

Moongate Farm was not what he'd expected. The way Cami talked about her mother, he would have expected some kind of new age paradise, with sun dials and rainbow wind chimes.

Instead, the house was well-kept and orderly, the gardens thick with bright flowers and lush vegetables.

A big stone patio with seating for probably twenty or more was ringed by hanging baskets and plants spilling from containers. It was an appealing spot on a summer morning.

His family had a long connection to Moongate Farm, though back in the day when his great-great-grandfather ran cattle here, it had been called simply the Double R.

The large two-story farmhouse had been built by his ancestors. Years later, his grandfather, who was an attorney like Franklin and created a fortune in real estate, had built Rose Creek on what he considered a better spot. Moongate Farm was protected on all sides by the terrain. The wind didn't blow here, unlike at Rose Creek, which had been built to take in the magnificent views up and down the coast.

He couldn't remember the last time he had stepped foot on the farm, though of course he had always been aware of his family's connection.

As he walked across the patio to the back door of the house, he had the oddest sensation of calm.

A few places he had visited in his life had instantly called to him. The Caño Cristales river in Colombia, the Temple of the Great Jaguar in Tikal.

Oddly, he realized he could now add Moongate Farm to that list.

"I haven't been here for years," he murmured. "Your mom has definitely made some improvements."

"Yes. She loves this place."

Cami seemed strangely ambivalent about the house.

"You don't?"

"I don't have the same connection as my mother and sisters. It was never my home. Just a place where I visited them."

"You didn't live here with your mother?"

She looked reluctant to answer but finally did, her words

clipped. "My parents divorced when I was fourteen. My parents split us up. The twins came with my mother and I stayed with my father in Los Angeles."

He didn't have any siblings, but he couldn't imagine how tough it must have been to be separated from her mother and sisters.

"How long since you've been back to Cape Sanctuary?" she asked him.

He sensed she hadn't wanted to tell him about her parents' divorce, any more than he wanted to tell her about the rift with his father.

"Three years. My father and I…haven't been close. That's a polite way to put it. We had a falling-out. Both of us said angry words to each other. I swore I wouldn't come back. He told me he no longer had a son, yadda yadda yadda."

The pain of it suddenly felt as raw and difficult as those first few weeks after he had left.

He waited for her to press him about it, yet she only nodded. "Yet here you are, in time to stop the opportunistic neighbors from taking advantage of your father in his vulnerable condition."

He could feel a muscle tighten in his jaw and tried to relax it. "I didn't know about my father's condition. If I had, I would have come home much sooner."

He knew he would be living with that guilt for a long time. His father might have been the one to push him away, but Jon could have pushed back and returned earlier.

"You're here now, when he needs you," Cami said. "That's the important thing."

Why did he find so much comfort from her words? He hadn't even known this woman a few days ago.

She had come looking for him when she had no obligation to do it. He wouldn't have blamed her for letting him stress all morning, especially after the way they had left things the day before regarding the campground lease.

"Thank you for coming to find me. I might have been searching for him all day."

She smiled and he wanted to drink it in like *quezalteca*.

He liked her. Against his better judgment, he was drawn to Cami Porter. He couldn't stop thinking of the kindness she had shown his father the day before after his social gaffe, when others might have shied away from dealing with him.

"Come in and have some breakfast," she said. "Then someone can give you both a lift back to your father's house."

He had no intention of eating at the house. His plan was simply to go inside and retrieve his father so they could go back to Rose Creek. When he walked into the kitchen, however, it was obvious Rosemary Porter had other ideas.

She beamed. "Jon Rafferty. Look at you, all grown up. And so handsome."

She hugged him, smelling of lemon and mint.

Though she had always been kind to him, he wouldn't have expected this kind of reception. Not when he so strenuously objected to her developing a luxury campground on Rafferty family land.

"Jonny!" His father stared at him. "What are you doing here? I thought you were in Central America?"

He had spent the past forty-eight hours with the man, but apparently that hadn't made an impression. "I was. I came home, remember?"

"What did you do to your arm?" Rosemary asked. "Is it broken?"

"Machete," Cami answered before he could.

"Machete! Oh my word."

"Dumb mistake on my part. I had an injury that became infected and required surgery to clean it out and repair some of the tendons and ligaments. It's on the mend. I probably don't need the sling, but I don't want to tear open my stitches right now."

"I have some salve you should use. It works wonders on cuts."

He wasn't sure a homemade salve would be quite the thing for a six-inch machete slice that went almost to the bone, but he wasn't about to argue with her.

"Thank you."

"First, sit down and have some breakfast. Cami, fetch Franklin's son a coffee."

He wanted to tell her he was fine and didn't need coffee or breakfast. But the whole kitchen smelled heavenly and he was suddenly famished.

When his father pointed to a chair around the big oak table, Jon finally gave in, feeling more than a little bemused. He couldn't remember the last home-cooked breakfast he'd had. Breakfast at the dig site was usually fruit and maybe an empanada.

Cami brought him a cup of coffee and slid over some cream and sugar at the same time her mother placed a plate overflowing with croissants and a healthy triangle of quiche.

"Make sure you have some of my huckleberry jam on your croissant," his father ordered.

"Your jam?" he asked.

"I didn't make the jam. But I did pick some of the huckleberries myself last summer. Rosie took me to all her favorite patches in the mountains east of here. We spent a nice day, didn't we?"

To Jon's shock, Rosemary beamed at his father. "We certainly did. And every time I open another jar, I think of how hard you worked."

"Not as hard as when you and Lily helped me clean up after that tree blew down on the garden shed in January."

"You know we were happy to help you."

"When are we going after huckleberries again?"

"They won't be on for a few more weeks, but I'll be sure to give you a call."

The interchange left him disoriented. He had assumed the worst of Rosemary Porter and her daughter Lily. He thought they had taken advantage of his father. Right now, though, they sounded like friends of long standing.

Perhaps he needed to reassess his perceptions.

He was listening to Rosemary and his father talk about other trips they had taken together into the mountains near Cape Sanctuary when the door opened and a woman walked in. She was tall and slender, with blond hair and lovely features. But she also had an indefinable air of sadness about her.

She stopped and smiled at Jon's father. "Mr. Rafferty. Hi! How are you?"

Franklin's face lit up. "Hello, my dear Lily. I haven't seen you in forever! Why haven't you been by to visit? I miss our poker games."

The woman seemed to freeze for an instant, and he saw Cami give her arm a comforting squeeze.

"I'm not Lily," she said quietly. "She was my twin sister. I'm Violet."

Franklin looked astonished. "Are you? My word. You are the spitting image."

"So I hear."

She had lost a twin sister. That must be terribly difficult for her.

"Do you remember Frank's son, Jon?" Rosemary asked. It was clear she wanted to change the subject away from her deceased daughter.

They had all suffered a difficult loss. He knew what that was like. He still felt vaguely nauseated when he thought of his mother, and that had been nearly twenty years ago.

Violet's smile returned, though it appeared somewhat forced. "Of course. The adventuring archaeologist returns. Hello."

"Hi."

"Those croissants smell delicious. Can I have one?" she asked.

"Of course."

Rosemary pulled a delicate plate out of the cupboard, plopped one of her flaky croissants on it and handed it to her daughter with a flourish.

The sisters weren't at all alike, he couldn't help but notice. Violet was cool, elegant, almost, while Cami was small, dark-haired, curvy.

Gorgeous.

He couldn't afford to indulge this unwanted attraction. He had too much to do here.

"What brings the Rafferty men to call today?" Violet asked.

"Breakfast, for me," Franklin said, taking another bite. He inclined his head toward Jon. "I don't know why he's here."

"Checking on you. That's all. If you're going to leave the house, you really need to let me know. At the least, you should take your cell phone with you."

"I thought I had it." Franklin patted his pockets, brow wrinkled with concern. "I guess I must have forgotten it again. I'll remember next time."

"Tell me when you want to make a visit. I'll come with you," Jon said.

Franklin didn't look thrilled at that offer but said nothing.

"Thank you for breakfast," Jon said after an awkward moment. "It was delicious, but we should probably get out of your hair."

"No need to rush off," Rosemary said.

"You heard her." Franklin took a long, slow sip of what looked like orange juice. "We don't need to rush off."

Jon needed to. Despite that initial feeling of peace, he now felt uncomfortable in this warm, cheerful kitchen that smelled delicious, of huckleberries and croissants and women.

He hadn't been with a woman in a long time, since before heading into the jungle for the dig.

Available women were few and far between on a remote archaeological expedition. He certainly couldn't indulge in something with a graduate student or the interns who flocked to an important discovery like Tikal.

Maybe that's what left him feeling edgy and almost painfully aware of Cami Porter.

"We really do have to go. Mrs. Porter has been kind enough to feed us, but we have things to do today."

Including an appointment with Robert Layton, who would be helping him pursue legal and medical power of attorney for his father.

"Before you leave, would you like to see the campground up close?" Rosemary asked quickly. "You can even go in one of the tents, if you'd like. The guests in the Jewelflower tent checked out early this morning and the new ones won't be here until late this evening. I would love you to see what we're doing there, so you can see firsthand how environmentally conscious we are trying to be."

As persuasive tactics went, it was as transparent as a newly washed window.

Rosemary wanted to convince him to honor the verbal lease agreement for Wild Hearts.

Jon wasn't about to do that. He might have been weak enough to give them a grace period of a few months, but he wasn't willing to bend more than that.

"We have appointments today," he said.

He didn't count on his father's obstinacy. "I want you to see one of the tents," he said.

"Camellia can drive you there before she takes you home. It's on the way."

Cami raised an eyebrow at her mother's suggestion, phrased more like a command.

"We can walk," Jon said quickly. "It isn't far."

He wasn't sure he wanted to be in such close proximity to her.

"I can give you a ride. I'm an expert now at the golf cart."

Jon did not want to come off as a jerk to these women who had fed him and his father—and who apparently had been opening their kitchen to Franklin for months, if not years.

Backed into a corner, he finally nodded. "Sure. A quick trip should work."

"I call shotgun," his father said quickly, as if they were teenagers heading out for a joyride.

That would at least solve the issue of proximity.

Jon climbed into the back seat. Once his father was settled, Cami drove up the trail that led to the Rose Creek headland.

He didn't know what he was expecting. It wasn't the small collection of canvas tents, each nestled in a stand of trees.

She parked the cart in front of a tent that was very similar to the one he had lived in for the past six months in Guatemala.

Funny. He hadn't felt like he had been glamping when they had spiders as big as dinner plates in the tent and snakes slithering on the roofs.

He counted ten tents, each on a wooden base that served as a deck of sorts.

Jon was certainly no expert on luxury camping. He spent plenty of time living outdoors but in fairly primitive conditions. Still, he could see how some people would find this appealing, especially with the stunning ocean views from up here.

"My sister wanted Wild Hearts to fit into the landscape as much as possible. As my mother said, she also worked to make the campground environmentally responsible, with composting toilets and solar-powered appliances."

A woman lying in a hammock in the trees waved at them. Another couple sat at a table going over what appeared from here to be a topographic map, likely in preparation for a hiking trip.

"This feels friendly," his father said. "Don't you agree, Jonny?"

He didn't know how to feel about his father's new habit of

calling him Jonny, a name Franklin hadn't used since Jon was out of grade school.

"Sure, Dad. It's nice."

"Looks like this is the Jewelflower tent." She gestured to the structure in front of them. "I haven't seen this one yet. But then, I've only seen inside one other tent."

She unlocked the door with a key her mother must have given her, then stood back for them to see.

So this was where the term *luxury camping* came from. It appeared to him like a fancy hotel room had been raided to furnish the tent, with colorful rugs on the floor, comfortable-looking chairs and a couple of trunks that looked antique.

Dominating the space was an oversize king-size bed, piled high with throw pillows. It looked plump and inviting.

He had a sudden mental image of messing up those thick pillows with the woman standing next to him.

The random thought horrified him.

Good Lord. What was *wrong* with him? He was not some kind of sex-obsessed fraternity boy who couldn't think about anything else.

"It's very nice," he said abruptly, heading for the door without risking a glance at her.

After a moment, she and his father followed him onto the small porch where the deck stretched out another four feet from the tent structure.

"Yesterday was the first chance I had to see the tent cabins," she said. "I have to admit, I was surprised and impressed. Lily thought of everything a person might need for a comfortable stay."

"Why does that surprise you?"

She paused for a long moment, her features distant, before she answered him. "My late sister was fantastic at coming up with ideas but not always so great at the follow-through. When she told me this grand idea a few months before she died, I thought this would be another of Lily's wild starts. I'm glad to see I was wrong in this case."

She sent him a sideways look. "I only wish she had made sure all the details were squared regarding the lease agreement with your father."

"A small but fairly significant detail."

"I cannot disagree."

Her wry tone almost made him smile again. He liked this woman, far more than he should.

"It does seem like a comfortable escape," he said.

"The view certainly doesn't hurt."

This time he was the one who could not disagree. The bluff jutting out into the Pacific had always been one of his favorite places on his family's property, which might explain some of his instinctive opposition to someone else using it.

"Thank you for indulging my mother and coming to take a look," Cami said. " She's very proud of what she and Lily created here, as you can probably tell, and I get the impression she likes to show it off."

"I imagine she's also hoping that once I take a look at it, I'll change my mind and extend the lease to next year and beyond."

Her laugh rippled through him. "You can't blame her for trying, can you?"

"I won't change my mind," he said firmly.

"I never thought you would."

The drive back to his father's house passed swiftly. He was aware of her the entire way while his father kept up a running conversation, telling Cami about a case he had argued in front of a superior court. Franklin seemed eloquent enough, but when Cami would ask him a question about the case, he would only gaze at her with a confused look before taking the conversation toward an entirely different aspect of the case.

In only a few moments, Cami delivered them to the massive front doors of Rose Creek. "Here you go."

Franklin jumped out. "Goodbye, then," he said, already on his way into the house.

Jon climbed out more slowly. "Thank you again for feeding him this morning. I'll try to figure out some alarms on the doors or something, but it may take me a few days. Let me know if he stops by again."

"I expect my mother would say he's welcome for breakfast anytime. You, as well."

Jon did not think he would be popping by Moongate Farm again soon for breakfast.

"We should probably exchange numbers, just in case he wanders down to Moongate Farm again."

"Good idea," she said. "Tell me your number and I'll text you. Then you'll have my info."

He gave it to her and she texted a simple message, with only her name.

It seemed oddly intimate to have her as a contact on his phone.

"Got it."

"I'll be sure to let you know if we see your dad out and about."

He nodded, suddenly reluctant to say goodbye to her. What the hell was wrong with him?

"I'm meeting with my father's former partner this afternoon to start the guardianship process. I've asked him to work up a temporary lease agreement as well. I'll try to have it ready by the end of the week for your mother to sign."

"Sounds good. You know how to reach me now."

He nodded and watched her drive back on the path until she was out of sight in the trees.

12

VIOLET

A MORNING SPENT GOING OVER THE ACCOUNTS for Wild Hearts left her with gritty eyes and a slight tension headache, but at least the bills were all paid for the month.

"Finished already?" Rosemary looked startled when Violet walked into the kitchen. "That job usually takes me the better part of the day."

"It wasn't so bad. I like working with numbers."

"That's because you're good at focusing on details, while I tend to go off on tangents like a hamster on crack."

Her mother smiled as she pulled a tray of thick, chewy oatmeal raisin cookies out of the oven. "Thank you so much for doing that. Why don't you take a break this afternoon and go do something fun with Cami? Go shopping or catch a movie."

Vi and her sister didn't have the sort of relationship for casual outings. Not yet, anyway. She planned to work on that.

"Are you sure you don't need my help with anything else?"

She was coming to learn there was always some task to finish when it came to campground administration, whether organizing the recreation schedule or taking reservations or purchasing the brand of paper products that fit the company's environmental focus.

Rosemary shook her head as she slid another tray of cookies into the oven. "I don't have anything to do myself. As soon as these cookies are done, I'm going to put my feet up for a half hour on the porch swing and read a book. It looks like a lovely day. You should enjoy the sunshine while we have it."

She did have somewhere she needed to visit. She had been here several days and had yet to go to the cemetery.

"If you're sure, I think I will take a few hours off."

"Take that dog with you. He could use a walk," Rosemary said, gesturing to Lily's cross little schnoodle.

Violet gave Baxter a baleful look and earned a snarl in return.

"Yeah. I don't like you either," she muttered. Still, when she reached for the leash, the dog thumped its tail against the leg of one of the kitchen chairs.

"We're not going far," she informed the bad-tempered creature. "Don't get your hopes up."

She stopped at the bunkhouse long enough to grab her backpack with her wallet and a few supplies, as well as her water bottle, which she hooked onto the pack.

She could hear Cami talking to someone in a virtual meeting. She heard a bunch of lawyerly words she didn't know, probably in Latin. Cami sounded firm, decisive, in complete control of the conversation.

Baxter seemed to perk up when he heard Cami's voice, straining a little against the leash. In contrast to how he treated Violet, Baxter adored Cami, which seemed to baffle her sister as much as it did everyone else.

She thought about waiting until Cami might be free to go with her, then discarded the idea. This wasn't for anyone else. Only for her.

"Come on, Bax."

The dog followed her, though gave a backward look of longing toward Cami's voice that did nothing for Violet's ego.

She stopped to pick a handful of her mother's peonies and lavender, creating a richly scented bouquet she knew Lily would have loved.

The day was gorgeous, with high streaky clouds reaching across the azure sky.

The ocean stretched out to the horizon, vast and undulating.

Vi never tired of that view. She had a picture of the ocean in her classroom, and on the days when it felt like every single one of her students had the "zoomies"—her word for days when nobody seemed able to settle down and their restlessness fed off each other—she would focus on that picture and transport herself here to her mother and Lily.

Home.

Tears burned but she fought them down. The day was too lovely for tears.

By the time she traveled the half mile to the Cape Sanctuary cemetery, Violet had worked out most of the kinks in her back and neck from hunching over the desk paying bills.

The cemetery was on a hillside overlooking downtown. It was shady and cool, covered in coastal pine and Douglas fir.

Violet paused outside the iron gates to look at the No Dogs Allowed sign. She should have thought of that.

She gripped the flowers. It was too late to turn back now.

She flirted with the idea of leaving Baxter tied up outside the gates of the cemetery. She would only be a moment, but with her luck, the dog would break free, run into town and cause all manner of trouble.

She looked around and couldn't see anybody else here on this slow, lazy summer afternoon. What would be the harm in taking him to visit his beloved mistress, as long as she carried him in so he wasn't disrespectful enough to strut through and pee on all the gravestones?

Without giving herself time to change her mind, Violet scooped him up and hurried through the gates, expecting any moment for the cemetery caretaker to come bursting out from behind a headstone, yelling at her for breaking the rules.

Rule breaking had always been Lily's job. Violet was the twin who toed the line, always trying to do the right thing.

Where had that gotten her? She was nearly thirty with no social life to speak of and she had just lost her sister and best friend. Following the rules wasn't working out so well for her.

Maybe it was time she started breaking a few once in a while.

Chin high, she carried Baxter through the rows toward Lily's marker.

Her sister had always said she wanted to be cremated, her ashes scattered in the ocean. Since the ocean had taken her from them, Rosemary put her foot down and refused to honor her wishes in this.

Lily was probably pissed about that and would haunt them all.

The headstone was small, tasteful, elegant, with a carved floral wreath and the words *Beloved Daughter and Sister* above her name.

Did it represent Lily at all? Not in the least. Still, it was something. If Lily had been cremated, Violet would have no physical connection to her twin.

A small vase had been cemented in place next to the headstone. Some older flowers with petals beginning to curl were there, so Violet removed them to a nearby garbage can before arranging her own hastily gathered bouquet in the vase. The bright, cheerful colors and heady aroma seemed almost garish against the gray and white stones.

Baxter whined, sniffing at the headstone as if he could sense some trace of Lily. With an ache deep in her bones, Violet sank down beside the grave and pulled the little dog onto her lap. For once, he didn't snarl at her.

Did he feel closer to Lily here, or was he only sensing Violet's own distress? She wasn't sure. For now, she decided to take comfort in the little dog's heat and soft, curly coat.

"Miss you," she said softly. The words seemed wholly inadequate. The world wasn't quite right anymore and she didn't know if it ever would be.

Would this pain feel as sharp if not for the distance that had been between them in the months before Lily died?

Her fault. The vast chasm would not have been there if Violet had not insisted on it.

You know I will always love you. But sometimes I don't like you very much.

That last bitter argument ran on autoplay in her head, as it had been doing since the horrible, life-altering moment she'd learned of Lily's death.

She would give anything to call those words back, to be able to remember only love and peace and joy between them.

Instead, she and Lily hadn't spoken for two endless months before her sister's death, the longest time in their lives they had been apart. Violet had set firm boundaries, and for once in her life, Lily had actually honored those boundaries.

Violet had planned to come up to the Cape to catch up with her sister's plans for the glampground and to begin the work of rebuilding a healthier relationship with her sister.

She hadn't had the chance. Lily had died before she could carve time away from school and life and obligations.

She made a tiny sound that made Baxter whimper and nestle closer.

Would she have to spend the rest of her life paralyzed by this regret?

Lily wouldn't have been living in Cape Sanctuary that fateful day if not for Violet. Vi had been the one to push her twin home after the holidays.

For six months before that, they had shared Vi's condo in Sacramento, the latest in several failed attempts to live together as adults.

The same patterns always emerged. Lily would start to take over, decorating the way she wanted, cooking the meals she preferred, insinuating herself into all of Violet's work relationships and friendships.

She never did it on purpose. Vi knew that. Lily simply always had been the stronger personality between them. The dominant twin. Technically, they were identical, but they really weren't. Lily knew how to do her makeup, how to flash her eyes, how to dress to play up her best assets.

Violet had always felt like a pale shadow compared to her sister, the poor imitation that hadn't quite come out of the mold the same.

It had been her problem. Not Lily's. Her sister hadn't done anything wrong. She had just been herself, fun and bright and effervescent.

It wasn't Lily's fault that all those traits that made her sparkle left Violet feeling as if she could never measure up, as if she would always fade into the background when Lily was around.

There had been a guy.

Wasn't there always?

In this case, the guy in question had been another teacher at her elementary school. Chris Nguyen taught fifth grade. He had been sweet, funny, great looking. An amazing teacher, the kind who won national awards for innovative methods and genuine caring for students.

All the other teachers, gay, straight, married, single, had crushes on him.

Chris had recently broken up with his fiancée and had asked Violet out a few times. She liked him and thought maybe once he was completely over his girlfriend in a year or so, their deep friendship could grow into something more.

And then Lily moved in with her and Vi made the mistake of inviting Chris out with them to watch a favorite local band performing in town.

After that, Chris only had eyes for Lily. In typical Lily form, her sister had strung him along, encouraging him to give more and more of his heart when she had absolutely no intention of keeping it.

Lily was never deliberately cruel. That wasn't in her nature. Only casual and thoughtless, which could be so much more devastating.

Her sister didn't seem to realize how people instantly adored her.

Vi had guessed what was coming.

Over the next few months, Violet had watched as a smart, compassionate teacher had been reduced to a lovesick puppy, following Lily around like Baxter did.

As she watched Chris barreling headlong into another broken heart when the scars were still fresh from his breakup, she had tried to warn Lily to be careful with him.

"We're just having fun," Lily had protested when Violet had asked her what she was doing. "It's nothing serious. Chris knows that."

But Chris obviously *hadn't* known. As Violet feared, he fell hard for Lily and invited her on a ski trip to Utah over the holidays.

She didn't know what happened on that weeklong trip. When they returned, Lily finally seemed to clue in that he wanted more than she did out of the relationship, so she started distancing herself from him.

When even that hadn't been enough to discourage him, she had finally told Chris she cared about him as a friend but that was all it would ever be.

The next day, Chris had come to Violet's classroom, devastated and broken. Vi had had enough. She had told Lily that since she was between jobs anyway, it would be better for both of them if she moved back to Cape Sanctuary. Violet needed space away from her for a while.

That final argument, the words she had said, haunted her.

"I meant them," she murmured at her sister's graveside now. "But I didn't tell you the rest. About how much I admire you for your creativity and your courage and spontaneity. All the things I don't have."

She would give anything to have the chance to pick up the phone and tell her sister everything in her heart.

She wiped away a tear and was shocked and more than a little freaked out when Baxter, her canine nemesis, angled his head and licked the tear off her cheek.

"Okay. Don't make things weird between us now."

The dog just looked at her, then licked at another tear.

A few moments later, Baxter jumped from her lap and bristled at something behind her.

Afraid the cemetery sexton had caught her, Violet looked over her shoulder, peering through a bush toward the pathway. Two figures walked toward her, one large and one smaller. Violet couldn't mistake that walk, though the pair were still some distance away.

Alex Mendoza and his daughter were heading toward the grave, with Ariana carrying a bouquet of flowers.

She didn't want to talk to Alex or Ariana.

Violet wanted to jump up and hide somewhere. Maybe behind that large statue of an angel with outstretched wings and a vacant expression.

Yeah, it gave her the creeps, but it was better than the alternative.

They probably hadn't seen her yet, since the leaves of a large shrub probably hid her from their view.

But she had nowhere to run except past them toward the gates. She was trapped—not to mention she had a small dog on a leash who wasn't supposed to be here. Baxter had stubby little legs and probably wouldn't be able to keep up with her.

Left with no choice, she decided to face the awkwardness head-on. She stood up as they approached Lily's gravestone.

At her sudden appearance, Ariana gave a shriek and dropped the flowers she was holding.

Violet winced. "I'm sorry. I didn't mean to frighten you."

"You might want to reconsider sneaking up on people at a cemetery," Alex said. "You're liable to give someone a heart attack. Especially when they're here to pay respects to your identical twin sister."

"Sorry," she said again, though she wanted to retort that she hadn't been sneaking anywhere, only sitting on the ground concealed by the bushes while she grieved for her sister.

"Hi, Baxter." Ariana, apparently quick to forgive, crouched down to pet the dog.

"Ari, why don't you put your flowers down, right there next to Violet's bouquet?"

Ariana extricated herself from Baxter's lavish affection and carefully arranged her flowers next to Violet's.

"They're very pretty," Vi said.

The girl beamed. "Thanks. We got them at the farmers' market last night. That's where we always buy them. Almost always. Sometimes we pick them from my *abuela*'s garden when she lets us."

From this, she inferred that Ariana and her father came often to bring flowers to Lily. For some reason, the notion touched her heart.

"Wherever you get them, I am sure my sister would love them. She adored all kinds of flowers."

"I hope so," Ariana said, then turned back to scratch Baxter between the ears. The little schnoodle promptly rolled onto his back in a shameless appeal to have his belly rubbed, which made Ariana giggle.

With the girl's attention firmly focused on the dog, Violet finally turned to face Alex. He was wearing sunglasses, which hid his expression. Her heart gave a sharp twinge when she remembered how very much she had loved him.

Alex had never seen her as the second-best twin. He once only had eyes for her.

"Thank you for remembering her. It…means a great deal."

"She saved my daughter's life," Alex said simply. "For that, I'll be here every week for the rest of my life, bringing her flowers."

It comforted her, knowing someone else besides her family wouldn't forget Lily.

"So," Alex said after a moment. "How long are you back in town? Your mom was vague when I asked her that."

She sent him a sidelong look. "Why do you want to know? So you can figure out how to avoid me?"

He frowned. "I wasn't thinking that at all. I have no reason to avoid you. If anything, it's the other way around."

How had they come to this awkwardness between them?

She looked away, her gaze resting on his beautiful child.

Violet was weary, suddenly, and felt as if her bones couldn't support the weight of all the pain inside her. "I don't hate you, Alex. I never did."

"You have every right," he said quietly.

She shook her head firmly. "We were high school sweethearts. That's all. You didn't owe me anything. I cared about you once, but I moved on a long time ago."

That was an outright lie. She had never really moved on. She had dated other men and even become serious with one or two. Still, she had never forgotten the man she had loved first and best.

She wasn't about to tell him that, though.

He gave her another searching look, then nodded. "Are you busy today with the campground? It's my mom's birthday and Tori is in town with her kids, so I took a half day off. We're having a late lunch and cake this afternoon to celebrate. I know everyone would love to see you."

Tori Mendoza had once been a dear friend, one Vi hadn't seen since that fateful summer so long ago.

She had loved his entire family. His mother, Renata, plump and pretty, cooked like a dream and taught piano lessons. His father, Jorge, was one of the hardest-working men she had ever known, but he always made time for the important things in life. His younger brother, Javi, always flirted with her shamelessly.

Despite her awkwardness with Alex, she had a sudden, almost overwhelming urge to see his family. To be around people who weren't lost in grief.

"I don't want to infringe on a family get-together."

"Are you kidding? You have no idea how many points I would score if I brought you by so everyone can hug you in person."

Yeah, she wasn't thrilled about that part of it. She didn't want his family's gratitude. She hadn't done anything.

"Sure," she said before she could change her mind. "I could stop by for a minute."

His face lit up. "Excellent! My truck is outside the gates. We can give you a ride."

The entire way to his parents' house, Violet sat in the passenger seat of Alex's crew cab pickup, listening to Ariana chatter and trying to figure out why on earth she had agreed to go with them.

Maybe being home in Cape Sanctuary was making some of Lily's bold, sometimes brazen courage rub off on her.

Or maybe he had simply caught her in a weak moment, when she had been raw with sadness for her sister.

Maybe it wouldn't be so bad, especially if she had the chance to see his family again.

From the very first time Alex had brought her home with him, when she was a starry-eyed fifteen and he was seventeen, his family had welcomed her into their home and their lives.

She ate dinner at his house at least once a week. They went on trips down the coast. They sat together at his baseball games. They all went to the movies on Saturday night, sharing a jumbo popcorn.

She had felt completely comfortable at their home.

After everything happened between them, she sometimes thought she missed those times with his family almost as much as she missed Alex.

"The house looks nice," she said when he pulled up in front of the ranch house not far from the marina.

"Javi and Sean, Tori's husband, helped me put on a new roof and siding last summer. We also put in new tile and appliances in the kitchen."

His clear love for his family had been one of the things that first drew her to Alex.

That and his dark eyes, broad shoulders, sexy smile and a hundred other appealing details.

She frowned at herself. That was a long time ago. She had no business noticing any of those things now.

When they walked inside, memories poured over her. The scents were the same, fabric softener mixed with vanilla potpourri and roasted tomatoes.

"Hey, *Mamacita*," he called. "We're here."

"I'm in the kitchen," Renata called back, her voice so dearly familiar Violet almost wept again.

"Do you have room for one more at dinner?" Alex asked as he led the way.

"Always," Renata answered, her back to them as she stirred something on the stove. When she turned, she gave a small cry, dropped her spatula with a clatter and rushed toward them, arms open.

"Violeta. Oh. Violeta. How wonderful to see you."

Renata squeezed her tightly and all the chaos of the world seemed to still for now.

The hug lasted a long time. Then Renata gave her a small shake. "Why have you stayed away so long?"

Violet glanced at Alex, who was popping an olive from a Fiestaware bowl into his mouth.

"Reasons."

Renata only nodded. "You're here now. That's the important thing. Let me look at you."

She held her away from her with a tender look. "You're too thin. And your eyes are sad, *mija*. You're missing your sister, aren't you?"

She nodded, feeling that constant lump rise again.

"Tori will be happy to see you. She's gone to the store but will be right back."

"Where's Emily?" Ariana asked.

"Out in the backyard with her brother."

"Can I take Baxter out to play?" Ariana asked Violet.

The dog was acting suspiciously good-natured, giving her no real reason to refuse. "Sure."

"Now." Renata spoke as soon as Ariana and the dog had left, her voice firm with no room for arguments. "Sit down and tell me what you've been up to since I saw you last."

She had to laugh. How could she encapsulate a decade in a few moments? "Where should I start?"

"How about your school? Alex tells me you're a teacher now. What do you teach?"

She gave Alex a sidelong look, wondering why he might have had a conversation with his mother about her. "I teach special education at an elementary school in Sacramento."

Renata beamed, giving her a look brimming with pride. "Do you? How wonderful. Any boyfriend? Husband? Significant other?"

"Mom," Alex said, his tone exasperated. "She came for dinner, not an interrogation."

"What? I haven't seen her in years. It's a natural question."

Violet could feel herself flush but forced a laugh. "None of the above. At least not at the current time."

Distraction always worked with her students, so she decided to try the same tack now. "How can I help you with dinner? Happy birthday, by the way. I can't believe your family is making you cook on your birthday."

"Making her? You want to be the one to try stopping her?" Alex asked, his voice dry. "We all suggested going out to dinner, but she said cooking a big meal was the only way she wanted to celebrate."

That tracked. Renata was always happiest when she was taking care of someone else. She and Rosemary were similar nurturers.

"What are you making? It smells delicious."

Renata gave her a look that told Violet she knew exactly what she was doing but was going to indulge her anyway.

"I'm making tamales. You always liked those, if I recall."

"I did." She hadn't been able to eat tamales in a decade, since it reminded her so much of him and his family and the life he had created without her.

"How perfect that I decided to make them when I didn't even know you were coming. You can help me by cutting up that watermelon there. Alexandro, go help your father. He's supposed to be straightening up the patio and wiping down the chairs. I'm willing to bet he fell asleep in the hammock again."

Alex gave Violet an apologetic look and a shrug, but he obviously didn't want to disobey his mother.

As Violet settled in at the kitchen table with the watermelon and a knife while the contents of the pans on the stove burbled away and Renata hummed softly, she decided this was exactly where she needed to be.

13

VIOLET

THE NEXT FEW HOURS WERE THE PERFECT distraction from the sadness at Moongate Farm.

They ate on the patio of the house, surrounded by blooming gardens, with the Pacific in the distance and the dying sun sending long shadows through the trees.

His family was warm, noisy, welcoming. Tori had squealed with delight to see her. While they were connected on social media, it was great to see her in person and catch up, like they had simply resumed a conversation that had been interrupted by life and circumstances.

His father, Jorge, had wrapped her in a big bear hug and actually shed a tear or two, which made her cry, too.

She loved her own father but couldn't imagine Ted crying with happiness over renewing an acquaintance.

Alex's younger brother, Javi, five years younger than Violet, buff and sexy now, flirted with her shamelessly as he always had, which amused her to no end, especially because it seemed to annoy Alex.

The children—Ariana plus her cousins Emily and Matt—all clamored to sit by Violet at dinner out on the patio.

Still, she knew it was a mistake to spend more time with the Mendoza family when her feelings for the oldest son were still so conflicted, even after all these years.

Like eating too many tamales, which she had also done, she knew she would pay the price for the evening in more ways than one.

"Thank you for dinner," she said after enjoying a small slice of a gorgeous birthday cake Tori had produced. "It was really great to see you all again."

"And you, *mija*." Renata gave her another tight hug. "You must come visit us again while you are living here in town."

"I'll try." She would, but only if Alex wasn't there.

"I'll give you a ride home," Alex said.

She shook her head, feeling a little flare of panic. She didn't want to be alone with him. "Not necessary. It's a lovely evening and not far to Moongate Farm. I'll enjoy the walk."

"Then I'll walk with you."

He gave her a look that made it clear that arguing would be a waste of time for both of them.

She glowered but went to where the children were playing so she could grab Baxter. The dog seemed to revel in the attention of the children. He was currently lying in the grass under a willow tree, chewing a tennis ball one of the children had provided.

When she reached to hook the leash on his collar, he gave her his usual baleful look but begrudgingly rose from his belly.

"You're leaving already?" Ariana asked with a pout.

"Yes. But thank you for inviting me. I enjoyed it very much."

The pain in her heart would always be there, but today it seemed almost bearable.

"I'm glad you came." To her shock, Alex's daughter reached around her waist and hugged her, much as Renata had done. The spontaneous embrace touched something deep inside her.

Violet loved children. She wouldn't have become a teacher if she didn't, especially of students with special needs who could sometimes have challenging behavior and cognitive issues.

She didn't remember ever feeling as instinctive a bond with another child as she did with Ariana. She didn't understand it and wasn't sure she liked it very much.

This was Alex's daughter. The child he had with another woman who had always despised Violet.

"Can I tell you a secret?" Ariana said quietly before Violet could walk away.

She drew in a shaky breath, not sure she had room inside her to hold anyone else's secrets.

"Of course."

"Promise you won't tell anyone, okay?"

"Okay," she answered, a little apprehensively.

Ariana looked around, as if to make sure her cousins weren't close enough to overhear.

"Your sister Lily is my guardian angel," she said, her voice low.

"Your…guardian angel?"

Ariana nodded. "I talk to her sometimes and I think she hears me."

The words floored her. She gripped Baxter's leash, not trusting her voice. She suddenly longed for her twin and all the secrets they used to share in the dark.

I need space from you. Not forever, only for now.

Not this. She never meant this much space.

"I'm glad," she finally said softly. "Thank you for telling me."

"If you want, I can tell her I saw you today and that you're as nice as she is."

She gave a watery smile. "That would be great. Thank you."

Tell her I miss her and I'm sorry.

Baxter seemed subdued as they walked in silence toward Moongate Farm.

"Are you okay?" Alex asked after they turned onto Seaview Road. "What did Ariana say to you to put those shadows in your eyes suddenly?"

She couldn't tell him. She had promised. "Nothing," she lied. "She's a great kid."

"Agreed. The very best thing to come out of my marriage."

She didn't know how to answer that and focused her attention on Baxter, sniffing at a rock as they walked up the hill to Rosemary's house.

"I'm sorry things didn't work out with you and Claudia," she finally said.

"Are you?"

"Do you think I'm the kind of person who would want someone's marriage to fail, especially when a child is involved? You know I'm a child of divorce myself."

He was silent for several more steps. Then he stopped and faced her. "I hate that I hurt you, Vi. I would say I'd like to go back and change all those decisions I made after you left. But that would mean no Ariana and I could never wish for that."

"No."

"But I am sorry you were hurt in the process."

She had carried so much anger inside her all these years toward him. It was easier to believe herself the wronged party than to acknowledge her own role in everything that had happened.

He had loved her, too. She knew that hadn't been a lie.

She had been eighteen, he twenty, when he proposed for the

first time when she came home for the holidays after the first semester of her freshman year.

She could picture him now. Earnest. Sincere.

I can't. Not yet, she had said.

She was too young and not at all ready to settle down. She wanted to finish college first and she knew Alex couldn't leave Cape Sanctuary. His father had just had the first of what would be three serious heart attacks and Alex had responsibilities here at the boat charter company.

They had tried to keep their relationship alive long-distance with phone calls and sporadic visits, but it had been hard from three hours apart. Making matters more complicated, Lily had a frenzied social life and frequently wanted Violet to double-date with her.

You've only ever dated one guy. How will you know he's your soul mate if you never even kiss anyone else?

As usual, Lily had been the stronger twin and had persuaded her to go along a few times. Alex had been furious, both at her and at Lily. They had fought fiercely, for the first time ever, and she had told him she needed a break, that she wanted to date other people. He should, too, so that they would both be absolutely certain of what they wanted.

She did not want a marriage that ended in divorce and heartbreak, like her parents' had.

Oh, how disastrous that argument had turned out to be. In the end, she had tried to date but ended up comparing every guy unfavorably to Alex.

Claudia Crane, on the other hand, her high school nemesis, had swooped in the moment she heard the two of them were taking a break. And why not? Alex had dated her a few times before he and Violet started going out and Claudia made no secret that she wanted him back.

Three months later Claudia was pregnant, the two of them

were engaged and Violet was quite positive her heart would shatter into a million pieces.

It hadn't. She had survived and was stronger because of it.

"The mayor has reached out to me about naming Lily the Citizen of the Year during Summer Sanctuary. She would like Ariana to present it personally."

"What did you say?"

"What else could I say? That it would be an honor. Ari is excited. She and Tori are going shopping this weekend for a new dress. She's only sorry her friend Ella can't be there. Her father was transferred to Japan shortly after…everything happened or else I'm sure she would be."

"How exciting for Ari."

"You'll be there, won't you?"

She didn't want anything to do with the ceremony that would make her more painfully aware of how much she missed her sister.

"I don't know yet."

He was silent the remainder of their way. At Moongate Farm, he walked her up to the door. For some ridiculous reason, her mind filled with the times they had parted here with all the passion of two teenagers who couldn't get enough of each other.

Would he still taste like cinnamon Certs and mint ChapStick?

She would never find out.

"Thanks for walking me home."

"You made my mother very happy for her birthday. I probably won't need to get her a present for years."

"It was good to spend time with your family again."

Not you, though.

She had spent ten years telling herself she was completely over Alex. How humbling, to spend one afternoon in his company and realize she had been fooling herself.

"I'm glad you're home, Vi. I've…missed you."

He brushed her cheek with his mouth and she had to catch her breath at the familiar scent of his skin.

"Good night," she said curtly, hating herself for her weakness around him.

She turned and walked away from him, Baxter's leash twisted around her hand like those memories twisted around her heart.

14

CAMI

SHE WAS SITTING AT THE KITCHEN TABLE OF the bunkhouse answering emails when Violet hurried in, Baxter panting along beside her.

The dog immediately went to his water bowl and slurped noisily, then plopped down next to Cami's feet. Violet went to the refrigerator and poured water into a glass with hands that trembled.

Cami folded her laptop, concern pressing in. "Everything okay? You were gone a long time and you didn't take your car. I was going to give you another hour and then go looking for you."

"I'm sorry," Vi snapped. "I didn't know I had a curfew."

Cami's mouth firmed at the sharp tone.

"Sorry," she said tightly. "You're right. None of my business. I was worried about the dog."

And you, she thought.

She was even more worried now, but she wasn't about to say that to her prickly sister.

"Everything okay?" she couldn't resist asking.

"Fine. I took a walk to the cemetery and bumped into Alex and Ariana. They invited me to Renata and Jorge's place for dinner. It's Renata's birthday."

Cami's gaze sharpened. Ah. No wonder her sister seemed edgy and upset. "I'm surprised you went."

Violet sipped at her water. "Why? I love Renata. She was always wonderful to me."

"Her son, on the other hand, broke your heart into tiny little pieces."

Violet wrapped both hands around her glass. "That was a long time ago. Ten years. Another lifetime."

She spoke in a dismissive tone that told Cami she didn't want to talk about her childhood sweetheart or the betrayal that must still sting, especially when his daughter was living proof.

And when that daughter was the reason Lily was gone.

"It still feels like yesterday to me. You came to LA to stay with Dad for a few weeks that summer. Do you remember?"

To her surprise, Violet sat across from her at the small kitchen table of the bunkhouse. "Yes. For the first few days, I mostly listened to emo and cried. I wanted to do nothing else but lay by the swimming pool and get a tan and forget Alex Mendoza ever existed. Instead, you dragged me out with you and Sterling and some of your law school friends."

Cami had cherished that time, when Violet had turned to her for solace.

Lily had been overseas, she remembered, doing a modeling assignment for a photographer friend.

Cami knew she was a poor substitute but she hadn't cared. She and Violet had talked into the night as they worked through all the cartons of Ben & Jerry's Chunky Monkey they could find at the supermarket.

She winced at the memory. "I'm sorry. Going out with boring law students was probably the last thing you needed at the time."

Vi shrugged. "You were trying to help. I got it at the time and I get it even more now."

"I didn't know what else to do, especially since my heart had never been broken."

Violet pressed her lips together. "At the time, anyway. And then you and Sterling broke up."

Was her heart broken then? She knew it should have been, but by the time her engagement ended, she had known what a disastrous mistake she had almost made.

"I should have come bearing Chunky Monkey the moment I heard you and Sterling split. I am ashamed to say it never even occurred to me. You always seemed so…self-reliant. Like you didn't need anyone."

She would have welcomed her sister's visit, even if it would have left her feeling ashamed that she needed it. She had been a mess for a couple of months, moving numbly between work and her new condo, where she would change out of her attorney suits into her jammies, climb into bed and not move again until the morning.

Only learning that Sterling had started dating the daughter of one of the senior partners in his new firm had finally shaken her out of her funk. The man certainly had a pattern. She had simply been unlucky enough to fall for it.

She didn't want to talk about their breakup and she opted to change the subject.

"So. How is Alex these days?"

Vi gave a casual sort of shrug that didn't fool Cami for a moment. "Fine, I suppose. I don't really know. I spent most of the time catching up with his mother and sister."

"I understand he and Regina split up."

As she hoped, Vi made a sound that could have been a laugh. Cami knew that was the nickname Vi and Lily used for Claudia Crane, comparing her to Regina George, the Queen Bee character played by Rachel McAdams in the movie *Mean Girls*.

"Yes. Renata told me Claudia lives in Redding now with her second husband and they have a couple of kids. She and Alex share custody of their daughter. Ariana told me she lives with her mother most of the year but spends summers with her dad."

"That can be hard on a kid, can't it?"

During high school, Cami used to come to Cape Sanctuary for a month in the summers and then the twins would go to LA. Sometimes because of their busy schedules, that time would overlap and they would only see each other for a few nights at a time.

No wonder their lives had taken such different paths as adults, so that they now were virtual strangers.

She had a few weeks to change that, but Cami didn't have the first idea how to start, especially when Violet seemed a jumble of conflicted emotions.

15

CAMI

FRANKLIN RAFFERTY SHOWED UP AT MOONgate Farm again the next morning. Cami spotted him walking down the path from his house while she was in the middle of an early phone call.

"I've got to go," she said abruptly to Joe.

"But—"

"Talk to you soon."

She tapped her earbuds to end the call before he could press her further about the hundred things on their mutual to-do list. Throwing on her shoes, she hurried out to meet her mother's neighbor, the dog at her heels.

"Mr. Rafferty. Hi. What brings you here this morning?"

She thought he might be unfocused and confused, as he had been the last time he stopped by. Instead, he looked bright and alert.

"What are my chances of having another one of those croissants? I woke up thinking about how flaky and delicious they were."

"No croissants today, I'm afraid. But I think my mom is making pancakes with lemon butter. How about one of those?"

"Pancakes would be delicious. Thank you."

She probably should have checked with his son before issuing the invitation. For all she knew, Franklin might have some specific dietary requirements.

Rosemary's pancakes were thick, fluffy and addicting. Cami suddenly remembered that when Vi was eight or nine, her sister had once eaten ten of them in one sitting, mostly because Lily had dared her.

One or two would probably be fine, but she should probably check in with Jon first.

"Can you give me a minute? I need to send a friend a message."

Wearing an amiable expression, he sat down on a bench formed out of willow branches that looked like part of the lush landscape in the garden.

She quickly texted Jon, grateful she had thought ahead and obtained his number.

Your father is here. Can we feed him pancakes?

His answer came back swiftly and made her laugh out loud. Sure, as long as you nail his damn shoes to the floor while you're at it so he can't wander off again.

Can't promise the nails, she replied. My mom loves her wood

floors. But we will keep him here for a while. I'll take him back after he eats.

Thank you, he responded. I'll call off the search party.

She slipped her phone back into her pocket and turned to his father, who was petting the dog and looking perfectly at peace.

"Okay, Mr. Rafferty. Let's get you some breakfast."

She hooked her arm through his and walked into the house.

He stopped and sniffed appreciatively before they walked into the kitchen.

"Wow, Rosemary. It smells like some lemons have died and gone to heaven in here." He sounded perfectly lucid. That up and down of his condition must be frustrating for him and for Jon, not certain which version of himself he would be at any given moment.

"Good morning!" Rosemary sang out, looking delighted to see him.

Cami's relationship with her mother was definitely complicated, but she admired Rosemary's warmth and openness, the genuine affection she held for most people and the fearless way she showed it.

Lily had inherited that generosity of spirit. Cami certainly had not and she had a feeling Violet hadn't either.

Again, Franklin ate as if he hadn't had a meal in days. She knew that certainly wasn't true.

He all but licked the plate clean before holding it out again. "Could I finagle a few more off of you? That was delicious."

"Of course. And if you don't mind waiting a moment, I'll have more turkey sausage ready."

He made a face. "Turkey? You don't have any of the good stuff?"

"Ours is locally sourced from a farm up on the Oregon border. It's delicious. I actually like it better than the pork kind."

"I suppose I could wait a few moments," he said, as if doing her a favor.

"You won't be sorry," Rosemary promised, flipping the sizzling sausage patties on the stove.

While he enjoyed the sausages and two more pancakes, Cami stayed busy pouring fresh coffee and juice for the glamping guests and replenishing the fruit bowl.

"Looks like you're out of cantaloupe," she told her mother when she returned.

"Do you mind cutting more?" Rosemary asked.

"Not at all." She had other calls to make, but they could wait.

She was slicing the fruit with one of her mother's sharp knives when Franklin rose abruptly. "I need to use the bathroom."

Cami set down the knife. "Sure," Cami said. "I'll show you where to find the guest facilities."

He waved her off. "I know the way. I don't need a tour guide." He slipped through the door before she could answer.

"Where's Violet this morning?" Cami asked as she suddenly realized Rosemary was handling the breakfast on her own. "I thought she told me she was helping you this morning with breakfast. I would have come earlier if I'd known you were on your own."

"I sent her back to bed. She has one of her migraines and I know how those knock her flat. It was a bad one. I even insisted on helping her back to bed to make sure she made it there."

"I didn't hear you come in."

"We tried to be quiet. It sounded like you were in the middle of important business."

"It wasn't. Just a call with my paralegal. It easily could have waited. Next time, knock on my door."

Rosemary looked astonished at the suggestion. "Oh, I could never do that. Your father used to hate when I interrupted him while he was working. As you can imagine, since he was always working, that made it tough to have any conversation at all."

Ted Porter hadn't made Porter, Garcia & Sheen one of LA's leading legal teams by spending evenings and weekends at the beach. He had been focused on work, almost to the exclusion of everything else.

Rosemary's cheeks turned rosy. "I didn't mean to speak ill of him. I understood him perfectly well when I married him. Even when he was still in law school, I knew he would be brilliant. Being an attorney is not simply a job for him. It is his passion."

Cami knew that to be true. She admired that in her father, even as she felt guilty that she didn't have the same drive. Maybe that was the difference between practicing life-and-death criminal law and her more prosaic intellectual property law.

"Your father is the smartest person I ever met," Rosemary said with a soft sort of look. "I always found his brain the sexiest thing about him."

Cami wasn't sure she wanted to be having this conversation with her mother, especially not in the morning when her own brain wasn't yet working at full capacity.

"He's quite amazing at what he does," she answered. "I didn't realize how good until I went to work for him."

"Is he…dating anybody right now?"

Oh sweet Lord. Was her mother actually asking her about her father's love life?

The knife came down onto the cutting board with a hard thwap. "I have no idea. We don't talk about his social schedule, on the rare times we meet up for lunch."

She continued transferring the cantaloupe chunks into a bowl, carefully not looking at her mother. "I think after two failed marriages, he's not in a hurry to get serious with anyone else."

Her father had married again about three years after the divorce, a short-lived marriage to a kind woman Cami had liked. Cami had been a senior in high school and sometimes she thought Ted had married Julie mostly because he felt guilty that he wasn't able to spend more time with Cami and didn't want her to rattle around in that big house by herself.

"Dad said after the divorce that he was better off sticking with his strengths. Work is what he's good at."

Her mother gave a wistful-sounding sigh. "Not all he's good at."

Yeah. She didn't want to be having this conversation.

"I'm going to take this out to the dining room," she said. As she started to leave the kitchen with the bowl of fruit, she suddenly realized it had been at least ten minutes since Franklin had gone to the bathroom.

In a sudden panic, she hurried out of the kitchen and found the door to the guest bathroom open, the light out and no sign of Jon's father.

Oh, shoot.

She was responsible for keeping him safe. Maybe he had started back home without her.

Instantly, she rushed for the front door, then realized she still held the bowl of melon and shifted in midstride so she could drop it off first in the breakfast room.

Nerves jumping with panic, she burst through the door, then stopped short.

Franklin Rafferty hadn't left the house. Instead, he sat at one of the tables with a few other couples. He was munching on another piece of turkey sausage and chatting.

"My great-grandfather ran two thousand cattle on our land. My father remembers helping him round them up and said his grandfather claimed the sea air and the grasses made the beef extra juicy. A lot of people had dairy farms along the coast. Still do, up in the Ferndale area. In fact, they still call it Cream City because they make the best butter in the state."

"It is delicious," one of the guests said.

"My great-great-great-grandfather Angus Rafferty came out from Massachusetts looking for gold during the gold rush in '47. He was one of the few lucky ones who actually had a strike. Instead of wasting his gold on fancy women and beer, like so many did, he bought land. Paid top dollar for it, too. Everyone called him crazy, but he fell in love with the spot and wouldn't consider anywhere else."

He appeared to be in his element, relaxed and at ease as he talked about his family history.

She could see why he once had been a good attorney. He spun a fascinating story, his voice low and melodious.

Three couples were listening with obvious fascination.

"I can certainly understand why he stayed," one of the female guests said. "This whole area is stunning."

"It is that," Franklin agreed. "But it's not only the beauty that has been drawing people here since the earliest inhabitants of the area. The trees on the headland are ancient and holy, with one bristlecone pine being thousands of years old. The Fairy Tree, my wife called it," he said with a soft smile of remembrance.

"Oh, that sounds delightful," one of the women said. "I would love to see it. Where can I find it?"

"I'm afraid I can't tell you that," he said, his smile winsome. "The Raffertys have sworn to protect it. If we don't, a curse will fall on our family."

"A curse?" One of the men raised a skeptical eyebrow. "Really?"

"Swear it on my mother's grave. Which, by the way, is at one of the most haunted cemeteries along the California coast. Want to hear about the lady in white who walks along the cliffs of the Cape, crying for her sweetheart lost at sea? Or the soldier who died of malaria and is said to wander the town, looking in windows?"

"Definitely," another of the guests said with an avid expression.

Franklin appeared to consider, then shook his head. "Maybe another time," Franklin said with a mischievous smile. "Stories like that wouldn't have the same effect on you here over pancakes with sunlight streaming through those big windows as they would if we were sitting around a campfire with clouds drifting across the moon."

A wild idea came to her, like the first gentle snowflakes of winter fluttering to the ground.

No. It was impossible. Franklin suffered from dementia. While he seemed perfectly lucid right now, she had seen him become confused in a blink. She didn't want to trigger anything.

On the other hand, maybe a little socialization and stimulation would be good for him.

She could always ask Jon what he thought.

He would tell her no, too protective of his father to even consider it. She was suddenly certain of it.

As if on cue, the front door chime rang out. Her pulse skipped. It was Jon. She was even more certain of that.

She had told him she would bring his father home shortly, but even after only knowing him a short time, she was already learning the man liked to do things his own way.

She set down the cantaloupe on the long antique serving buffet and returned to the entryway. As she'd expected, when she opened the door, she found Jon standing on the other side, lean, dark, dangerous.

"Hi." She felt suddenly awkward, as if she were at a school dance with all the boys lined up on one side of the gym and the girls lined up on the other.

This attraction was so ridiculous. They were worlds apart. He was an archaeologist who lived on the edge and she was a boring IP attorney whose fiancé left her as soon as she had outlived her usefulness.

"I could have brought him back."

"I didn't want to trouble you further. I'm sorry about my dad. I'm going to have to shower at 3:00 a.m. in order to make sure I'm done before he wakes up."

Thinking about him in the shower again did nothing to help her regain her composure.

"I'm glad he feels comfortable coming here."

"Is he in the kitchen?"

"No. Breakfast room, actually. He's regaling some of the Wild Hearts guests with stories about the history of the area."

A look of alarm crossed his features. "Is he?"

"Yes. He's keeping everyone entertained. He seems to be having a good day."

"I'm glad. Yesterday was the opposite. He kept talking to my mother all day as if she were standing right next to him, and he had bouts of tremors so intense, he could hardly lift a glass of water to his mouth."

Oh, how tragic for both of them.

"Have you seen the neurologist yet?"

He shook his head. "Not yet. Our appointment was rescheduled. We go this afternoon. I guess it's good he had a solid breakfast."

He handed her a legal-size envelope she had been too distracted to notice earlier. "I've also got the signed lease agreement. My dad and I both signed it already at our attorney's office."

She had almost forgotten their conflict over the lease. Oh. Right. He was supposed to be the enemy, the one shattering all her sister's dreams.

"Great," she said, without conviction.

"Your mother needs to sign a copy for me, in the presence of a notary. I guess that's you. You can return it to me at your convenience."

He held the envelope out for her. As their hands brushed, she thought a spark of *something* bounced between them.

He tensed, looking suddenly wary, as if he felt it, too.

"Your father is a great storyteller," she said, mostly to distract herself. "He makes the past come alive."

"He's always loved history. He's been on the local historic committee as long as I remember. They fought to preserve the character of several older buildings downtown when developers wanted to raze them and start over. One of his favorite sayings is that our culture and society will be preserved not only by the things we create but by the things we refuse to destroy."

"He probably has a hundred great stories. Do you think he might be willing to stop by and share some with the other Wild Hearts guests? I was thinking a sort of campfire chat some evening."

He stared at her, clearly shocked. "You want my father, who has early dementia and suffers hallucinations, to perform for a bunch of strangers?"

When he phrased it like that, in those stark, no-nonsense terms, Cami could see all the glaring flaws in her idea.

"Not perform. Just be himself. He seemed to come alive while he was talking about the history of the area. I thought he might enjoy it and it might provide a little mental stimulation for him."

He didn't look convinced. Maybe he needed to see for himself.

"Whatever else he might be losing," Cami said gently, "he seems able to hang on to the past. Come see."

16

JON

CAMI HEADED DOWN THE HALL, TOWARD A room where he could see morning sunshine spilling through windows.

Left with no choice, Jon followed her, still mentally shaking his head at her outrageous suggestion.

It was impossible. He might have only been here a short time, but he was quite certain his father wasn't at all capable of that kind of thing.

"One of the most famous shipwrecks in these parts was the *Evelyn Riddle*, a steamer coming from New York through Panama and up the coast during the worst of the gold fever days. It was carrying a hundred passengers when it crashed in the fog."

Jon listened to his father go into detail about the ship that went down, what it had been carrying, how the survivors clung to debris for hours until the storm abated enough for locals to make it out to them.

His father always could spin a good story. Jon used to love listening to him around the campfire as he talked about the history of the area.

That was before his mother's death, anyway. After Elena died, his father became withdrawn, melancholic, prone to sudden bursts of temper.

The two of them had lived in the same house those last few years before Jon left for college, but they were like roommates who rarely interacted beyond a terse nod or quick conversation about necessary details of sharing the same house.

It was as if the heart had gone out of the house. Or at least out of his father.

He missed the father of his youth. The one who used to take him camping into the hills above town, who instilled a love of history in him, who even took him on his first archaeological dig, volunteering for a week with a team from one of the local universities at the Ross Colony, a multiethnic community in the early 1800s that served as a Russian trading outpost.

He hadn't realized exactly how much he missed those times until this moment.

"He's been going like this for several minutes. He knows so much history about this area. Amazing, isn't it?"

He swallowed down the lump in his throat, especially at the realization that this man was slipping further away every day.

"Remarkable."

"I've read stories about people with dementia who can't remember where they live or their birthday or their spouse's name, but they can pick up a violin and play like a virtuoso, relying on those old ingrained pathways in the brain. Maybe that's happening here. All those stories are locked inside there, waiting for some trigger to act as the key."

"Perhaps." He didn't know what else to say.

"The mental stimulation of sharing those stories might be good for him." She paused. "If nothing else, you could record him telling them so you would still have his stories in the future when…when things get worse."

He didn't want to think about that, though he knew it was inevitable. His father would only go downhill from here.

Jon couldn't believe how the direction of his life had shifted in a matter of days. Two weeks ago, his days had been filled with exploration on the dig.

He had imagined spending years in Guatemala savoring that thrill of discovery as he helped document each new insight into a lost civilization.

Now he was back in Cape Sanctuary, a place with so many painful memories, contemplating his father's difficult future.

Shouldn't he try to grab any chance to reclaim the good parts of the father he had loved?

"You don't have to decide anything today. You can think about it," Cami said.

He couldn't believe he was actually considering this.

Ultimately, the decision belonged to Franklin. For all he knew, his father wouldn't want to talk to a bunch of strangers anyway.

He opened his mouth to tell Cami that, then closed it again. Who was he kidding? He only had to look at Franklin now, aglow as he talked to a bunch of strangers, to know what his father would answer.

Franklin had always loved any chance he had to spout arcane tidbits of events that happened eons ago.

"When would you want to do it?"

"Whenever he wants. I haven't even talked to my mother or

sister about this. It was a totally random idea, but I'm sure they'll be excited about it."

He really didn't need their lives to become more entwined with the Porter females.

"What about tomorrow night?" she suggested.

He studied her. "Considering that only a few days ago you didn't know anything about the glampground business, you've certainly jumped in with both feet. Serving breakfast, giving tent tours, arranging campfire programs."

"I'm only trying to help out my mother. She's passionate about making this a success for Lily's sake, especially if this is the only season they can have the glampground at its current ideal location."

She gave him a pointed look that should have annoyed him. Instead, he had a ridiculous urge to smile. She was relentless.

And adorable.

His sudden urge to lean down right now and kiss her came out of nowhere.

He frowned, annoyed with himself. He had to get this attraction under control soon before he did something they would both regret.

"The decision really belongs to my father. If you want him to deliver some kind of short campfire program for your guests, you can go ahead and ask him."

Excitement burst across her features like the sun rising above the mountains on a spring morning. "I'll do that. I hope he agrees. Everyone will love it, I'm sure of it."

Everyone except Jon. The last thing he wanted to do was spend the evening hanging out with a bunch of strangers who were misguided enough to think they were actually enjoying nature from inside their luxurious tents.

But this version of his father, engaged and active, left a sharp pang in his chest. He hadn't been here for his father the past three years, had let anger and harsh words keep him away. He could blame Franklin, but Jon knew his own stubbornness was as much responsible as his father's.

If there was any chance, however slight, that something could help his father hold on to himself a little longer, Jon couldn't let the chance slip away.

17

VIOLET

WHEN IT CAME TO STUBBORNNESS, ROSEMARY could give lessons to every single one of Violet's students who threw tantrums over homework.

By the exasperation on her mother's face, Violet had a feeling Rosemary would say the same about her right about now. Like mother, like daughter.

They were in the kitchen of Moongate Farm, Rosemary at the sink washing dishes while Violet and Cami sat at the table. The other two women were both gazing at her like she was an unexploded ordnance that had been thrown into the house.

"You have to go, Violet. I won't hear any arguments. I'm

not sure you understand what a great honor this ceremony is. I don't remember a single time when the Citizen of the Year was awarded posthumously."

"I'm sure it is an honor." Violet forced a smile. "It's lovely of the mayor and city council to want to memorialize Lily this way. She certainly deserves it."

"Yes, she does. And everyone will expect her entire family to be there, especially her twin sister! Even your father is making the effort to come up for it."

Yes. She knew. Being named Citizen of the Year was a lovely honor for Lily and no less than she deserved.

Violet had planned to attend, but over the past few days, she had realized she wasn't at all ready to put her grief on such public display.

She wanted to remember Lily her own way, not at some stuffy ceremony attended by people who hadn't even known her sister.

She should have simply come up with some kind of excuse and bowed out the day of the ceremony. That would probably have been the better choice. Instead, she had made the mistake of telling Rosemary in advance she wouldn't be going.

Her mother was treating the news as if Violet were abdicating the throne or something.

"They're having her name carved into the Lost at Sea memorial also down at the park and plan to announce it that day. You have to come with us."

"I can't, Mom. I'm sorry but I just can't."

The only thing worse than having to smile and be gracious while everyone lauded Lily's actions would be to break down in front of everyone and let the hounds of her grief loose.

Her loss was too deep, too private, to share with the world right now.

"You're her twin sister. If you don't attend, everyone will be sure to wonder where you are."

"You can make up some excuse for me. You can tell people

I'm sick. Or quarantined. Or on vacation. I don't care what you tell people."

"Don't be ridiculous. I'm not going to lie for you. If you don't go, I will simply tell people you refused to attend."

"Fine."

"Is that what you want? For everyone in Cape Sanctuary to think you don't care about your sister's sacrifice?"

"What I don't care about is the opinion of people who would think that."

"I care! These are our friends. Neighbors. *Lily's* friends and neighbors. How will it look?"

Since when had Rosemary cared a fig about appearances and following conventions?

"Nobody will even notice I'm not there."

"I'll notice. Your father will notice and so will Cami."

At her name, Cami fidgeted, looking uncomfortable. "Leave me out of this. I think if Violet doesn't want to go, that's her choice. We all are grieving Lily in our own way."

Violet stared, shocked to have her sister on her side, defending her position. She would've thought Cami would be the first one to tell her to suck it up and do it for Lily.

"This is important," Rosemary exclaimed. "Everyone in town will be there."

"And if Violet chooses not to be among those ranks, that's her right."

"But people will think she doesn't want to celebrate what a hero Lily was!"

"That's not it," Violet exclaimed. "You know that's not it."

"Then what?"

Because I'm afraid part of me died when she did. Because I still don't know how to get along without her.

Before Violet could come up with an answer she could actually say out loud, the phone rang from the small room Rosemary used as an office.

Rosemary frowned but moved to answer it. "I know you're grieving your sister and you miss her," she said on her way out of the kitchen. "But sometimes you have to think about more than your own feelings. Lily saved the lives of two children and I'm grateful the community is recognizing her for that. I hope you'll change your mind."

Violet could hear her muffled greeting as she answered the phone. "Hello. Wild Hearts Luxury Camping."

While her mother was occupied with what sounded like someone trying to change their booking, Violet picked at her salad. She hardly tasted it, though it was made with fresh cucumbers and strawberries from the garden.

"I don't blame you for not wanting to go to the ceremony next week. It's a lot."

Again, Cami's support surprised her, but she was grateful at the same time. "Yeah. It is."

"I've said it before and I'll say it again. Everyone grieves in her own way. For Mom, seeing Lily celebrated by the town will help her. If you don't feel the same, I'm sure everyone will completely understand."

"Not Mom, apparently."

"She will. Give her time."

Violet was suddenly immensely grateful Cami had stayed in Cape Sanctuary for a few extra weeks. "Thank you."

"For what? I didn't do anything."

"You took my side. That means the world."

To her shock, Cami reached out and covered Violet's hand with hers. "We're sisters. Sisters should stick together."

They hadn't, though. She and Lily hadn't stuck by Cami. They used to talk about her behind her back, believing she thought she was too good for them.

Cami had always been…Cami. Their older sister who didn't seem to need them much.

She suspected now that hadn't been true, that Cami had needed them as sisters and friends.

Violet swallowed against the lump rising in her throat. She flipped her hand over and squeezed her sister's fingers. "You're right. Thank you. I needed that reminder."

Cami smiled and Violet was struck by how lovely she was beneath her usually serious expression. "You're welcome."

"I'm still not going to a stupid ceremony."

"I believe you've made that clear," Cami said.

Vi had to smile at her dry tone, her first genuine smile in far too long.

She withdrew her hand and reached for her water glass. "I understand from Mom that you invited Mr. Rafferty to give a campfire lecture for our guests on local history."

A slight flush suddenly blossomed on Cami's cheekbones. "Yes. I invited him this morning after he regaled the breakfast crowd with one fascinating story after another. I probably should have talked to you and Mom first."

Violet waved a hand. "No. It's a great idea. Everyone is always fascinated with local lore. The stories about the gold rush and the lumber industry and the tribes who first inhabited this area. I hope he knows all the spooky stories about ghostly shipwrecks and mysterious otherworld sightings on the beach, the ones our friends always shared when we would have campfires on the beach."

"I don't know how much of that Franklin will offer."

"No matter. Whatever he shares will be great. Do you think he's up to it?"

"I think so. Jon was reluctant but I persuaded him. I hope we all don't regret it."

"I'm sure it will be great." She paused, giving her sister a closer look. That was twice now that Cami's color rose when Jon's name was mentioned. She thought she had noticed a subtle tension between them.

"Jon is hot, isn't he? Danger and geekiness in the same gorgeous package."

Cami rose abruptly and carried her salad plate to the sink. "I wouldn't know. I hadn't noticed."

Violet almost laughed out loud at the outright lie. "He's always been good-looking with those dark eyes and long eyelashes. Lily and I both had crushes on him when we were girls. He was much older, of course. Four years. Ancient to us. But he was nice enough to us whenever we would bump into him at Rose Creek Beach or down at the marina. Once we missed the bus after school because we both tried out for a play. Mom was gone somewhere and couldn't pick us up. Jon saw us walking home through the rain and fog and gave us both a ride in the beat-up old Jeep he used to drive."

"Did he?"

"Yeah. Best day of our lives. When he left for college a few months later, we were both heartbroken."

Cami didn't answer, focusing on rinsing off her dish and loading it into the dishwasher.

"He always had this sexy tragic air about him. Probably because of his mother."

Cami met her gaze and Violet could see her sister's natural curiosity vie with her attempts to appear not interested.

"What about his mother?" Cami finally asked.

Oh, right. Cami probably didn't know all the old gossip around town. Sometimes she forgot this had never really been her sister's home.

"She died in a car accident a year or two before we moved here. I think Jon was fifteen or sixteen."

Cami's features softened. "I had wondered what happened to her."

"I don't know all the details. Mom would probably remember better than I do, but I think that she was driving somewhere on a rainy night and lost control on the slick roads. Her car went over a guardrail, over the cliffs. It took days for divers to find it. The search was called off several times. You know how dangerous the water can be there."

"Oh. How sad."

It seemed even more sad to Violet now that she had also lost someone she loved to the sea.

"Elena Rafferty was beautiful. I only met her a few times, but I remember thinking she looked like a Spanish contessa or something. I don't know if it's true or not, but I heard she was an actress in Spanish soap operas before she married Franklin. I only know everyone in town seemed to love her."

Rosemary returned to the kitchen before Cami could answer.

"Okay. I finally have that sorted," she said with an exasperated sigh. "A couple from Texas want to push back their reservation by a week to go to Yosemite first, but we don't have any free tents available for their new dates. We tried to come up with alternate dates but couldn't make anything fit. I thought they might cancel, but they said they would rather change their Yosemite reservations than miss out on a chance to stay here, after all the glowing reviews they've read. Isn't that wonderful?"

"Great," Violet said.

She was grateful for the couple's indecision, especially since it seemed to distract her mother from their argument.

18

JON

AS HE WALKED WITH HIS FATHER THROUGH THE trees toward the glampground, the sunset slanting through the dark trunks to light up the trail, Jon almost turned around a dozen times.

He wasn't at all convinced this was a good idea. Franklin seemed too fragile and the neurologist's words that day weren't reassuring.

They did have a few answers. Tests had ruled out a brain tumor or signs of a stroke. The diagnosis they were given was tentative, but because of his father's hallucinations, the occasional bouts of tremors and his fluctuating cognitive abilities, the neurologist suspected he was suffering from Lewy body dementia.

The past few days had been among his most lucid since Jon had returned, but that state of affairs seemed nebulous at best.

What if Franklin stood in front of the crowd and panicked? What if the pressure of people waiting for him to speak, all those eyes watching, sent him tumbling back a step?

He should never have agreed to this. What had he been thinking?

He knew the answer to that. He hadn't been thinking. Cami Porter only had to look at him out of those big, serious blue eyes for him to completely lose any hint of common sense he might once have claimed.

The last time he let a woman shift him off course like this had ended in disaster.

When he had been a naive twenty-one-year-old graduate student, he had spent a summer on a dig at a small ruin in the Yucatán Peninsula with a team from various North and Central American universities.

Jon had been foolish enough to fall hard for another graduate student from Boston University, Teresa LaGrange. She had been smart, driven, passionate about the work and, he thought, about him as well.

That summer had seemed magical, with each day another exciting find and nights spent with Teresa. He had even started inquiring about what he would need to do to transfer to Boston for his final year of grad school and then his doctoral studies.

And then her husband showed up—the husband she had never bothered to mention to him.

To make the betrayal more complete, a month after the dig ended, he discovered Teresa was publishing some of Jon's discoveries as her own.

The manipulation and betrayal had been a bitter pill to swallow, but he hadn't forgotten the lesson.

In every relationship since then, Jon had been careful to keep some part of himself separate.

"I'm sure nobody will come," Franklin said suddenly, yanking Jon out of the past and back to this moment, a walk through the pines at dusk while gulls cried on the wind currents and the ocean murmured below.

"Why do you say that?" Jon said. "Sure they will."

"Who wants to listen to a bunch of boring old stories?"

Jon did, suddenly, with an intensity that shocked him. He didn't care much about the history of Cape Sanctuary. He did care about his father and Franklin's health and sensed he wouldn't have many other opportunities to listen to him talk with eloquence about anything. Heeding Cami's suggestion, he had brought along a digital recorder and planned to also record the evening with his phone for redundancy.

"Plenty of people will want to hear you," he said gruffly. "I saw you entertain a whole room full of people yesterday. This will probably be many of the same guests."

Franklin was quiet, leaving Jon to worry again that this would be too much for him, especially after the extensive testing of the day before.

His father hadn't seemed to comprehend what the neurologist had told them, the finality of his condition. He had merely thanked the man for his time and returned to the book he had brought along.

Today he had been more quiet than usual, spending most of the day watching classic movies on TV.

"What if I forget what to say?" Franklin said when they were nearly to the campground.

The raw fear in the question pierced Jon's chest like it had been fired from a crossbow.

How terrible must it be to know more pieces of yourself were slipping away with every passing moment?

Instead of the anger he had nursed against his father for so long, all he felt now was compassion and, yes, love.

"You'll be great, Dad. Don't worry. You have all those notes we wrote down this afternoon to remind you of the stories you wanted to tell. You only have to look at those to remember what you wanted to say. And if you forget, just signal to me and I'll step in with what little I know about the area's history."

"You're a good boy, Jonny," Franklin said softly.

Jon forced a smile, wishing fiercely that he could turn back the clock and have the past three years back so that he could have spent more time with his father before the symptoms of his dementia started to manifest.

Franklin's sudden attack of nerves should have been yet one more indication that this whole thing was a mistake. He ought to turn right back down the hill and take his father back to the house.

But Cami was counting on them, and despite his reservations, he didn't want to let her down.

As the trees thinned, the forest turning to meadow, the tents came into view, lights inside making the canvas glow.

The sun was beginning its daily slide into the water and Jon could see little twinkling bulb lights in some of the nearby trees. As he couldn't see any cords, he assumed they must be solar or battery powered.

It was a cozy spot, he had to admit, amid the tall trees and wildflowers of the meadow.

About a dozen people had pulled chairs around a small fire ring. Propane, not wood, probably because of the area's strict rules banning campfires during most summers, as forest fires could devastate entire communities.

A few people were roasting marshmallows, he saw. Others were chatting in little groups.

The evening was one of those rare perfect summer nights

along the coast, with only a few high clouds to add texture and interest to the dusky sky.

If not for his nerves about his father and the sudden certainty that this whole thing was a mistake, he would have thoroughly enjoyed being on the headland, listening to the waves and tasting the salt in the air.

How many evenings had he spent like this on digs, sitting around a fire with camp stove coffee while discussing the day with his fellow researchers and the locals hired to help them?

That was one of the best parts of any dig, the camaraderie and cooperation among his peers.

Most of them, anyway. There were a few outliers, like Teresa, not there for the sake of research or the thrill of discovery but for personal and professional gain.

He was going to miss those evenings.

His arm throbbed harshly, a constant reminder of a part of his life that seemed to be slipping away as surely as his father's memories.

Would he ever have the chance to return to Guatemala? Right now, that did not seem likely.

Before he could dwell on it too long, Cami disengaged from a crowd and hurried over to them. She was wearing jeans and a hooded UCLA sweatshirt against the cool coastal evening and looked as if she had just stepped out of her dorm for an evening with friends in the mountains.

A sharp, hungry ache prowled through him like a feral cat.

Her smile was aimed at his father, Jon reminded himself. Not him.

What would he have to do to earn a smile as bright and welcoming as that?

He didn't want one, he reminded himself. And if she did ever smile at him like that, he would inevitably question her motives, wondering if she was only manipulating him so that he would change his mind and let her family's campground enterprise remain on Rose Creek land.

"Hi, Mr. Rafferty." Her voice was as bright as her smile, incandescent in the orange glow of the sunset on the water beyond the campground.

Apparently, his father was also susceptible to that smile.

"Hello, my dear," he said, taking her hands in his.

Any trace of nerves in Franklin's voice had completely disappeared.

"Thank you again for agreeing to do this. Everyone is so excited to learn more about the history of the area."

"My pleasure."

"Can I get you something to drink? We have ice water or soft drinks."

"I'll have a whiskey. Straight," Franklin said, just as if he were bellied up to the bar down at The Sea Shanty.

Cami gave him a startled look, then turned to Jon with a question in her expression.

He gave a subtle shake of his head. "Your meds don't interact well with alcohol, Dad. The neurologist was clear about that."

His father gave him a disgruntled look. "Like I care what some fancy doctor has to say. I'll drink if I want to drink."

"I'm sorry. We aren't serving anything alcoholic tonight, Mr. Rafferty."

He huffed out a breath. "Fine. I'll have a Coke, then."

"Great. I'll grab one for you."

Cami turned to go, but Franklin held out a hand to stop her. "I'll find my own. I want the coldest drink you've got. I like to check the temperature myself."

"Okay. The drinks are all in ice in that metal bin on the picnic table."

"Got it."

Franklin headed in the direction she pointed, leaving him alone with Cami.

"How is he?" Cami asked after Franklin walked away. "Is today a good day?"

The globe lights reflected tiny sparks in her eyes and he wanted to sink into the compassion he saw there.

For one wild moment, he wanted to rest his head in her lap and let her fingers caress all the tension out of his shoulders. He wanted to wrap his arms around her waist and hold on tight…

Where the hell had that come from? He jerked his attention away from that completely inappropriate train of thought. It took him a few beats to remember what she had asked.

"So far," he answered. "This afternoon, we sat down and made some notes about the stories he wanted to tell, in case he gets a little lost."

"Great idea." She gave him an approving smile that was almost, but not quite, as warm as the one she had bestowed on his father.

"We'll see. He was a little nervous on the way up here."

Her approval slid into distress. "Oh no. I'm sorry. I didn't want to make him anxious."

"He seems fine now. Perfectly relaxed." He inclined his head toward his father, chatting away with a couple who looked about Franklin's age.

"If that changes, let me know. We can improvise something else. I can always give a lecture on how to write non-compete clauses into your employee contract boilerplate."

"Wow. That *would* be a treat."

She laughed, a low, throaty sound that instantly made him ache.

While he tried to conceal it, he had a feeling some of his hunger must have filtered through to show on his features. Cami froze, her gaze locked with his and he saw unmistakable awareness flare in her light-spangled eyes.

Her gaze flicked to his mouth, for only an instant. Then she turned away, color rising in her cheeks.

Jon released a slow breath, cursing to himself. This would have been so much easier if she didn't share this attraction. He could have ignored his awareness, the aching hunger, and simply gone about his business.

She would be leaving Cape Sanctuary soon to return to LA, while he should be focusing on his father and what treatments and therapies Franklin might need, moving forward.

"We told everyone we would start at the top of the hour. About ten minutes from now. Did you want something to drink?"

"I'm good."

He didn't add that he would be better if he could grab her hand and tug her into the darkness of the surrounding trees. Her mouth would be sweet, warm, inviting…

To his relief, Franklin returned before Jon's brain could go completely off the rails.

"I found the coldest pop they had. I grabbed one for you, too, son."

Franklin held a can out to him and Jon took it. He didn't usually like sugary carbonated drinks but might make an exception tonight.

It was either that or pour the whole ice-filled beverage chest over his head to cool this ache he didn't want.

19

CAMI

SHE GAVE AN EXCUSE A FEW MOMENTS LATER and walked away from the two Rafferty men, her insides twirling as if she had just rolled end over end down the hillside to the beach.

Her breath seemed to catch and she couldn't manage to gather her scattered thoughts.

Jon Rafferty. Attracted to *her*.

It seemed utterly impossible, as unlikely as snow here along the temperate coast. He couldn't be.

And yet. She couldn't have mistaken that wild heat in his gaze. The edgy hunger that made her feel hot and breathless and tempted to dig her hands into his hair and kiss him right there in front of everyone.

He didn't even like her. He thought she was part of a family that had manipulated his father into agreeing to a multiyear lease when he clearly had cognitive issues.

She was a boring contract law attorney whose own fiancé claimed he only slept with her because he wanted to use her father's influence to further his legal career.

Why would someone like Jon Rafferty possibly be interested in her?

She frowned. Even if he was, so what? People were attracted to each other all the time without doing anything about it.

They wouldn't act on it. Neither of them was in a good place. He was busy dealing with his father's failing health and uncertain future, while she was only in Cape Sanctuary for a brief respite from the hectic pace of her life in LA.

She let out a shaky breath and reached for the water bottle she had left in the holder of her folding chair.

"I can't wait for this!" Rosemary approached her carrying a tray of fresh-baked chocolate chip cookies, still gooey and warm. "What a great turnout. Almost all of our guests showed up to listen to Franklin tonight. Isn't that marvelous?"

"Amazing," she said, still feeling shaky.

"If it goes well, maybe we can make it a regular thing. He can come a few times a month to speak to our guests."

She didn't want Rosemary to count on anything. If her mother didn't get her hopes up, she wouldn't be disappointed when it didn't happen.

"I'm not sure that's possible. He's having a good day today, but who knows what will happen next week or next month? You should probably consider this a one-off."

Her mother sighed, clearly disappointed. "You're right. I keep forgetting. Who knows? Maybe I'm going senile, too."

Though she knew her mother meant the words as a joke,

Cami couldn't bring herself to smile. Though her relationship with Rosemary wasn't as close as she would like, she would never wish the kind of future that Franklin faced on her mother, or anyone else, for that matter.

The harsh reality almost made her throat close and she took another sip of water.

"I told Jon we would be ready at the top of the hour. Do you want to introduce Mr. Rafferty? I should have talked to you about the format before."

"An introduction is a great idea. It will make the evening feel a little more official."

A few moments later, Rosemary moved closer to the fire ring, her dangly earrings and bracelets sparkling in the glow.

"Hello, friends and guests of Wild Hearts Luxury Camping. I am delighted tonight to introduce you to a dear friend and neighbor. Franklin Rafferty lives down the hill, in the big house you can see peeking out through the trees from certain angles."

She gestured around to the campground. "All of this is actually on his property, which he was kind enough to let us lease for our campground."

One of the campers spontaneously started clapping and the others soon joined in. Franklin, Cami saw, beamed at the assembled group.

"It's my pleasure," he said.

Jon, she noticed, looked anything but pleased.

"Franklin Rafferty basically wrote the book about the history of Cape Sanctuary," Rosemary went on. "He knows everything there is to know about the early tribes that lived here, about the Russian settlements in this area, the mining we saw here after the gold rush and about the logging industry that took its place."

Her mother smiled at Franklin and held out her hand. "Please give a warm Wild Hearts welcome to our dear friend, Franklin Rafferty."

The campers applauded again and the man she had seen Franklin speaking with earlier patted him on the back.

Mr. Rafferty moved forward and Cami was utterly charmed when he lifted Rosemary's hand and kissed the back of it.

"Dear Rosemary. Thank you for that kind introduction."

"I meant every word. I'll turn the time over to you now. You don't have to stand the whole time. Please. Sit down."

She pulled over one of the empty camp chairs. "I want this to feel like friends chatting around the fire."

Franklin sat down and faced the group. He gave a tentative smile, and in the fading twilight, she saw sudden confusion flare in his eyes.

He opened his mouth to speak, then closed it again, looking around with a furrow between his eyes.

Oh no.

Cami was about to step in and improvise what little she knew about Cape Sanctuary's history when Jon hurried to his father and handed him a stack of index cards.

He murmured something to Franklin, then stepped away.

His father immediately and visibly relaxed. He looked down at the cards, then back to the group with a smile. "If you were to visit this area five hundred years ago, you might find settlements dating back hundreds of years. This area was originally home to various tribes, mostly gatherers, who were later called by Europeans the Pomo."

He launched into stories about the first Europeans to the area, Russian trappers coming down from Alaska who hunted sea otters nearly to extinction and then others who came with gold fever in the late 1840s and 1850s.

All of the campers looked as enthralled as the group that morning in the breakfast room. After an hour, when she could see Franklin was beginning to tire and lose focus, Cami stepped forward.

"Thank you very much, Mr. Rafferty. I'm sure we could go

on all night. You've been amazingly informative. Wouldn't you all agree?"

The campers clapped with enthusiasm. "So interesting!" an older woman Cami knew was celebrating her fortieth anniversary with her husband exclaimed. "We've been coming to this area to vacation for years and I never knew half of this stuff."

"Neither did I," her husband agreed.

"Fascinating stuff," the gentleman Franklin had been speaking with earlier said with a hearty smile.

Mr. Rafferty looked flustered, though pleased, at the praise. "If you would like more information about the area, there is a small historical museum next to city hall. It's worth a visit, if only to see the collection of sea glass collected from Glass Beach."

Rosemary spoke from the refreshments table. "I have makings for s'mores here along with roasting forks and s'mores wire baskets. You can make them the traditional way, with marshmallows, chocolate and graham crackers, but we also have the ingredients and instructions for some savory s'mores, which are delicious. Try the goat cheese tomato bruschetta, trust me."

Some of the guests opted to return to their tents, but there were at least five couples who either stayed to talk to Franklin or moved to the refreshments table to look at the offerings.

Cami worked her way through those who were asking follow-up questions. She saw that Jon had moved to stand near his father. His protective stance touched something deep inside.

His relationship with his father might be strained, yet Jon was still focused on his welfare.

Franklin answered the questions patiently, and she was happy to see he appeared to be enjoying himself, his features relaxed and easy. He even smiled a few times as he spoke.

She couldn't resist approaching them.

"He did great," she said to Jon, while his father was busy telling the anniversary couple about the early fishing industry.

In the fire's flickering glow, his features looked lean and dangerous. "He has always been a student of local history. I'm grateful he can hang on to something he loves. For now."

"My mother would like to make this a regular event, maybe once or twice a month, for as long as he's still willing and able."

He looked down at her, his expression difficult to read in the darkness. "I don't want to push him."

"Right. Totally understandable. But if he's interested, he would be more than welcome."

"I'll talk to him about it," he finally said.

"Can I make you a s'more? I can vouch for the tomato/goat cheese/bruschetta one or the prosciutto/pear one."

"I'm good. But my dad has always been a sucker for anything with prosciutto."

"You've got it."

She hurried to the fire and looked over the recipe cards until she found the one for prosciutto, Brie and pears. Rosemary had set out all the necessary ingredients, and it only took a moment for Cami to throw a few together on herb crackers and load them into one of the small wire s'mores baskets on the table.

Rosemary beamed at her when she approached the fire ring, where a few other guests were enjoying their creations.

"That was all so fascinating," her mother said. "Everyone loved it. What a fabulous idea."

"I'm glad it worked out. It could have gone either way."

Jon had saved the day by providing note cards to help his father stay on task.

Thinking about him going to all that trouble to help Franklin with something Jon didn't wholly support left her feeling as soft and gooey as the Brie roasting on the flame.

"I learned so much about this area. You think you know a place, but Cape Sanctuary constantly surprises me."

Her mother met her gaze with an expression Cami couldn't read in the pale light of the fire and the globe lights hanging in the trees. "People can be like that, too, can't they? Sometimes you have to dig a little to work your way through the layers."

"Lovely evening, Mrs. Porter," a woman staying there with her sister for a girls' week said with a smile. "Thank you."

"You're welcome, Edie. I'm so glad you enjoyed it."

"And the s'mores were terrific," her sister Barbara added. "I loved the margherita, especially the fresh basil touch. I'm definitely making those at home with my kids."

"I'm so glad," Rosemary said, sending them back to their tent with a bright smile.

As Cami finished preparing the snacks for Franklin and Jon, she had to admit there was something calming about being here with the ocean's murmur down below and an owl hooting in the trees.

The gas fire ring might not have the crackling, evocative appeal of a wood-burning fire but was infinitely more safe in this fire-prone area.

She carefully divided the concoction between two plates and added a drizzle of raw local honey to each, then carried them over to the men.

Franklin definitely looked tired now, his shoulders drooping and his mouth turned down. When she held out the plates, some of his fatigue seemed to seep away.

"What's this?" he asked.

"Jon said you like prosciutto. This is melted Brie, chopped pears and prosciutto on toasted herb crackers."

"That sounds delicious," he said, taking the plate from her with hands that suddenly trembled.

Oh. She hoped they hadn't pushed him too far. "If you want, you can have it to go," she offered. "Or you can finish it and then I'll take you home in the golf cart."

She could see Jon wanted to protest, but he was also looking at his father with concern.

"Thank you," he said. "We would appreciate a lift back to the house. Right, Dad?"

"Yes. That would probably be good. I'm not used to all this excitement."

They finished the crackers with obvious enjoyment. Franklin even smacked his lips.

"That was so good. Rosemary will have to give me the recipe," he said.

"Sure thing," Cami said. "She has printed cards all ready for the guests to take home. I'll grab one for you."

She picked up a card from the table and returned to the men.

A moment later, they loaded up into the golf cart, with Franklin in the back this time and Jon next to her. Feeling like something of an expert now at driving this trail, Cami turned on the headlights and headed toward the Rafferty house.

"What do the campground guests do the other nights when you don't have guest lecturers?" Jon asked. "I didn't see TVs in the tent you showed me. There's not much to do out here. Don't they get bored?"

She shrugged. "I assume people know what they're getting into when they sign up to stay in a tent. However luxurious, it's not going to be a high-end hotel room."

"What about Wi-Fi?"

"My understanding is that Lily did not want internet up here at the campground because she wanted people to talk to each other and to enjoy nature instead of being hunched over a screen all the time. We do have Wi-Fi down at Moongate Farm they can use anytime, and people obviously have data plans on their cell phones."

Though she was already going at turtle speed, she slowed down to make one of the hairpin turns. "My mom has an extensive library down at the house. You might have seen that when you had breakfast there. She's also got a large puzzle and board game library where guests can borrow things and take them back to their tents."

Franklin spoke from the back seat. "You young people. Who needs puzzles and games? You're talking about romantic tents in the woods, with the ocean nearby and a sky full of stars. I imagine most of the couples, at least, don't have time to get bored."

Cami instantly felt hot, fiercely aware of Jon beside her, all rangy muscles and sexy geekiness. Her mind filled with plenty of things she would thoroughly enjoy doing in a tent under the stars with Jon Rafferty.

She let out a breath, trying to focus on the trail.

One of the sticking points of her engagement was the bedroom. Sterling had rarely been interested in sex, and when he was, it was a rushed affair, as if he were only interested in racing to the finish line.

He complained she was too tense and couldn't relax, even in bed. There was probably some truth to that. She had also been a junior associate working sixty hours a week and trying desperately not to disappoint her father, all while managing the housework, the grocery shopping and the cooking.

Of all the ways their relationship had been lousy, the worst had been the way Sterling had ground down her self-confidence. She had never been enough for him. Not thin enough, not witty enough at parties, not aggressive enough professionally.

For a woman who had half-healed scars from her childhood, feelings of not being enough when her mother chose to bring the twins to Cape Sanctuary and not Cami, Sterling's disappointment in her had been hard to combat.

Emotionally, professionally, sexually. She had come away feeling like a failure in every single arena.

She hadn't been. It had taken hard work and introspection, but she was finally coming to see that the only thing she had really failed at had been trusting the wrong man.

She still didn't know why she had.

What would an affair with Jon Rafferty be like?

Hot. Intense. Glorious. A tangle of bodies and mouths.

"You're lost in thought."

She was grateful for the dark evening so he couldn't see the blush she knew was probably covering her cheeks.

"It's, um, been a busy day. That's all. I had some virtual depositions, as well as a mandatory associates meeting for the law firm where I work."

"I'm an attorney." Franklin spoke up suddenly as she pulled the golf cart in front of their house.

"A good one, I hear," she answered.

"Was I?" he asked.

The tired confusion in his voice broke her heart. "You were fantastic. Everyone says so."

"Good. That's good."

In the porch light from the house, she could see Jon's jaw tighten. He climbed out and reached a hand to help his father out. "Let's get you to bed, Dad."

"I don't need your help," Franklin said, his voice sharp. "I'm not a child."

"Of course you're not," Cami said, her voice calm and even. "It's dark out here, though. I wouldn't want you to stumble on the steps going in."

"Why didn't you leave the outside lights on?" he snapped to his son. "You knew we would be home late."

"I didn't think about it. Give me a moment."

Jon hurried up the steps and unlocked the door. A moment later, the recessed can lights of the courtyard switched on and he came back out.

Franklin started up the steps but stumbled a little on the second to the top one. Cami reached for his arm to help stabilize him.

Far from appreciating the assistance, Franklin gave her a scorching look. "Stop fussing over me. I'm fine," he said abruptly, pulling his arm away like a toddler who didn't want to hold his mother's hand crossing the street. "I'm going to bed."

"Thank you again for speaking to our guests," Cami said, taken off guard by his abrupt rudeness. He had been kind and amiable to her since she arrived in Cape Sanctuary. These quicksilver mood swings must be another symptom of his condition.

Franklin didn't acknowledge her words, only walked away toward the back of the house, where she guessed he must have a bedroom overlooking the sea.

Jon stood inside the door, eyes murky. "Sorry about that. I'm learning his moods can be mercurial, especially when he's tired."

"I can't begin to imagine how frustrating it must be, feeling the pieces of himself slip away."

Grief spasmed across his face, and Cami had to stop herself from reaching out to comfort him, sensing he would be uneasy with it.

"My father was never an easy man," he said. "My whole life, he has had strong opinions and hasn't been shy about sharing them. He...became much worse after my mother's death."

"Grief affects people in different ways. I've certainly learned that since my sister died."

"True enough. It didn't help that we both blamed ourselves. And each other."

His eyes looked bleak now, like storm-tossed waves.

"Why would you blame yourself? My sister said something about a car accident."

He looked away. "It was a long time ago."

"Why would you blame yourselves for an accident?"

She thought for a moment he wasn't going to answer her. Then he sighed. "I blamed myself because my mother had insisted on coming to one of my high school basketball games across the county. And I blamed my father because he was too busy with work to take her, though he knew she didn't like driving at night. If he had been driving, she probably wouldn't have crashed."

"You don't know that. If he had been driving, you might have lost both your parents that night."

"I did, in all the ways that mattered. We lived together in this house for two more years but rarely saw each other except in passing. He drank too much and worked even more. I graduated high school early and left Cape Sanctuary as soon as I could."

"And now you're back to take care of him, because he needs you," she said, her voice soft.

He gazed at her with an odd, intense expression.

She should leave now. She had no real reason to stay, but she couldn't seem to make herself head for the door.

"Cami."

That was all he said, only her name, but the intensity of his voice made it feel like a caress down her spine.

She shivered. She couldn't seem to help it. He caught the gesture, though, and something hot and needy kindled in his gaze.

They stared at each other as the moments ticked by. She seemed to hear each pulse of her blood, each beat of her heart.

She wasn't sure which of them moved first, but then his mouth was on hers, warm, firm, delicious.

Unable to believe this was really happening, that a man as alive and adventurous as Jon could want someone staid and boring like her, Cami froze in his arms, beset by her demons of self-doubt.

Then biology kicked in, all the attraction she had been trying to suppress for days bubbled to the surface and she kissed him back. Right now, she didn't care that it made no logical sense for the two of them to ignite such fire in each other.

That didn't matter, as long as he didn't stop.

20

JON

AFTER THAT FIRST BURST OF SPONTANEOUS heat and delicious madness, he came to his senses gradually, like the sun creeping over the Andes.

This was a mistake.

He liked Cami Porter very much. She was smart, compassionate, beautiful, though she seemed completely unaware of it.

Under other circumstances, he might have been tempted to indulge in a fling with her.

With the passion he saw her bring to her dealings with her family, he knew they would be perfect together.

They already were. He was more aroused from a simple kiss

than he remembered being in his life. He wanted to scoop her into his arms and carry her up the stairs to his bedroom, where he could spend all night exploring all the things that made her shiver.

He let his thoughts explore all those possibilities for only a moment before he reined himself in.

He wouldn't be scooping her up and carrying her anywhere, as much as he wanted to.

He couldn't let his unexpected and inconvenient attraction to Cami Porter distract him from his entire purpose in coming back to Cape Sanctuary. To take care of his father, to protect his family's interests, to settle things so he could return as quickly as possible to his work.

He couldn't afford to be distracted from those goals. Nor could he let this inconvenient but overpowering attraction to Camellia Porter lead him into making foolhardy decisions about the Rose Creek headland, no matter how tempting he found her.

He reluctantly eased his mouth away, wishing things could be different—that she was just a lovely woman he happened to meet who challenged him, intrigued him, attracted him.

She gazed at him, eyes huge. Her mouth was swollen from his kiss and it took everything he had not to pull her back into his arms again.

Instead, he released her slowly and had to hope she didn't see the hunger in his eyes.

"I'm sorry about that."

"S-sorry?" Her breath hitched in a little, her expression dazed. He had to fight with everything inside him not to tug her back into his arms and start all over.

Instead, he forced himself to take a step back. "It's probably not a good idea to spend much time alone on a romantic summer night with an archaeologist who has been on a jungle dig for the past six months, where the few women there were either married or off-limits interns."

For a few seconds, she gazed at him, those eyes still wide. Then she shuttered her expression.

"Right. My mistake," she said with a brittle smile. "I'll keep that in mind next time and bring my pepper spray."

He was an ass to make her think the only reason he wanted her was because she was here and available. He opened his mouth to correct her, then closed it again. Better she think that than for her to have any clue how much he burned to pull her back into his arms.

"Please tell your father thank you again for the wonderfully informative lecture," she said, in that same brisk tone. "I know all the guests enjoyed it. If he wants to make it a regular thing, you can reach out to my mother or my sister Violet."

"What about you?"

"I won't be here. I'll be leaving right after Summer Sanctuary, when my sister Lily will be honored."

Lily. Right. The sister she was currently grieving, who had died saving two lives.

He didn't like thinking about Cape Sanctuary without her in it. He tended to forget she wasn't part of this community. She had a life in Los Angeles that didn't involve tents or prosciutto s'mores or men who kissed her even though they knew damn well they shouldn't.

She swallowed again, looking as if she wanted to say something more. When she didn't—when she only turned to walk outside—he wasn't sure whether he was relieved or disappointed.

The night air was cool, with a steady breeze that smelled of pine and the sea. It danced through her hair, rippling the ends.

He walked with her to the golf cart, hands shoved into his pockets. "Will you be all right driving home in the dark?"

She didn't meet his gaze. "Sure. Why wouldn't I be?"

He had no answer to that, so he merely watched her start the golf cart, turn on the headlights and drive toward the path that led to Moongate Farm.

He watched until she was absorbed into the night, wishing things could be different between them.

21

CAMI

IT WAS ONLY A KISS.

Only a few moments out of time when she had shared the same two-foot radius with Jon Rafferty, when his skin had touched hers, when his arms had wrapped her in warmth and hormones.

Their kiss couldn't have lasted longer than a few minutes.

Afterward, he had made it quite plain he considered it a mistake.

By the next morning, as she helped her mother fix breakfast for the Wild Hearts guests, Cami was still trying to convince herself their embrace hadn't been the pivotal, crucible moment it had felt at the time.

"Can you turn the bacon?" Rosemary asked as she poured fresh-squeezed orange juice into narrow glasses. "There's nothing worse than burnt bacon."

Cami could think of a few things. Including a man who kissed a woman like she was his salvation, then acted like it was nothing.

Why had he kissed her?

She didn't buy his "any port in a storm" explanation.

He had been attracted to her. She had seen that look in his eyes earlier in the evening, the one that had left her achy and restless.

Heat had been building between them since the day they met.

She hadn't exactly pushed him away. Surely he could tell she had been into the kiss, too. She had wrapped her arms around him and kissed him right back.

She was glad he stopped before they could go further because she wasn't sure she would have been capable of stopping. She had been completely caught up in the moment, in the thrill and heat and wonder, and would have surrendered any last hint of common sense.

Cami let out a breath. Yes. Good thing he stopped when he did. Any more kisses like that and she might completely lose her head and do something disastrous like fall for the man.

She wouldn't do that. She was too sensible, too centered, to act like some kind of dreamy-eyed adolescent over a man with blue eyes and long eyelashes.

Or at least she wanted to be.

"Is the bacon done?" Rosemary asked briskly, flipping another pancake.

"Almost," she said, focusing again on the task at hand instead of the man living on the other side of the bluff.

She was transferring the bacon from the pan to a plate when

Violet hurried in, throwing on an apron. "Sorry. I overslept again."

Violet wasn't sleeping any better than Cami was right now. As she tossed and turned, her mind filled with that kiss, she had heard the shower running, then her sister moving around in the kitchen.

Guilt pinched at her. She should have gone out to check on her sister, but she hadn't been certain she could talk to Violet without spilling every detail about that earthshaking kiss.

She wasn't sure what she would even say about it.

I kissed the enemy and now I can't forget the taste of him.

And I want to do it again.

She wasn't ready to share that yet. At least not until she'd had time to sort through her own chaotic feelings. Who knew? She might never be ready.

"Not to worry," Rosemary assured Violet. "You must have needed your sleep. We managed fine. Didn't we, Cami?"

"Sure."

"Anyway, I'll remind you both that for nearly a decade now, I've been running this kitchen by myself for the yoga retreats. Somehow I figured out how to manage without my daughters."

Violet rolled her eyes. "That involves hosting six or seven people for the occasional event. This is twenty strangers every day, all summer long. You can't keep up that pace by yourself."

Rosemary frowned. "Well, I won't have to after this season, right? I'm going to have to shut the whole thing down and sell the tents."

She didn't say the words with any kind of recrimination in her voice, but Cami felt the sting.

Rosemary still thought Jon might change his mind and sign a formal lease for the use of the headland.

Her mother didn't say it, but Cami knew Rosemary wanted her to use her best lawyerly powers of persuasion to press the point.

How could she now, when their relationship had become as tangled as old kite string in a drawer?

"If you don't mind taking out the last of the pancakes and bacon and the juice, that should take care of breakfast. Nearly all the guests have eaten by now."

"Sure." Violet picked up the plates and carried them out to the breakfast room. Cami followed her with the tray of orange juice.

Her mother was right—only a few lingerers were sitting in the breakfast room, a couple Cami hadn't seen at Franklin's history lecture the night before and the two women on a sisters' getaway, Barbara Greco and Edie Linsky.

"Tell your mother everything has been delicious, as usual," Edie said with a smile. "I think I've gained five pounds from breakfast alone this week. I just can't stop eating."

"Good," Barbara said firmly. "You need every ounce."

Cami thought that an odd thing to say. Edie wasn't overweight, but she wasn't particularly scrawny either.

"I might grab another few pieces of bacon."

"I can never say no to bacon," the man at the other table said.

Cami and Violet left them to it and returned to the kitchen, where they found Rosemary pulling a tray of sugar cookies from the oven. "A little early to be making the afternoon snack, isn't it?" Violet asked.

"Normally, I would agree, but six of our guests have chartered a whale watching and coastal exploration trip with Alex today, and I offered to make box lunches for them and the crew."

Violet, she noticed, had turned stony-faced at the mention of Alex Mendoza and his boat.

"Can I help?" Cami asked.

"Don't you have a video conference this morning?"

"Oh. Right."

Good thing her mother remembered her schedule. Cami had nearly forgotten she had arranged an off-hours discussion with one of her clients, one who traveled for work all week and only had time to chat on weekends. She had even told her mother about it when she first walked over from the bunkhouse.

She could blame Jon Rafferty for her scattered thoughts, too.

She checked her smartwatch, which would have reminded her of the appointment in ten minutes anyway. "I can help you for another half hour," Cami offered. "What kind of sandwiches?"

Her mother checked a list posted on the refrigerator. "Looks like I need five ham and four turkey and one PB and J."

"This should be easy, then. Vi?"

Her sister didn't look thrilled about working on anything that had to do with Alex Mendoza, but she forced a smile and reached into the refrigerator for the sliced turkey and ham.

"What bread do you want us to use?"

"I picked up some hoagies from the bakery. You can use those for all but the PB and J. You can slice off the bread I made yesterday for that."

"Got it," Cami answered.

"Maybe one of you could make the sandwiches while the other one helps me package the lunch bags with the cookies and carrot sticks."

"I'll do the sandwiches," Cami offered.

Violet moved across the island to help Rosemary.

For a few moments, the kitchen was silent as they each worked on their respective tasks.

"I talked to Dad this morning," Cami said into the easy silence.

A clatter rang out as Rosemary fumbled the metal spatula she was using to remove the cookies from the pan to a cooling rack.

"Did you?"

She immediately regretted bringing it up. "Yes. We were just finalizing plans for next week. He's flying into Redding Friday. I told him I would pick him up at the airport."

"That will be nice."

Rosemary's features suddenly looked as wooden as her cutting board.

It made her wonder again about her parents' relationship. Cami had long suspected her father was still in love with Rosemary and regretted the end of their marriage.

Rosemary had been the one to leave and the one to file for divorce. She knew that much, though her parents had presented a united front to their three daughters and gave the impression it was a mutual decision.

After her father divorced his second wife, he didn't seem to date much. Or if he had, he didn't share those details with his adult daughter.

Instead, he worked long hours, outperforming every other attorney in the firm, partner or associate. He was considered the attorney to the stars but also took on many cases pro bono, working to free people he considered wrongly convicted.

She did not know all the reasons for her parents' divorce and had tried to stay out of it over the years.

She suspected Ted's long hours and busy court calendar hadn't helped anything.

"He's looking for a hotel room. I wondered whether he could stay here."

Rosemary gave her a startled look. "Where?"

Maybe one of the four empty guest rooms you have here in the house?

She didn't dare say that, especially given her mother's odd mood. "We have one more room in the bunkhouse. He can stay there, if Violet is okay with it."

"Fine with me," her sister said.

The twins had always had a good, though distant, relationship with Ted. She supposed it was similar to the one Cami had with Rosemary.

Her mother didn't seem as sanguine. "I'm sure there are plenty of other places he could stay for that weekend."

"Not with Summer Sanctuary going on. He said his secretary tried and the few hotels in town were already booked. He could stay in Eureka or Ferndale, but that would be fairly inconvenient, especially when we have room here."

Rosemary still looked reluctant, which surprised Cami. What was behind it? She thought her parents were getting along better than ever. They had leaned heavily on each other during Lily's funeral services and the aftermath with shared grief over losing their child.

"It's fine with me if he stays here," her mother finally said, though her body language conveyed an entirely different message.

Cami decided the conflicting emotions were Rosemary's to deal with. "Great. I'll let him know."

"We have time to decide what room we'll put him in."

"Definitely," Cami said as she finished the last sandwich and wrapped it in paper like the others.

Her mother picked it up and put it in one of the paper lunch bags. "There. That's the last of them. Thank you."

"You're welcome," she and Violet both said at the same time.

Her mother smiled as she loaded everything into a small box. "Violet, would you mind running these down to the marina for me?"

Her sister sucked in a breath. "The marina? Why me?"

Rosemary gestured to Cami. "Because your sister has an important client call in a few moments and I promised the couple from San Francisco I would show them how I make my croissants. They're meeting me here in the kitchen in fifteen minutes, which doesn't give me enough time to make it down to the marina and back."

Violet didn't appear in the least appeased by that explanation. In fact, she looked fairly panic-stricken.

Was it really that hard for her to see Alex?

"Sorry," Cami said. "I wish I could run them down for you. I could take care of it later, but my call will take at least an hour."

Violet looked very much like a bird trapped inside a house, trying to fly against a window that simply wouldn't open.

"Fine," she finally said, scooping up the box of lunches.

"Thank you, dear," Rosemary said cheerfully, apparently oblivious to how difficult it must be for Violet to interact with the man she had once loved.

22

VIOLET

SHE REALLY HATED BEING BACKED INTO A corner.

She would rather be preparing for ten IEP meetings in one day than find herself driving the short distance to the marina with some sack lunches.

With any luck, maybe Alex wasn't there. Maybe Javi or Jorge were handling the charter.

She wasn't sure why she was so reluctant to see him, but she could feel the tension crawling across her shoulders like giant spiders.

She shouldn't be feeling this way. Alex had been nothing but kind to her since she returned to Cape Sanctuary for the summer.

Maybe that was the problem. He had been *too* kind. How was she supposed to keep up her defenses against the man when he was so sweet to her mother, took flowers to her sister's grave and invited Violet to have dinner with his family?

Ridiculous. She was not about to go down that road again, especially not with Alex Mendoza. She had enough heartache in her life right now, losing Lily. She certainly did not need to sign up for more.

With that in mind, she loaded up her car and drove the short distance between Moongate Farm and the Cape Sanctuary marina.

The Mendoza Charters office was in a low-slung building with white shutters and flower planters she guessed were cared for by Renata.

She had hoped she wouldn't have to go in, that some kind of employee might be outside to meet her. When that didn't happen, she sighed, parked her car in an empty space and walked into the office carrying the box.

Inside, she found herself in a small waiting area with comfortable chairs and pamphlets about the marine life and fishing tours the company offered.

Through a doorway, she could hear Alex on the phone, his voice tense.

"What do you mean, you can't come in? I've got a tour starting in twenty minutes. I was counting on you."

Could she be a total chicken and dump the lunches on the coffee table in the waiting area? The idea was tempting. Unfortunately, she was lowering the box when Alex spied her. Still on the phone, he gestured for her to come into the office.

Left with no choice, she hefted the box of food and moved through the doorway. His office was neat and orderly, though several fishing poles were clustered in the corner and stacks of Mendoza Charters brochures were stacked on the desk.

"No. I get it," Alex was saying. "You can't do anything about your son's broken arm. You're right where you need to be. With him. Give him a hug for me. Don't worry. I'll figure out something for today. Thanks for calling to let me know, Kim."

He hung up the phone and raked a hand through his dark hair in a painfully familiar gesture. She could picture him, ten years younger, doing the same thing while he worked on a boat motor or tried to go through their business accounts.

"Sounds like you've got a problem."

"You could say that. Do you remember Kim Phillips? Now she's Kim Harrison. She was a year or two older than me. She teaches science at the middle school and helps me as a tour guide during the summers when she can. She was supposed to go with me today with the charter from Wild Hearts, but apparently her son broke his arm an hour ago at the skate park. She's at the ER with him now and doesn't expect to be done for at least a few hours."

"Poor kid. A broken arm stinks anytime, but especially at the beginning of summer."

"Yeah. Been there. I broke my arm in eighth grade surfing at Sunshine Cove on the last day of school. That blasted cast itched all summer long."

"Will you have to reschedule the charter?"

"Not if I can avoid it. The Wild Hearts guests have had this booked for a month."

"Can you handle it without Kim?"

He sighed and that hand went through his hair again. "I don't know. Maybe."

He gave her a careful look. "I only need someone to talk about some of the local points of interest and the behavior of our resident orca pod and the various migrating whale populations that are moving through the area. You could do it."

Panic suddenly flared through her, wild and fierce. She had barely been able to *look* at the ocean since the Pacific claimed her sister.

She used to love the water. Now even being this close at the marina made her feel shaky.

"No. No way."

"It will only be a few hours. Kim has written out a script so she doesn't miss any of the high points when she's talking about the local marine life. It's ready to go on the boat. You can read from that."

"I can't."

He looked disappointed. "Understood. I'll just have to explain that we have to cancel and issue refunds. Too bad Kim didn't call me fifteen minutes earlier so I could have contacted your mother to let her know not to send the guests this way. It's too late now."

The door to the office opened and she saw several of the Wild Hearts guests enter the office wearing hats and windbreakers.

Violet wanted to whimper. Of *course* the first two to come through the door would be Edie and Barbara, her two favorite guests.

She stood frozen as she felt her options shrink to only one.

"You can't cancel," she whispered.

"It's a pain but it happens. I could push it back a few hours, but we're supposed to have some high winds this evening and I want to be back at the marina before that starts."

Why couldn't Cami have acted as Rosemary's delivery person? Violet didn't want to do this. With every fiber of her being, she wanted to dump these lunches on his desk and rush out of the office.

But then she saw the excitement on the two older women's features and knew she couldn't disappoint them. The night before, when she had chatted to them at the fireside after Franklin's history lecture, they had talked of nothing else but today's tour Rosemary had arranged for them and two other couples.

"You can't cancel," she said, louder this time. "Edie, the one in the blue hat, has cancer. Ovarian. She's having surgery next week, back home in Nebraska, then likely will be having radiation treatments."

His eyes widened and he swore in Spanish. "Rosemary didn't tell me that."

"She's so excited about the chance to see a whale. I would hate to be the only thing keeping her from realizing her dream."

He gazed at her with a warm look on his features she did *not* want to see.

"You are remarkable. In case no one has told you that lately."

No one had, in a very long time. Probably because it wasn't true. She wasn't remarkable. She held grudges and lashed out at those she loved most.

Oh, Lily.

Her sister would want her to do this. She could almost picture how Lily would look at her out of eyes drenched with compassion. *She has cancer, Vi. She might not even make it through the surgery next week.*

Violet screwed her eyes shut, wishing she could block out the ghost of her sister that seemed to haunt everything she did.

"Let's get this over with."

He grinned at her so broadly, her heart seemed to kick up a beat. He rose from his desk. She thought she was going to have to keep him from hugging her, but instead he went to a wooden cabinet, reached in and pulled out a hoodie that read Mendoza Charters, emblazoned with a stylized logo of a sleek cruiser with a whale tail in the background.

"You want to work for the company, you have to wear the uniform."

Instead of simply handing it to her, he gathered the shirt and tugged it over her head. Left with no choice, she pushed her arms through the sleeves and tugged down the waistband, intensely aware of him.

He was so close, she could see the slight pulse of blood through a vein in his neck, smell the pine-and-citrus scent of his soap.

She couldn't breathe suddenly. He looked down at her, that pulse beating more rapidly.

He leaned down and she held what little breath she had in her lungs, certain he was about to kiss her.

He did, but to her astonishment, only a kiss on her forehead.

"I'll try to make this as painless for you as possible," he promised.

Too late, she thought. It was far too late for that.

He walked out to greet the guests. "I'm Alex Mendoza. You can call me Captain Alex. You all probably know today's crew, Violet Porter."

The guests all greeted her with enthusiasm.

"I didn't know you helped out on the boat tours, too!" Barbara exclaimed. "You should have told us yesterday."

"I don't usually. But *Captain Alex* is in a bind."

"The boat is ready and waiting. I'm expecting one more, but I think she just pulled up."

Violet thought only three couples from the campground would be there. She looked over his shoulder and was startled when Ariana came running in, wearing a bucket hat and a Mendoza Charters hoodie that was at least three sizes too big.

"Sorry I'm late. I couldn't find my hat."

"You're only five minutes late."

"Hi, Violet!" the girl suddenly exclaimed, catching sight of her finally. At least she had stopped staring at Violet like she had suddenly materialized through the walls. "I didn't know you were going with us!"

Before Violet could answer, Ariana looked around. "Where's Kyler? Is he already on the boat with his mom?"

Alex shook his head. "Bad news, kiddo. Kyler broke his arm

this morning at the skate park. Kim is at the ER with him. Violet has agreed to pinch-hit for her."

"Oh no. Is he okay?"

"His mom said he has some bruises but mostly the broken arm. I know you were looking forward to hanging out with him today on the boat while his mom gave the tour."

She shrugged. "Kyler is cool, but you know I'm all about the whales."

He smiled and tugged Ariana's hat down on her head with clear affection.

For all the pain between them, Alex was a wonderful father. She had always known he would be.

Of course, she had expected him to be a good father to the children they would have had together.

"Everybody have binoculars and cameras?"

The assembled guests held up their packs.

"I've already got drinks on board and Violet has brought lunch for us. Let's go."

He grabbed the box of sandwiches and led the way toward the marina, filled with sailboats, fishing craft and a few expensive-looking pleasure cruisers.

He stopped at a deck beside a sleek, beautiful cabin cruiser with the name *Second Chance* written in curling script along the side.

Violet stood on the dock, her heart pounding. She didn't want to do this. She didn't know if she *could* do this. All she could see was Lily, silent and cold. Gone.

"What's wrong?" Ariana asked. "Did you forget something?"

"No. I..." Her voice trailed off.

The girl looked confused. "Aren't you coming?"

"Yes. Right now."

She couldn't put it off any longer. Feeling vaguely nauseated, she stepped onto the narrow gangplank. At least there were polished wooden railings along either side. She gripped them tightly, certain that she was shaking enough she would have trembled herself right off the side without them.

Alex waited on the boat, his hand outstretched to help her take that final step.

"Everything okay?" he asked as his warm fingers closed around her and he tugged her onto the boat.

"Yes. Great," she lied. She slid her hand away from his as soon as her feet were safely on the deck of the *Second Chance*.

"Here's the script," he said, handing her a clipboard with notes on it. "Ari is great at spotting and identifying marine life. She can be your eyes. Okay, kiddo?"

"Sure thing." His daughter beamed.

"Do you need me to do anything as we leave the marina?" she asked.

He smiled and this time her shakiness had more to do with the impact of that smile than her nerves. "Just enjoy the ride."

Right. Like that would happen.

She found a chair inside the spacious cabin with the other passengers as Alex gave them a quick lesson on safety and handed out life vests.

A few moments later, he went out the side door and climbed up to the wheelhouse above their cabin.

Violet watched as a young smiling marina worker who looked about twelve pulled the gangplank back to the dock and unmoored the vessel.

Violet's stomach lurched as Alex steered the boat carefully away from the dock.

What was she thinking? She should have come up with any excuse to extricate herself from a situation she absolutely did not want to find herself in.

She had never been particularly seasick. Spending her teenage years in Cape Sanctuary, especially dating Alex, she had been out on the water plenty of times.

But she hadn't been on the water since Lily drowned not far from where they were right now.

As the boat crawled slowly through the water, seagulls cried overhead. Sea lions barked at them as they passed the mouth of the marina.

The boat's speed picked up now and Violet forced herself to relax. She was perfectly safe. Alex was good at what he did, she reminded herself.

He had always loved being out on the water, working with his father after school and on weekends. After Jorge's health issues, Alex had been glad to take over running the family's charter business with Javi.

He would keep them safe. She knew that. Nothing to worry about.

"It's so fun to see you here!" Edie spoke loudly to be heard over the boat motor. "I had no idea you helped out on the whale watching tours in addition to working with your mother at Wild Hearts."

"I don't, usually," Violet admitted. "The captain was in a bind today, so I agreed to help out. Otherwise, he would have had to cancel your excursion."

"How nice of you!" Edie beamed at her. "Isn't that nice, Barbara?"

"Thank you!" Her sister, who seemed a little more formal and always seemed to be watching Edie with concern to make sure she didn't tire herself out, gave Violet a nod. "Can you tell me how soon before we might have a chance of seeing whales?"

"I'm not sure, to be honest. I haven't been on the water in a few years and I know the patterns can change. We're probably a little late for the gray whale migration, since that's usually done by early June, but we will probably see humpback whales and possibly minke whales. There's a resident population of orcas that tend to hang out in certain areas. We also might be able to find blue whales, the largest mammal on earth. They're fairly rare but it's possible."

"I don't care what we see," Edie said, eyes bright with excitement. "I just can't believe we're here on this beautiful boat with a scrumptious captain."

Vi couldn't disagree about that part, at least. Alex was definitely scrumptious. The past decade had only heightened the natural good looks of his youth.

"There are lots of things to see besides whales," Ariana informed the group. "You should watch for dolphins, porpoises, seals and, of course, sea otters. Those are my favorites."

"Sea otters are adorable," Jane Allen said. The young YouTube travel broadcaster from Las Vegas and her videographer partner, Tony, had been at the campground for only a few days, but Violet instinctively liked her. She had checked out the woman's channel and thought she approached every location with sensitivity and a passion that came through in her work.

"Right?" Ariana said. "I love them so much. I hope we also see puffins. They're so adorable. There are a couple of little islands we'll pass by where they hang out a lot."

"Oh, that would be amazing," exclaimed Donna Howe, the female half of the third couple. "We saw puffins on our Alaskan cruise. Remember, Jim?"

"You'll want to keep your binoculars handy," Ariana informed them knowledgeably. "You never know what we'll see."

Just then from the loudspeaker, Alex's voice rang out.

"We've got a pod of Risso's dolphins coming up on the port side."

"That means left," Donna said. "We learned that on our cruise. I remember it because *left* and *port* both have four letters."

Everybody grabbed binoculars and headed out of the cozy cabin to the deck that circled the boat. They found a group of at least fifteen of the large gray dolphins near the surface about a few hundred yards away.

Violet scanned the notes until she found a section on the dolphins and shared what she read with the group as they watched them dive and surface again playfully.

"How old do they get?" Edie asked. "I read that whales can be over a hundred years old. What about dolphins?"

Violet looked down at her notes but couldn't specifically find the answer to that.

"I'm not sure," she answered. "What about you, Ari?"

She shook her head, though she looked interested in the answer. "I don't know. My dad might, though. He knows all kinds of things."

Violet hesitated. She might have made some excuse, but Edie asked her a second question about how the dolphins communicate with each other.

"I don't know that either," she admitted.

"Do you want me to go ask my dad?" Ariana asked.

She had no doubt Alex could answer all those questions. He had always fascinated her with his vast knowledge of the sea and all the creatures who lived in and around it. On the other hand, she thought it would be more safe for Ari to stay here on deck than to climb the ladder to the wheelhouse.

"I'll go ask him. Hold on a minute."

"Ask him when we should start looking for whales," Barbara said.

She walked to the back of the boat. Gripping the rail tightly, she climbed to the wheelhouse, where Alex was standing, looking out to sea.

He gave a surprised look when she climbed up to join him. "Hey. How's it going down there?"

"I have no idea what I'm doing," she admitted. "I haven't been out on open water in years. People are asking questions I can't answer."

"Most things are on the script."

"Yes. It does seem to be fairly comprehensive. Edie asked me about the Risso's dolphins we saw. Their life span and how they communicate with each other."

"Tell her they can live to be older than thirty and they communicate like most dolphins, with a combination of echolocation, whistles and social communication like clicks."

She made a mental note of his answers. "Got it. Thanks. Also, they've asked when they should start looking for whales."

"Now," he said with a smile. "I've had reports from buddies who were fishing earlier in this area that there were several humpbacks breaching earlier. Possibly a mother and a baby in the group. Tell everyone to keep their binoculars handy."

"I'll do that."

He gave her a careful look. "Are you doing okay? You seemed upset earlier."

She gave a slightly hysterical-sounding laugh and the words seemed to spill out before she could stop them. "Sure. Why wouldn't I be okay? My twin sister drowned four months ago, which has left me deathly afraid of water. Yet somehow here I am, out bobbing around in the middle of the Pacific with a man who once broke my heart into tiny pieces. I'm perfectly fine."

"Oh, Vi," he exclaimed, looking stricken.

"Don't worry about it. I'll be fine."

She hurried back out of the wheelhouse and down the ladder toward the deck.

Why had she said that? She should have kept her mouth shut.

She hadn't told anyone about her new fear of the water, deeply ashamed of the weakness. The last person on earth she wanted to know about that vulnerability was Alex Mendoza.

She loved the ocean and had always found peace there. She had lost so much when Lily died. She hated losing the solace of the water, too.

And now she had revealed that to Alex, giving him one more thing to pity her about.

She reported what he had told her about the dolphins to the group.

"Also, the captain said we are entering an area where humpbacks were seen earlier today."

Everyone lit up, lifting binoculars and scanning the rippling surface. It took another fifteen minutes before Alex came over the loudspeaker this time, his voice more muted than it had been earlier.

"Look to the horizon, straight ahead of us. We're approaching the pod. We follow the rules of the Marine Mammal Protection Act, which means we'll slow down to no more than seven knots and will not approach closer than two hundred yards, especially since this pod has a calf. I'll still put you in position for a great view, especially from the aft deck."

The guests all hurried to the back of the boat. It was a pod of six humpbacks, sliding gracefully into the water, then surfacing again, their blowholes spewing air and water. He stayed near the whales for about twenty minutes. One even breached, leaping straight out of the water, then twisting to dive again.

Seeing the sheer delight on the guests' features, especially Edie, pushed most of Violet's anxiety to the back of her subconscious.

To Violet's surprise, Ariana was a fount of information, talking about how they were a species of baleen whales, how males can sing a complex song lasting ten to twenty minutes, about their migration patterns and their diet of krill and other small fish.

Alex's daughter easily could have run the tour herself, without Violet's input at all.

After everyone on the boat seemed to have seen enough, Alex turned back closer to shore. He piloted the *Second Chance* with skill through the rough waters, then pulled into a small protected cove north of Cape Sanctuary, one of those "dog hole" harbors Franklin had talked about the other day that logging companies had used, the name coming from the fact they were considered barely large enough for a dog to turn around in.

The small, nimble *Second Chance* had no trouble navigating it.

This was a rugged area, with hardly any beach and mountains rising up from the sea. Violet passed around the sack lunches for the guests.

"I can't get over how beautiful this is," Edie said, eyes shining. "Funny, how a bad diagnosis can shift your perspective. Every morning I wake up, only to find a world that seems to be more beautiful than the day before."

Lily would have adored Edie, Violet thought. The woman was facing a tough challenge with grace and gratitude.

The group seemed to enjoy their lunches. The conversation shifted around between grandkids and children, other trips during other times.

When she could no longer avoid it, Violet quietly asked Edie and Barbara to keep an eye on Ariana, then carried the remaining lunch bag and a soft drink up the ladder to the wheelhouse.

Alex looked surprised to see her. "What's this?"

"My mother made lunch for passengers and crew. I guess that means you."

"Did I ever tell you that your mother is one of my favorite people in Cape Sanctuary?"

Violet wasn't at all sure how she felt about the new bond between Rosemary and Alex. "She's obviously fond of you, too."

He reached inside and pulled out the ham sandwich and carefully unwrapped it. The boat bobbed on the waves as he took a bite with a sound of appreciation.

"I was starving. Thank you."

"Don't thank me. It was my mom," she said, though she didn't add that she had helped make the sack lunches for the group.

"This is a beautiful boat," she said instead. "Quite an upgrade from the seventeen-foot Boston Whaler you used to take me out on."

"We have a bigger one we use for larger groups, but I like the speed and agility of the *Second Chance*. She works great for fishing charters and whale watching trips."

"That's good."

He studied her. "How are you doing? Did you eat something?"

"I'm not hungry."

He frowned. "Feeling a little seasick?"

That would be the easy explanation. But she had already told him about her anxiety. She could see no point in lying to him.

"Nerves," she admitted. "I told you I'm not thrilled about being out on the water these days."

"I'm sorry, Vi. I wasn't thinking when I asked you to come. I should have realized."

She shrugged, lifting her face to the sea breeze. "I haven't told anyone but you. I'm sure I'll get over it eventually. I'm already feeling less panicky than I did when I boarded the boat."

"That's good."

"I'm embarrassed about it," she admitted.

"You shouldn't be. It's completely understandable. Lily was part of you. Your best friend."

"I miss her every minute of every day." Her voice cracked on the last word. To her dismay, she could feel tears begin to seep out as the compassion in his eyes shattered what remained of her composure.

"Oh, Vi. Sweetheart. I'm so sorry."

He pulled her into his arms. He smelled of sunshine and sea and the past, all entwined together.

She knew she would regret leaning on him, but at this moment, she needed the familiar comfort of his arms. She wrapped her arms around his waist and held on while the boat at anchor bobbed on the light waves and gulls cried overhead.

Against her cheek, she could hear the beat of his heart.

How could she be finding such peace here, with Alex? It made no sense at all.

His hand smoothed down her hair and it was only natural that she lifted her gaze.

He was looking at her with an expression so fiercely tender, she had to swallow.

His kiss seemed inevitable. It was slow, gentle, a quiet reunion.

His mouth felt the same, as if those ten years between them hadn't existed. While she could sense heat below the surface, his mouth was undemanding, straightforward.

She wanted to close her eyes and pretend she was nineteen again, in the arms of the man she loved, without all the pain and heartache.

She sighed, her hands grasping the front of his shirt, and he deepened the kiss.

She kissed him back, then heard a small splash out of the corner of her subconscious. She didn't know what it was. Maybe a seal slipping into the water or a cormorant diving for a meal. Whatever it was, it distracted both of them.

She stared into his eyes, shocked that he had kissed her and that she had allowed it. Not just allowed it. Fully participated.

He dropped his hands from her waist and stepped back against the railing, dark eyes filled with a strange mix of heat, tenderness and regret.

"I'm sorry. I shouldn't have done that. Not yet, anyway."

She chased the chaos of her thoughts around until she could come up with something coherent in response. "What do you mean, *not yet*?"

He looked as if he regretted saying anything. "Forget I said that. In fact, why don't we just forget the past few minutes ever happened?"

"Can you forget?" she demanded. "I doubt I can. What did you mean?"

"This isn't really the time or the moment, when I have six passengers below deck. Not to mention my daughter." He reached for her hand. "I might as well tell you, though. You have always been in my heart. I have never been able to get over you."

"You slept with Claudia Crane two months after we broke up," she replied sharply. "I certainly wasn't in your heart then."

"*We* didn't break up. You dumped me. I wanted to marry you, if you recall, but you told me we should date other people, that you weren't ready to settle down."

"I was nineteen years old! Still in college. You weren't much older. Neither of us was ready for marriage. I didn't think you would turn around two months later and sleep with someone else. Especially not Claudia!"

He was right—this really wasn't the time for this. Among the people below deck was that daughter he shared with Claudia.

She pushed away from the railing. "I need to get back to the passengers."

He reached out and rested a hand on her arm. "Vi. We need to talk about this."

The heat of his fingers seemed to burn through the fabric of the Mendoza Charters hoodie she wore, straight to her skin.

He could still affect her with a simple touch. After all these years. After everything else.

She flexed her biceps and he instantly dropped his hand. "I think we said all we needed to say ten years ago. Don't you?"

"Not by a long shot. Look, Ari is staying overnight with her cousins tonight at my mom's place. Can I meet you somewhere? We could grab a drink at The Sea Shanty or a piece of pie at the Sand Dollar Café or even just take a drive, like we used to do."

She didn't want to go anywhere with him, when his touch could send her spiraling back through the years. But she also didn't want to leave all these unresolved feelings between them.

Lily had died before she and her sister could work out their issues. Violet would always regret that she had left things unsaid between them and had vowed not to do that in other relationships in her life.

"I don't see the point in rehashing the past. It's done. But fine. We can grab a drink tonight."

She had a feeling getting completely hammered would be the only way she would ever forget that Alex Mendoza had kissed her again.

23

CAMI

SHE WAS BORED, A FEELING SO UNUSUAL SHE almost didn't recognize it.

Cami sat at the kitchen table in the bunkhouse, the spot she had taken over for work since her bedroom only had a small desk with an uncomfortable chair that left her feet dangling about six inches from the ground.

The problems of shorter people. Most furniture was designed for people of average size. Since she was only an inch over five feet tall, her feet never seemed to touch the ground and she always needed a footstool.

Here, she had room to fit a small ottoman under the table.

The other bonus was the window overlooking the beautiful gardens at Moongate Farm, overflowing right now with blossoms and bounty.

It was quiet. The mystical, proverbial state of being *too* quiet.

Violet had taken the sack lunches down to the marina and, surprisingly, had texted back that they shouldn't worry about her, as she was going out to help Alex with their guests on the whale watching excursion.

That left Cami here, alone with her thoughts.

She sighed. She usually enjoyed being alone with her thoughts. But then, her thoughts weren't usually consumed with remembering the kiss she had shared the night before with Jon Rafferty.

Why had he kissed her?

Hours of pondering had found her no closer to figuring that out.

Finally, she sighed and closed her laptop. After her call with her client, she had written up notes on their conversation and sent a long email to her paralegal with instructions for Monday. She had also somehow managed to clear her inbox and check off three other tasks from her to-do list.

Baxter whined at her from his new favorite spot on the small rug by the sink in the kitchen, where he could rest in comfort and still keep an eye on her.

She rose, muscles stiff. They both could use a walk.

She had come to love the little schnoodle, with his furry face and dark stern-looking brows.

What would Rosemary think if Cami offered to provide him a home? Would her mother be grateful, or would she feel as if Cami was trying to take away some kind of link to Lily?

It didn't make much sense for her to take him, as much as she loved him. What would she do with a dog, really? She had a busy career and worked long, tiring days. She couldn't give a dog the attention it needed.

She certainly didn't have a beautiful farm for a dog to run through.

The sad reality was, Baxter was better off here with Rosemary. She could still come visit him. She would just have to make more frequent trips back to Cape Sanctuary.

The prospect did not fill her with the uncertainty and discomfort it might have a few weeks ago.

She was coming to love it here, as much as the rest of the women in her family did.

"Want to go for a walk?" she said to the dog.

The answer was an obvious and resounding yes. Baxter jumped up from the rug and started dancing around the kitchen, tail wagging furiously. Cami threw on her sneakers and found Baxter's chest harness and leash, laughing as she struggled to hold him still long enough to put it on.

Finally she managed to work all the buckles and clipped on the leash and Baxter danced to the door.

The day was sunny, with a few high, plump clouds. She would have liked to walk down to the beach, but she deliberately set out in the opposite direction from Rose Creek.

They walked down to the marina, where Baxter scared up a few magpies in the parking lot.

By the time she returned to the house, her restlessness had eased and she felt more centered and comfortable in her own skin.

A little exercise always did that for her. Sunshine helped even more. In LA, she tried to swim and work out when she could in the exercise room of her condo development.

Still, a half hour on the treadmill wasn't the same as thirty minutes outside on a gorgeous summer day with a cool breeze and the ocean glinting in the sun.

She should spend the afternoon doing something completely selfish and irresponsible, for once, she thought as she approached Moongate Farm.

Read a book or browse through the shops downtown or just hop into her rental car and take a drive down the coast.

She was still trying to decide what appealed most when she walked up the driveway toward the bunkhouse and discovered a figure bent over in the garden.

Rosemary, she realized.

She was momentarily tempted to try sneaking into the bunkhouse without drawing her mother's attention. Their relationship was still so tangled, a mix of love and resentment, respect and old hurts.

As soon as she had the thought, Cami discarded it. Her relationship with Rosemary would never get better if she ran away from any chance she had to work on it.

More clouds had moved across the sky since she and Baxter set off and the temperature seemed to have dropped a few degrees.

Her mother stood up when she saw Cami approach, a small spade in her hand.

"You've been on a walk. Lovely. Where did you go?"

"Down to the marina. No sign of Violet and the campground guests yet."

"Alex will keep them safe," Rosemary said with perfect certainty.

"What are you working on out here?" Cami asked.

"Picking the spoils. I've got peas, new potatoes and strawberries that need to be harvested. I usually like to do it first thing in the morning or in the evening when it's cooler, but the past few days have gotten away from me."

"Can I help?"

Rosemary pushed back her wide-brimmed straw hat. "Certainly. I never turn down help in the garden."

Cami let Baxter off his leash and slipped him out of the chest harness. He immediately went to plop in the shade of the big oak tree.

"What should I do?"

"Why don't you pick the strawberries? There are a bunch that suddenly ripened in the past few days. I've got an extra pair of gloves in my garden cart you can use."

She pointed to the little wheeled seat Cami had seen her mother use to move along rows of produce without getting up and down a hundred times.

Cami found the gloves and pulled them on. She went to work lifting the leaves and finding all the hidden berries underneath. It was a little like a treasure hunt, with a delicious bounty at the end.

As they worked together, Cami felt something tense and tight inside her begin to uncoil.

"Thank you for helping me," Rosemary said after several minutes. She smiled at Cami. "And for everything else you've done since you came to Cape Sanctuary. It's been so nice to have you home."

"Except this isn't my home, Mom. Not really." She shouldn't have said it and regretted the words as soon as they were out, especially when her mother's gaze shifted.

"I suppose not. That wasn't the way I wanted things. I hope you know that."

She said nothing, not wanting to make things worse.

Rosemary set down her spade and perched on one of the willow benches scattered through the garden. "I hated leaving you behind, darling. But would you have been happy here if things had been different? Cape Sanctuary is a sleepy little town with one public high school for miles around. You would have been bored after the first day."

"It was good enough for Lily and Violet," she felt obliged to point out.

Rosemary gazed into the distance. "That was different. I love your sisters dearly. You know I do. But you needed more."

"Did I?"

"You were always so smart, it scared me. So much smarter than I was."

She stared, shocked at Rosemary's bluntness.

"I was an average child."

"You were never average," Rosemary corrected. "You were reading storybooks to your baby sisters by the time you were three years old. I didn't teach you how. You picked it up entirely on your own. And reading chapter books by kindergarten, when other children were learning how to spell CAT and DOG."

Rosemary gave a short laugh. "What was I supposed to do with you? I had no idea. You were so much like your father. He was always scary smart. I never quite knew what he saw in me, a former catalog model who barely graduated from small Cape Sanctuary High School."

Rosemary gave another short laugh, this one bitter with self-deprecation. Cami didn't know what to say. She would never have thought her tall, beautiful, self-assured mother would feel inadequate about anything.

Before she could press her, Rosemary went on briskly. "Anyway, your father would have been lost without you, rattling around in that big house in the hills by himself. In the end, it all worked out for the best, right?"

Cami wasn't sure she agreed. During those three years between when her parents divorced and when she left for college at seventeen, she had missed the rest of her family desperately.

She had been busy struggling through the cutthroat world of a competitive Los Angeles prep school and coming home to a housekeeper while Ted worked long hours.

When she would talk to her mother or sisters on the phone, they would bubble over with talk of how much they loved living by the ocean at Moongate Farm, with the chickens and the neighbor's milk cow and the rich vegetable garden.

It had seemed an entirely different planet.

"I would have liked to have more choice of where I lived,"

she finally said as she plopped a few more strawberries into the basket.

Rosemary looked at her, startled. "Would you have picked Moongate Farm?"

"I might have. We'll never know, will we? You and Dad told us you were getting divorced one minute and in the next breath you both told me that of course I would be staying in LA with him while the twins were coming here."

"It was the best possible option. You had been accepted into Vinehurst! Your father's alma mater. You had been on the waiting list basically since you were born. You couldn't just turn your back on that kind of opportunity."

It had never felt like a fair compromise. She had traded her mother and sisters for a snooty education at a prep school where she had always felt like an ugly duckling among all the tall blond swans with perfect teeth and plastic-surgery-enhanced noses.

What was the point in belaboring that? None of them could go back and change the past. Cami would probably always feel that her destiny had been chosen for her by her parents. For all she knew, maybe the twins resented that they hadn't had the chance to attend that exclusive prep school.

Her parents had wanted the best for them. She accepted that. She knew they loved her and never would have intentionally done anything that would cause harm.

The Vinehurst social jungle had certainly prepared her for the equally cutthroat world of law school and then working as a junior associate at Porter, Garcia & Sheen.

Still, she couldn't help the wistfulness curling through her as she plucked more strawberries and dropped them in the bucket with a satisfying thud. She would have liked the choice. Maybe she still would have picked Vinehurst. But she might have liked the chance to get her hands dirty more as a teen. To surf and have bonfires on the beach with friends and do yoga at sunrise with her mother and sisters.

"I'm sorry," Rosemary said softly, as if she could read her mind. "The hardest part of being a parent is accepting that not every decision you made for your children benefited them as much as you hoped it would. You do your best and pray it's enough to help them become decent, well-adjusted humans making a difference in the world."

Was she? That was certainly debatable. She helped companies protect their intellectual property. She wasn't sure that was exactly on par with saving the lives of two children like Lily had done or, like Violet, helping special-needs children learn and grow.

"So. Jon Rafferty. He's certainly grown up, hasn't he?"

The question from Rosemary seemed to come completely out of the blue.

"I never knew him as a boy, so I have no frame of reference to compare to."

"I didn't either, really. He was a teenager when we moved here. But I remember him being always quiet, with his nose in a book." Her mother gave her a knowing smile. "Kind of like someone else I know."

She didn't want to think that she had that in common with him.

Jon Rafferty was a sexy adventurer currently battling a machete injury, while she was a boring intellectual property attorney who hadn't taken a vacation since starting law school.

Why had he kissed her?

"Be honest with me. Do you think we have any chance of convincing him to change his mind about booting out the campground at the end of the season?"

Cami sighed. Her mother wasn't going to give up. "I think you would be better off exerting your energy toward trying to find a new location, rather than holding your breath that Jon will come around."

"You never know. He might see reason. He seemed perfectly nice last night when his father was speaking to our campers."

"The two things aren't mutually exclusive," she was compelled to point out. "He can be perfectly nice yet still not want a bunch of strangers traipsing through his backyard."

Rosemary gave her an affronted look. "What's not to like? I'm sure he saw for himself last night that our guests aren't a bunch of...of rabble-rousing hooligans."

"I don't think anything we do or say will change his mind," Cami said, trying for a gentle tone. "You need to prepare yourself that at the end of the season, Wild Hearts is either going to have to close or move to a new location."

Her mother yanked a few more peas off their plants, clearly annoyed. "What if I don't like either of those options?"

"Then the choice will be made for you," Cami said, somehow managing not to point out the irony.

24

VIOLET

"HOT DATE?"

Violet gave an inward groan as she glanced over her shoulder at her sister. So much for slipping away without anybody noticing.

She thought Cami planned to be preparing a brief all evening. Instead, she was standing in the door of Violet's bedroom, her sharp gaze missing nothing, from the Mendoza Charters hoodie Violet was still wearing to the makeup she was putting on for courage.

"No," she said reluctantly. "Not a hot date."

She wished she could leave it there, but she really didn't want to hurt Cami's feelings, when her sister had been so kind to her all week.

"I'm meeting a…friend."

Cami sat down on the edge of the bed.

"Does this friend happen to be a man named Alex Mendoza?"

Her lipstick smeared and she cursed, reaching for a makeup wipe. "Why would you say that?" she asked, trying for a casual tone.

"Call it a lucky guess," Cami said dryly. "Or at least an educated one. I know you ended up going out with Alex and some of the guests on a whale watching charter earlier today. I also know you seemed upset when you came home."

"Did I?"

She couldn't stop replaying those moments in the wheelhouse, when the past and the present had collided in his arms.

"I also know you hardly said a word during dinner. Being the logically minded attorney that I am, I have to ask myself whether there is any connection between your mood and your boat trip with Alex. Which is it? Correlation or causation?"

She made a face. "Smarty-pants. What if it's both?"

Cami studied her. "Are you sure meeting up with him is a good idea?"

She didn't want to talk about it with anyone, especially as she still wasn't sure why she had agreed to see him that night.

She closed her eyes, reliving that kiss again. She still didn't feel as if she had caught her breath.

"I have no idea. He wants to…clear the air between us."

"Ah."

Violet narrowed her gaze. "What do you mean by that?"

"It's merely a sound denoting understanding."

She finished touching up her lipstick and closed the applicator, smacking her lips together. "I'm glad one of us understands what's going on. I certainly don't know why he wants to talk or, more importantly, why I possibly agreed."

She had been tempted a dozen times to text him and tell him to forget it. Every time she picked up her phone, she couldn't bring herself to do it.

"The two of you have unfinished business, I guess."

"We don't, though. Everything between us was finished a long time ago. Completely finished."

Cami raised an eyebrow. "Who are you trying to convince? Me, Alex or yourself?"

She had no idea about that either. She didn't have time to answer, anyway, before a knock sounded at the door.

Her nerves jumped and she was tempted to hide out here in her room and lock the door.

Alex had insisted on picking her up, though she'd told him she could easily meet him at the bar. If she didn't answer the door, she wouldn't have to go with him and the past could stay where she had buried it.

"Want me to get that?" Cami asked, when Violet stood frozen, panic swirling through her.

"No," she finally said. "I'm good. Thanks, though."

With a deep breath, she picked up her favorite small crossover bag and slipped her phone into it.

"You don't have to go anywhere with him if you don't want to," Cami said, clearly reading her hesitation.

"I'll be fine," she said, forcing a smile and wishing she believed that.

Her sister still didn't look convinced, her brows furrowed with a worry that warmed Violet, despite her own anxiety. "I'll be fine," she repeated.

"Call me if you need backup."

On impulse, Violet hugged her older sister, grateful beyond words for her steady support.

"I love you," she said.

"Back at you," Cami said, squeezing her tightly.

A knock sounded again. Vi knew she couldn't avoid him anymore.

She headed for the door and opened it to the cool summer evening beyond and to Alex, who stood on the porch.

How did he look more gorgeous every time she saw him?

She felt awkward, which was ridiculous, considering how many times he had picked her up for dates during the years they had been a couple.

"Hi."

"Hi back," he said. She couldn't read his expression. He looked over her shoulder at Cami, who was standing a few feet behind her, arms crossed and a scowl on her face, like she was some kind of diminutive bodyguard.

"Cami. How are you?"

"I've been better."

Violet didn't need her sister to fight her battles for her, as much as she appreciated the backup. She pasted on a cheery smile. "I'm all ready. See you later, Cam. Good luck with the brief."

She basically pushed him back out the door and closed it behind them.

The night air smelled sweet from the garden and the pine trees around the farm as she walked to his pickup truck. She didn't wait for him to hold the door open, simply opened it herself and climbed inside.

"I wasn't sure you would come with me," he said, after he had climbed into the driver's side.

"I didn't want to," she admitted. "I almost called you several times to cancel."

"Why didn't you?"

She should have met him somewhere instead of letting him pick her up. Neutral ground would have been better than the tight confines of his pickup cab, where she was surrounded by the familiar, intoxicating scent of him.

Get it together, she ordered herself, trying not to shiver.

She released a breath. “As you said. I’ll be here all summer helping my mother. I don’t see the point in things being ugly and contentious between us.”

“I’m relieved to hear that.”

He pulled out of the driveway. Instead of driving toward the marina and town, he turned in the opposite direction.

“Where are you taking me?” she asked. “I thought we were grabbing a drink?”

“We still can. But we’re twenty minutes from sunset and it looks like it’s going to be a gorgeous one. I don’t want to miss it while we’re stuck inside the windowless Sea Shanty.”

She knew in a moment where he was taking her.

Their place.

It was an overlook on the cliffs south of town, with sweeping views down the wild, rugged Northern California coast.

Always desperate for somewhere to be alone when they were dating and living at home, they used to park there to make out.

On warm summer afternoons, they would walk the narrow twisty trail to a small isolated beach that only appeared at low tide.

He didn’t suggest that now, much to her relief. Instead, he pulled off onto the side of the road to a narrow strip of land surrounded by wildflowers. Sea figs, fiesta flowers, coastal goldenbush.

They both climbed out and walked a short distance through coastal pine and brush on a well-beaten path toward the overlook.

“Oh. Someone’s put a bench at the overlook!” she exclaimed. “How perfect.”

He said nothing and she instantly knew who had put the bench there.

“You did this?”

He didn’t meet her gaze. “A view like this should be shared, don’t you think?”

Did he think of her at all when he came here? She wanted to ask but couldn't find the nerve.

"I'm glad you wore a hoodie. It can be cool here with the constant wind."

Yes. She remembered that. She also remembered they never seemed to have much trouble staying warm.

The sun, still probably a half hour from setting, hovered above the horizon, painting the ocean with pastels.

He sat down on the bench. She hesitated for only a moment before she sat beside him, hands shoved into the center pocket of her hoodie. His hoodie, actually, though she wasn't sure she wanted to give it back.

They sat in silence while the ocean washed against the beach far below and the wind whispered through the pines.

"I owe you so many apologies, I don't know where to start," he finally said, his voice low.

She curled her hands into fists. "You don't owe me anything. We've both moved on. I got over you a long time ago."

He gave a rough laugh. "That's good, I guess. Because I never got over you."

She stared at him, the fading light burnishing his features. "You were married for three years. You must have gotten over me a little."

"I tried, for Claudia's sake and Ariana's. I told myself I had. I wanted my marriage to work and grieved at my own failure when she filed for divorce. But I think she always sensed some part of my heart would never belong to her. How could it? It was yours. I suspect it always will be."

Violet caught her breath at the low emotions in his voice. In another man, she might have thought it some kind of a line, sweet words intended to seduce her into forgetting all the pain.

Not from Alex. He had never lied to her. Not once in all the time they'd dated.

She felt hot suddenly and had to be grateful he couldn't see the blush she knew would be coating her cheekbones. She lifted her face to the wind, grateful for its cooling power.

What could she say? *Some part of me has always loved you, too?*

The words hovered but she swallowed them. What would be the point? Yes, it was true, but she wasn't ready to say them. Nor was she ready to jump back into a relationship with him, after everything that had happened.

She let out a breath. "Ariana was amazing today. She knows more about whales and their habitat than I do. Why don't you have her narrating your sea life tours all the time?"

He looked down at her, his dark eyes murky, obviously aware she was deliberately changing the subject.

She thought he might press her into a discussion she wasn't ready to have. Instead, he sat back on the bench. "She's always been fascinated by the ocean. She wants to be a marine biologist when she's older."

"I think I wanted to do the same thing when I was her age."

Emotions crossed his features. "She loves going tide pooling. That's what she and her friend were doing down by the water that day. I had to run into the hardware store for something, so I told them to go ahead down to the beach and I would be there in a minute. It was low tide and I thought they would be perfectly safe."

The regret and guilt in his voice made her throat feel tight. "You couldn't know there would be rogue waves. They took everyone by surprise."

"Two nine-year-old children should never be allowed anywhere near the ocean alone. I know better."

A different decision and he might have been the one to drown.

"Even you can't stop a rogue wave."

"No. But I might have seen it coming and could have grabbed them and carried them up to the high water level before it could reach them. Thank God Lily was there."

She didn't want to think about that day, but she still had questions no one else had been able to answer. "After she rescued them, why couldn't she get out?"

The murky light in his eyes turned sharp edged with grief. He reached for her hand inside the hoodie pocket. She wrapped her fingers around his, not sure which of them was offering comfort to the other.

"Ari said another wave hit and knocked Lily down. The girls heard a crack and then she seemed to go limp and went under the water. They didn't see her again."

He was quiet. "I'm so damn sorry. I can say it a thousand times and it will never be enough."

"It's not your fault. Or Ariana's or her friend's. Or Lily's, for that matter. It was only a tragic accident."

Her voice broke on the last word, and to her horror, all the sadness and grief she had been battling for months seemed to come bubbling to the surface.

"Oh, Vi," he murmured.

He reached for her and, helpless, she sank into the familiar comfort of his arms and lost the battle.

She cried until she had nothing left, until her throat felt sore and his shirt was soaked.

"That felt long overdue," he said when she managed to retain some semblance of control.

Her eyes burned as if someone had tossed a handful of sand into them. Or maybe an entire beach.

They had come to enjoy the sunset but somehow she had missed it during her outburst. The sun was now only a band of orange and yellow on the horizon and a few stars had appeared in the sky.

How long had she been crying?

Embarrassment made her face heat again and she wanted to bury her head in her arms. "I'm sorry you had to bear the brunt of that."

"I'm not. I'm glad." His voice was fierce. "I can't do anything to bring Lily back, but the very least I can do is hold you while you grieve."

She had needed someone to do just that, she realized. These past four months, she had ached for someone to hold her.

Never in a hundred years would she have expected that to be Alex Mendoza.

They sat in silence as even that band of light disappeared. She was about to ask him to take her home when he reached for her hand again.

"There's no good way to say this, so I'm just going to come out with it. I want a second chance with you, Vi."

She stared, wishing she could read his expression in the darkness.

"You…what?"

"I never stopped loving you. Even with everything between us, some part of me always loved you."

She slipped her hand away, not sure she could trust herself to have that contact with him.

"I don't know what you want me to say."

"You don't have to say anything. Not now, anyway. I know the timing isn't right. You're grieving your sister. I just want you to know that when you're ready to think beyond that pain, I will be here in Cape Sanctuary, waiting. It doesn't matter how long it takes."

She screwed her gritty eyes shut, tempted beyond words to fall into his arms again and kiss that beautiful, familiar mouth. She wanted to tell him that she had never stopped loving him and that no other relationship ever felt right because those men weren't Alex Mendoza.

And then she remembered Ariana, the child he had created with Claudia Crane.

"Don't," she said quietly.

"Don't wait for you?"

"Don't love me. I won't ever be in a better place for that. You broke my heart. I know I told you we should date other people. That was on me and I own that. I still thought we would end up together. I never expected you to be married to someone else within six months."

"Again, I can't change the past and I wouldn't, even if I could, if that meant no Ari."

"I know you wouldn't. I get that. But you still broke my heart. I was a mess for a long time. I can't go through that again. Don't love me."

"Here's the funny thing about love, Vi. You have no control over other people's emotions. You can't tell me to stop loving you. It's too late for that."

"We were high school sweethearts. We didn't know anything about love. Real love."

He started to argue but she cut him off.

"You were cute and funny and popular, and I was flattered that you were interested in me instead of…"

Instead of Lily. She couldn't say the words.

"But that was a long time ago. We're different people. You're a father now. You have more important things to worry about than some girl you once loved."

She stood up. "Do you mind taking me home? I changed my mind and don't really feel like hanging out in a bar somewhere."

She did, however, feel like getting drunk. Truly hammered, which she had done only a few times in her life. Once when he'd called her to tell her Claudia was pregnant and wanted to keep the child, and once when she'd found out her sister had died rescuing that child.

He said nothing for a moment, but finally rose as well. He pulled a small flashlight from his key ring and turned it on to light their path back to his pickup truck.

He held the door open for her and extended an arm to help her inside, but she carefully avoided touching him. He didn't miss it. She could tell he was annoyed by the way his mouth thinned.

He climbed in behind the wheel but didn't start the vehicle immediately. Instead, he shifted toward her, his face a dark blur in the night. "I was hoping to clear the air between us, but I'm afraid I've only made everything worse."

She shook her head, though she knew he couldn't see it. "You haven't. You've made me realize something fundamental. I can't tell you I'm over you in one breath and then continue to be angry with you about the past in the next. I have to choose one or the other."

"Which one are you choosing?"

"I've decided not to be angry with you."

His mouth thinned again, but he started the pickup and focused on turning around, back toward Moongate Farm.

"I guess that's good. It will at least make everything a little easier this summer. Ariana has missed visiting your mom. She asked me yesterday why we hadn't stopped in for breakfast in a while."

Was her mother feeding everyone in town? No wonder Rosemary struggled with her bottom line.

No. She was just being neighborly and bringing in strays. It was one of the things her mother did best.

"Don't change your routine on my account. I wouldn't want to deprive my mother or Ariana of each other's company."

"They're pretty fond of each other. And Ari loves your mom's lemon butter on pancakes. She said it tastes like sunshine."

She could picture the girl saying that and almost smiled, despite the turmoil of her emotions.

He loved his daughter. She couldn't doubt that.

A moment later, he pulled up in front of the house. She thought she saw a curtain twitch in her mother's bedroom window but couldn't be certain.

Cami, she noted, wasn't making any effort to be subtle. Her

older sister was sitting on the front porch, watching them with interest.

"I wish I had at least had the chance to buy you a drink, after all your hard work today guiding the tour."

"You don't owe me anything."

"I wish that were true, but we both know better."

He exited the driver's side before she could answer. She started to open her door but he beat her to it, standing in the opening so she had no choice but to face him.

"I know you meant every word, Vi, but I also meant what I said. I love you. You can tell me not to all you want, but that's like telling the ocean to stop being so wet."

He stepped aside so that she could get through and she hurried to the bunkhouse without a backward look.

"How did that go?" Cami asked.

She knew her sister was concerned about her, just as she knew she would break down again if she had to go through the postmortem with Cami.

"I'm not in the mood to talk about it," Vi said. "Maybe sometime, but not tonight."

She hurried into her room, grimly aware she might have just destroyed all the progress she and Cami had made toward becoming closer.

25

CAMI

COLLECTING SOMEONE FROM THE SMALL airport in Redding was vastly different from an airport pickup at LAX.

No bumper-to-bumper traffic, no strict rules about where you could drive, no vast parking lots filled with people waiting on arrivals.

Here, she only had to take a leisurely drive, pull up roughly the time the plane was scheduled to land and then text that she had arrived.

A few moments later, her father came striding out of the terminal with his laptop case and a small suitcase.

She had already told him the color and make of her rental car and he headed straight for her, then opened the back door for his bags before sliding into the passenger seat.

"Thanks for picking me up, kiddo. My assistant tried to swing a rental car for me, but apparently there isn't one to be had anywhere in town."

"It's no problem at all. I guess I was lucky a few weeks ago. I didn't have any trouble. By the way, when Mom heard you couldn't get a rental, she said to tell you you're welcome to drive her car while you're here and she'll use the farm's pickup truck."

"That's nice of her," Ted said.

"It's a great car. A BMW. She didn't offer to let me drive it, which is why I'm still in the rental car."

He smiled at that as she pulled out of the airport and headed toward Cape Sanctuary.

"How are you holding up, Cam-bam?"

She smiled at the nickname the twins had given her when they were small. Her dad was the only one who occasionally used it these days.

"I'm good. It's been nice to take a little break from the commute and work remotely for a while."

"We miss you at the office. Did you hear we won the appeal for James Rowland? New trial and the justices threw out the testimony of his girlfriend's sister. As they should have, since it was complete hearsay."

"That's terrific. Just what you hoped would happen."

"Right. Without that testimony, the prosecution has no case. I expect it to be thrown out. With luck, he'll be home within the month."

That was one of her father's pro bono cases that he was particularly passionate about.

"And Carol and Pete Hernandez settled the suit against that delivery company in the fatal accident that killed their son. The company knew the writing was on the wall. Their driver was overworked and shouldn't have been on the road, and the company knew it."

"All in all, a good few weeks for Porter, Garcia & Sheen."

"We still miss you. Have you solved all of Rosemary's lease issues?"

She tried not to feel the sting of failure. "Only temporarily. Mom has permission to keep the campground at the Rose Creek headland for the rest of the season. Then she'll have to move the tents. That was the best I could do."

"I bet Rosie is not happy about that."

"She's still hoping her neighbor's son will change his mind, but I think she's finally starting to accept the inevitable and consider alternatives."

She and her mother had taken a drive along the coast a few days earlier, looking for a new location for Wild Hearts, without having much luck.

Neither of the Rafferty men had made an appearance at Moongate Farm, for breakfast or anything else.

Cami tried to tell herself she didn't care, but the truth was, she missed them both.

"I hope she'll come around. Your mother can be stubborn." He paused. "I'm confused, though. Why does the son get the final vote if his father's still alive?"

"Because his father is showing signs of dementia. The neurologist suspects from his symptoms it's Lewy body dementia."

"Oh no. That's a bad one."

It was. In the week since Jon had told her about their appointment with the neurologist, she had done a little basic research on the condition and had learned that it was the second most common cause of dementia, after Alzheimer's. Lewy bodies, she had learned, were protein deposits that developed on nerve cells in the brain, impairing thinking, memory and movement.

It was progressive, with no known cure.

"His son, Jon, is working on obtaining guardianship so he can have medical and legal power of attorney."

"Where does it stand?"

"I don't know. I haven't spoken with them in a week or so. I would guess they're going through the ad litem process right now."

"You could always sneak in and have Franklin Rafferty sign an ironclad lease agreement before any final guardianship hearing."

She knew her father didn't mean that, that this was just another way of testing her by playing devil's advocate.

"I would rather not be disbarred, thanks. Or, at the very least, face an ethics investigation."

Ted smiled. "Leave it to me to raise the only cutthroat attorney with principles."

She knew that wasn't true. Her father had principles. He fought hard for his clients but only within the law.

Ted had been her hero all her life. Though he wasn't prepossessing in any way—short, balding, with a mild-mannered smile—he still managed to fill any room he entered.

"Besides the campground, how's your mom doing?"

This was always a sticky subject between them. The casual way he always asked about Rosemary never quite rang true. Cami sensed he was far more interested in her answers than he ever wanted to reveal.

"She seems okay. Still grieving, of course. She and Violet both miss Lily desperately."

He nodded. "I don't know if any of us will ever figure out how to navigate a world without her in it."

His voice shook on the words and Cami suddenly had a hard time swallowing. Her father, always so even-keeled, hardly ever showed that kind of deep emotion. She found it as touching as it was heart-wrenching.

"True enough," she answered.

"You know, after Lily died, I expected your mother to give up this idea of running a luxury camping operation. I got the feeling it was Lily's dream, not necessarily Rosemary's. Your mom seemed happy enough with her occasional yoga retreats."

"She's really good at it, Dad. You should see the breakfasts she makes. People actually come for breakfast who aren't even staying at the campground."

He smiled a little. "She always did love to take care of people."

There was so much affection in his voice, Cami had to wonder again why they had divorced.

"No one is staying at the house this week, so Mom's offering you one of the fancy guest rooms. You should feel honored. Violet and I are sharing the bunkhouse, which only has hot water about half the time."

Despite her joking, Cami had actually quite enjoyed staying in the small, comfortable house. She had even become accustomed to the occasional icy shower.

"That's very kind of your mother." Ted gave a smile that looked slightly frayed at the edges. If Cami didn't know better, she would have thought he was nervous.

About what? Staying in the same house with her mother? What did he think would happen?

Did she really want to know?

She deliberately pushed that out of her head, and they talked about some of the cases she was working on until she drove through Cape Sanctuary and pulled up to Moongate Farm.

After she turned off the engine, Ted climbed out of the rental car and took a deep breath of the warm summer air. "That smell. It's unforgettable. Lavender and lemon balm and the ocean."

"It's nice, isn't it?"

She had become used to that, too. She would miss it when she returned to Los Angeles, where the air wasn't nearly as appealing.

"I always forget how beautiful it is here," her father said.

"Every time I come back, it's like reconnecting with an old friend I haven't seen in a long time."

She had started to open the rear door to grab his suitcase for him but had to do a double take at his words.

"I always thought you didn't like Cape Sanctuary."

Ted looked genuinely surprised. "Whatever gave you that idea?"

Because you let her go without us. Because you didn't chase after her.

"I like Cape Sanctuary fine. I've always thought it was a sweet little town with a beautiful setting. Just maybe not the best place to drum up business when you're a criminal defense attorney."

Baxter came around the house, barking furiously at the newcomer who dared invade his territory.

"Bax. That's enough," Cami said, her tone firm.

The dog shifted his attention from Ted to her and dropped his confrontational stance. His tail started wagging and he rushed toward her for some love.

She opened her arms and he jumped straight into them, as if they had been practicing. Cami laughed at the sweet, warm weight of him wriggling against her.

She scratched behind his ears. "There's my good boy," she cooed, earning a surprised look from her father.

"Since when are you a dog person?" Ted asked.

"Maybe I've never had one, but that doesn't mean I don't like them. Baxter is a sweetie. Baxter, this is my dad. And Lily's and Violet's, too."

The dog gave Ted a quizzical look but seemed perfectly content to stay in her arms. "He's only fierce until he gets to know you. Go ahead. You can pet him."

Her dad reached a tentative hand out and patted the dog's back. In that moment, the door of the house opened and Rosemary walked out on the porch, looking tall and stately and beautiful in the afternoon sunshine.

"I thought I heard a car. Ted. Darling. Hello."

She hurried down the steps and toward her ex-husband. The two of them embraced with clear affection and Rosemary even kissed his cheek, leaving Ted looking bemused.

"It's so good of you to make time for this. I know how busy you are."

"I would not have missed this. How wonderful of the town to honor Lily as part of Summer Sanctuary."

"Yes. I don't remember them ever picking a citizen of the year posthumously. Can I help you with your bags?"

"Not necessary. I didn't bring much. Only a carry-on and my laptop bag. You'll just have to point me in the right direction."

"I hope you don't mind, but I had to move you at the last minute. I was planning to put you in the Morning Glory room, our grandest suite, but I ended up giving that to a young couple from Idaho who eloped in Tahoe yesterday and then drove out to the coast for their honeymoon. They were hoping to stay in one of the tents, but those have been booked for weeks, unfortunately."

"I don't care where I sleep. I can take the sofa bed in the bunkhouse if that's all you have."

"It won't come to that. The Honeysuckle room is beautiful, if a little feminine."

"You know I never minded a little froufrou," Ted said gruffly.

Rosemary smiled. "I love a man comfortable enough in his masculinity to sleep surrounded by ruffles."

Ted gave her a wide smile that somehow left Cami feeling awkward and in the way.

A timer went off on Rosemary's phone and she frowned. "That's the muffins I'm making for tomorrow's breakfast. I need to take them out. Cami, you know where the Honeysuckle room is, right? Can you direct your father?"

"Sure."

"Thank you, darling."

Rosemary hurried back up the stairs, Ted watching after her

with an expression so raw with naked tenderness and yearning that Cami felt scorched just being in the vicinity of it.

Before turning back to her, Ted seemed to make an effort to compose his features into some semblance of a casual smile. "Thank you again for picking me up, Cams."

She was lost for words, still shaken by that look.

Did Ted still have feelings for Rosemary? He must. Cami had wondered a few times over the years by things he said or the careful way he asked about Rosemary, but she had never seen such blatant confirmation.

Her father was a ferocious adversary and cutthroat attorney. When he wanted something, he made no secret of it and did not rest until he had it.

If he had feelings for Rosemary, wouldn't he have acted on them before now?

More to the point, if he still had feelings for her, why would he have agreed to the divorce in the first place?

Her parents' relationship was not her business, Cami reminded herself. She had enough trouble figuring out her own.

She only had to make it through Summer Sanctuary this weekend and then she would be returning to LA, to her busy world of meetings, court filings, depositions.

The prospect held zero appeal.

She forced a smile. "No problem."

"I would love to take everyone out for dinner tonight, if you all don't have plans. I mentioned it to your mother on the phone the other day and she said she thought that might work."

"I don't have plans. I doubt Vi does either."

She hadn't talked much to her sister in the past week, after Violet returned so overwrought from going out with Alex Mendoza.

Violet had been staying close to home for the past week. She helped Rosemary with breakfast and then worked on the campground social media properties or paperwork, then would go for long walks on the beach each evening before crashing in her room.

Cami had tried to talk to her several times, but Violet was clearly not interested in sharing confidences. She was never rude about it; she just seemed determined to talk only about casual things and avoid any deeper discussions.

If Cami thought she and Violet were on track to forge a better relationship, this past week made her strongly question that.

They seemed like polite strangers who might have DNA in common but little else.

"Know of any good places around town?" her father asked.

"The Fishwife is always delicious, and I've heard good things about Melanzana's, if you're interested in Italian. There's also a new fancy hotel and restaurant down the coast. I can't remember the name, but I'm sure Mom or Vi can tell you."

"Okay. That's a start."

"I'm not the expert on Cape Sanctuary cuisine, though."

"We'll figure something out. Meanwhile, don't make other plans."

She snorted. Her social life here in Cape Sanctuary was nonexistent, especially with Violet keeping to herself.

For only an instant, that kiss she had shared with Jon flashed across her mind, but she quickly pushed it away again. He had made it crystal clear he didn't want to repeat the experience.

After showing her father to the lovely Honeysuckle room, decorated in pale yellow and rose, she walked back toward the bunkhouse with Baxter at her heels.

Before she reached the small dwelling, she could smell something chocolaty and delicious.

"Yum. What smells so good?" she asked as she walked into the kitchen, where Violet was paging through a magazine.

"Chocolate chip cookies," Violet said. "Here's something you might not know about me. When I'm stressed, I bake. I know this recipe by heart now."

"Does it help?"

Violet made a face. "Not really. Then I become stressed about eating an entire batch of cookies by myself. I started giving them away to any of my students who were struggling. I would drop them off and we would have a quick visit, which always seemed to help the situation."

Her sister seemed to be a compassionate, dedicated teacher. "That sounds nice."

"I thought I would make these for Mom to put out for the campground social hour tonight."

"Good idea. She'll appreciate that."

She hesitated, not wanting to be shut out again, when Violet seemed to be more inclined to chat than she had been all week. Still, what kind of an older sister would ignore Vi's obvious turmoil?

"Want to talk about what's stressing you?"

Violet gave a humorless laugh. "That would take more time than either of us has."

Cami poured a glass of water from the filtered pitcher in the refrigerator. "You've been upset all week," she dared to point out. "Ever since you met up with Alex last week. Again. Correlation or causation?"

"I'm not upset," Violet said sharply, rising with suddenly jerky movements to take the cookies out of the oven.

"No?"

"Why would I be? I'm completely over the man. Seeing him again doesn't bother me at all."

"Are you sure?"

Her sister released a breath as she set down the cookies on a trivet to cool and threw another prepared tray into the oven.

"I'm not sure of anything anymore," she finally said. "He wants the two of us to try again."

Cami sipped at her water. "I take it you're not interested."

This time Violet let the silence drag on longer as she transferred the cookies from the tray to a cooling rack.

"He was my first love, but that was a long time ago. We're not kids anymore."

"Sounds like you've thought things through."

"I feel like I've done nothing but think all week."

Violet set a couple of cookies on a plate and handed them to Cami. As peace offerings went, this one wasn't bad.

"I'm sorry I shut you out this week. I wasn't ready to talk about it."

"It's fine."

"It's not. You're leaving soon and I wasted an entire week acting like a total drama queen over a man I thought I had worked out of my system ten years ago."

"Some men are harder to shed than others."

"True enough."

"I totally understand that you needed to process things yourself before you could talk about it. I tend to do that, too."

She sipped at her water. "And I don't blame you for not wanting to talk to me. I'm obviously not the world's greatest expert on relationships. I spent four years with a man who cheated on me and undermined my confidence in just about every way."

"I'm so sorry. Sterling was an ass who never deserved you."

"True enough." She managed a smile. She didn't really want to talk about her ex any more than Violet did.

"I'm supposed to tell you Dad wants to take us all out to dinner tonight. He's looking for suggestions."

"I have a few," Violet said. "Dinner out will be a good distraction."

Cami bit into a cookie. "Oh my word. I don't need to go to dinner. I can just sit here and eat cookies. Those are possibly the best thing I've ever eaten."

Violet smiled, as Cami had hoped, looking brighter than she had seen her all week.

"I told you. They make everything seem better."

"Why don't you just plan on sending me those every week for the rest of my life?" Cami said, only half joking.

Violet smiled again. "Done. Then I'll have absolutely no stress left and you'll weigh four hundred pounds."

"I can live with that," Cami said and felt a huge sense of accomplishment when her sister laughed out loud.

26

JON

IN A SMALL TOWN LIKE CAPE SANCTUARY, IT was difficult but not completely impossible to avoid someone you didn't want to see.

Jon managed to avoid Cami Porter for the better part of a week, mainly by getting up early to fix his father's breakfast so Franklin wouldn't wander down to Moongate Farm looking for food and by keeping a close eye on him during the day.

By Friday, he was tired of his own cooking and ready to see something besides his father's house.

Franklin was having a good day, the latest in several good days in a row.

Jon didn't know if it was the new medication working or if his father's condition was simply momentarily stagnant. He could only be grateful that Franklin seemed more lucid, with fewer incoherent moments.

Franklin suggested they go out for dinner that night at The Fishwife and Jon didn't see any reason to refuse.

When he and his father walked out to the restaurant patio, surrounded by flowers in containers and overlooking the ocean, he should have known Cami Porter would be the first person he would see.

She was sitting with her mother and sister and an older man he didn't recognize. Something about the man's eyes looked enough like Cami's that he guessed this must be her father.

She didn't see Jon or Franklin at first. She was turned slightly away from him, laughing at something someone else said. In the glow from the discreet lighting around the patio, she looked animated and bright and lovely.

His mind suddenly filled with memories. Her taste, her touch, her scent, like wildflowers after a spring shower.

He had dreamed of that kiss every single damn night since.

He let out a breath. He was about to turn and make some excuse so he could ask the server to seat them inside when his father caught sight of the group.

"Look at that, Jonny. Our friends."

"Oh, you know the Porters?" The young hostess gave them a bright smile. "I can seat you at a table near them, if you'd like."

"Not necessary," he started to say at the same time his father eagerly contradicted him.

"That would be lovely. Thank you."

"Great." Her smile widened. "Follow me."

She led the way to the table next to Cami and her family. It was the absolute last place he wanted to be. Jon wanted to request a different table, but that would only make everything worse.

He knew the moment she spotted him. She was speaking animatedly to her sister one moment and then her eyes widened and she seemed to freeze.

Instantly, he was back in the entryway of his father's house, her mouth warm under his, her body soft and curvy.

He hadn't been able to get her out of his head, no matter how hard he tried.

Rosemary spotted them almost immediately. Her face lit up, in vivid contrast to her daughter's. "Franklin! Jon. Hello. Are you meeting someone?"

"No," Franklin said. "It's just the two of us. We were tired of eating our own cooking, if you want the truth. I've been telling Jon we should head down to Moongate Farm for breakfast, but he won't hear of it, for some reason."

Jon did not want to look at Cami, certain he would see a knowing look in her eyes. She had to suspect, correctly, that he was trying to avoid her.

"Why don't you join us? We have plenty of room at our table. You don't mind, do you, Teddy?"

Teddy. Ted Porter. As he'd suspected, this was Cami's father.

"Of course not. Please. Join us."

Jon was about to make some kind of excuse, not wanting to intrude on a family gathering, but his father took the decision out of his hands.

"Very kind of you." Franklin immediately pulled out a chair and sat next to Violet.

"Hi, Lily. I haven't seen you in forever," his father said.

Violet gave him a polite smile that didn't quite reach her eyes. "I'm Violet. Lily's twin."

He noticed she did not add the information that her sister was dead.

"Of course you are. My mistake. You two look so much alike."

"Yes. We do." Violet gave another smile, this one tinged with sadness.

Jon sat stiffly next to Cami while the hostess gave menus to him and his father.

"I guess you all haven't met," Rosemary said. "Franklin, Jon, this is my ex-husband, Ted Porter. Ted, these are our wonderful neighbors, Franklin Rafferty and his son, Jon."

"Pleasure to meet you. I understand you're the ones leasing the headland property for Rosie's glampground."

"Yes. That's right," Franklin said. "It's been a pleasure to have all the campers around. I've always said that spot is my favorite little stretch of land along the coast. Such a beautiful view from there, in all directions. And all the campers have been lovely. I gave a talk to them last week about some of the local history, and they were so kind and warm about it."

"Are you a history expert?" her father asked.

"Not really," his father said.

"Don't be so modest," Rosemary said. "You seem to know everything that ever happened in the area. Your lecture was fascinating. All the guests who heard you said it was the highlight of their stay."

"Oh, that's nice."

"We would love you to come again. Just say the word."

"I'll have to see," he said.

The waiter came just then to take their order.

"I see we've added a few people. Do you need more time?"

"We really don't need to intrude on your family dinner." Jon tried again, a little desperately. "We can grab our own table."

"Don't be silly. We're happy to have you," Rosemary said. "Aren't we, girls?"

Violet, whom Jon barely knew, nodded. "Of course."

"Thrilled," Cami said, her voice so dry he doubted anybody else noticed.

"We haven't even ordered our food yet," Rosemary said. "Why don't you two take a look at the menu and we'll all order together to make things easier for the kitchen staff."

"I'll come back in a few moments," the server said.

Jon pointed his father toward a moderately healthy option, grilled shrimp and vegetables, while he picked the wild-caught halibut.

After the server returned to take their order, her parents asked Franklin more about the history of the area, with Violet chiming in to ask questions of her own.

"How are you?" Jon said to Cami in an undertone.

She sent him a quick look under her lashes. "Fine. It's been a busy few days. We've missed having your father for breakfast."

"I've been trying to do a better job at keeping track of him. I had sensors installed on the doors and windows so I know when they're opened, and I also bought him a watch that doubles as a GPS locator."

"Smart." She paused, looking down the table where Franklin was telling everyone about one of the early mines in the area.

"He looks good," Cami said. "Better than I've seen him since I came to town."

Jon thought the same. There were even days when it was hard to remember his father had dementia.

"The new meds appear to be helping. I'm hoping we can stave off the inevitable a little longer."

"That's good. Any progress on the guardianship application?"

This, at least, was something he didn't mind talking about with her. "Robert Layton says a hearing should be scheduled soon. Everything seems to take twice as long as I expected."

She glanced down the table at her father. "If you need to hurry the process along, my father probably has connections in the court system up here. Friends who have friends. He knows everyone."

"I just need to be a little more patient, which has never been one of my strengths."

"I know you're anxious to get back to Guatemala and the dig."

He let out a breath, regret pinching at him more intensely than the puckered scar on his arm ever had. "I'm quitting the dig."

She gaped at him. "You're what?"

After a careful look to make sure his father wasn't paying them any attention, he spoke in a low voice.

"With the reduction of symptoms and the cognitive improvements in the past week, we've been able to have some tough conversations. Dad feels himself slipping away. It's killing him."

"Oh, Jon. I'm so sorry."

How did she do that? With only her look of compassion, he felt as if she had reached out and embraced him, soothing away all the uncertainty of the past few weeks.

He wanted to gather her into his arms and simply hold her.

More than that, he wanted to kiss her. To lose himself in the heat that always seemed to simmer between them.

"The bottom line is, Dad is vehement that he doesn't want to go into a care center until he absolutely has no choice. He wants to live at home for as long as possible, while he still has most of his faculties about him. He says he'll agree to any legal arrangement, if I promise to help him stay at Rose Creek."

"I can't fault him for that. Can you?"

He shook his head. "No. I would want the same. I just don't know how I'm supposed to make that happen. He certainly can't live on his own, and I suspect he won't be happy with some stranger I hire from an agency."

"You're in a tough spot."

"Not really. It all boils down to one thing. How can I selfishly travel across the world to delve into the past when my father needs help now, in the present?"

"What about your work? What will you do, if you leave the dig?"

He had thought extensively about this and still did not have any clear answers. "I've got a few projects I can do from Cape Sanctuary. I could teach some distance classes at my university in Austin. I could also document the work I've been part of so far at Tikal. Maybe finish writing the book I've talked about doing for years."

He looked down the table at his father again. "It won't be forever. Even with the initial success the medicine has had, the neurologist warned me the effects won't last. Eighteen months from now, maybe sooner, he likely won't know who I am."

After the bitter words and distance between them the past few years, Jon wouldn't have thought that would hurt so much.

He hadn't realized he had curled his fingers together on the table until Cami reached out and covered his fist with her hand. "I'm sorry," she said again. "This must be so difficult."

Why had he stayed away from her all week? He had no answer to that. All he knew was that he wanted to lean into her comfort, lose himself in the warmth and concern he saw in her eyes.

She was leaving, he reminded himself. Before long, Cami would be returning to Los Angeles and her busy law practice.

He missed her already.

"You're a good son," she said quietly.

He hadn't been. He had let resentment and anger and all the things he couldn't change drive a wedge between him and his father.

He was here now, trying his best to help his father.

What else could he do?

27

CAMI

DINNER WITH THE RAFFERTY MEN TURNED OUT to be an exquisite sort of torture.

After those quietly intimate moments with Jon, they were both drawn into the conversation with the rest of the table and didn't have the chance for any other private conversation.

Still, Cami was aware of him throughout the entire meal. The shift of his leg under the table, brushing against her skirt. The casual smile he gave her mother when Rosemary said something amusing. The way his eyes lingered on Cami whenever she offered something to the conversation, until she inevitably forgot everything she was saying.

Oh, she had it bad.

All in all, she was relieved when they all finished the delicious meal and her father settled the check.

"You really didn't have to pay, but thank you. It was a lovely meal," Jon said.

"Oh, it was our pleasure," Rosemary said. She kissed Franklin's cheek and then did the same to Jon, who looked startled.

He didn't kiss Cami goodbye. She told herself she was relieved at that.

Ted had driven them all there in Rosemary's BMW, and she and Violet climbed in the back for the ride home while their mother sat in the passenger seat.

"That really was lovely, wasn't it?" Rosemary said.

"Yes. Kind of like old times," Ted said.

"Almost." Rosemary sighed. "Being all together like this makes me miss Lily even more."

Cami was shocked when her father reached out and squeezed her mother's hand. She was even more shocked when they didn't seem in any hurry to separate, holding hands the rest of the way home.

In the back seat, Cami nudged Violet and gestured with her head toward their parents' linked fingers. Even in the darkness she could see her sister's raised eyebrows.

At the house, Ted climbed out and opened the doors for everyone.

"Thanks for going to dinner with your old man."

"Thanks for paying," Cami said. "It was nice of you to pay for the Raffertys, too."

Ted shrugged. "Who knows? Maybe the son will decide the Porters are all too nice for him to kick the campground off the bluff."

"I wouldn't hold your breath," Cami said.

Rosemary sighed but mustered a smile for them all. "Well, I'm beat and tomorrow's bound to be a stressful, er, busy day. At least for those of us going," she added, giving Violet a pointed look.

Cami could see Violet's mouth tighten, but her sister said nothing. As far as Cami knew, Violet was still insisting she couldn't endure the Citizen of the Year ceremony the next day.

"Don't worry about helping me with breakfast," Rosemary said firmly. "You should both sleep in while you have the chance. I've told the guests to expect only muffins and fruit tomorrow. If they want more, they can find it over at the fire department pancake breakfast."

"Sounds good."

"Night, then." Rosemary glided away, her wispy scarf trailing behind her.

Cami was quite sure she didn't mistake the way Ted's gaze followed her up the stairs and into the house.

"Good night, Dad," Cami said, giving him a hug.

"Yes. Good night," Violet said. Her usually graceful sister reached out rather awkwardly to hug their father, who was about the same height.

Did Violet feel the same awkwardness around Ted that Cami did around Rosemary?

It was a startling thought but made complete sense. Just as she spent more time around Ted, the twins had spent more time with Rosemary, so they would automatically feel more comfortable around their mother than their father.

Ted gave them one last wave and headed into the farmhouse behind Rosemary, leaving Cami and Violet alone in the evening, scented by flowers blooming wildly around them.

"It's barely ten," Violet said as they headed for the bunkhouse. "I'm not ready for bed yet. Especially since we've just been given permission to sleep in tomorrow. What about you?"

"No," she admitted. "Want to go into town and hit up The Sea Shanty?"

"Not really," Violet said with a grimace.

Before they could reach their guesthouse, her sister looked up at the full moon.

"I'm going to take Baxter for a walk down to the beach," she said suddenly.

Cami stared. "Are you kidding? It's pitch-dark."

"No, it's not. It's a full moon and I've got a good flashlight inside. Don't worry, though. You don't have to come."

"I've already lost one sister to the ocean. I'm not going to lose another."

"Don't worry about me. I'll be fine."

"I'm coming with you," Cami said, in the same implacable tone she used with demanding clients. "Give me five minutes to change into something more suitable for a late-night trip to the beach."

"Good idea. I'll do the same."

Half-worried her sister would leave without her, Cami changed with her bedroom door open, listening to Violet move around in her own room and then head to the kitchen with Baxter at her heels.

By the time Cami changed into yoga pants and a baggy sweatshirt, Violet had found the dog's leash.

"Look what I found," she said, holding up a bottle of wine with a label Cami didn't recognize. "I think Lily must have left it. Let's take it with us and raise a glass for her."

It would have been faster to drive one of the golf carts over the headland and down to the beach, but they took the trail that skirted the campground.

The strawberry moon lit their path, bright as twilight. In ten minutes, they were heading through the break in the chaparral to the sand.

Violet had shoved the wine in a backpack. To Cami's surprise, she pulled out a thin plaid blanket that she spread on the sand above the high water mark.

"This was a great idea," Cami said, settling in beside her sister. "Thanks for inviting me."

Violet, who hadn't invited her at all, snorted and reached into her backpack for the wine bottle. Apparently, she had thought ahead enough to bring a corkscrew as well as a couple of plastic cups from the bunkhouse.

She poured the wine into each cup and then set the bottle in the sand next to her.

"To Lily," Violet said, holding out her cup to Cami. "My partner in crime, my womb mate, my mirror image. You drove me crazy most of the time but, damn, I miss you."

"To Lily," Cami said. They tapped cups and a little wine sloshed over the sides.

Cami sipped at hers while Violet chugged a healthy amount, then made a disgusted face.

"Oh man. That's terrible."

Cami wouldn't have called it terrible. Just bland and uninteresting. "Maybe we're just comparing it to the fancy stuff Dad insisted on buying at dinner."

"No. It's awful. Lily always had lousy taste in booze, just like she did in men."

Violet immediately covered her mouth. "I shouldn't have said that."

Cami sipped again. The second taste wasn't quite as nondescript, but she still wouldn't have called it memorable.

"Did she have bad taste in men? I wouldn't know. She never shared much with me about the men she dated."

"Of course she didn't. You have a life and it would have taken weeks to go over the men in her life."

Violet winced again and chugged more of her wine. "I shouldn't have said that either. I usually try not to be so bitchy. I don't know what's wrong with me tonight."

"You miss her," Cami said gently.

Violet gave a rough laugh and held her cup up. "There you go again, Miss Smarty-Pants."

She didn't mind the nickname, under the circumstances. "I miss her, too."

They sat in silence for a few moments, listening to the waves and the night. Cami could hear peeping frogs somewhere in the distance, probably in the wetlands next to the creek that flowed into the ocean, and an owl hooted from the trees behind them.

"Did you ever wonder why Lily was living back in Cape Sanctuary with Mom in the first place?"

"I wondered," she admitted. "I take it you know."

"Yes. I know." Violet took another healthy swallow of her wine. "She was here because of me."

Cami waited for her to elaborate. It took a few moments but Violet finally continued.

"For about six months last year, she lived with me at my condo in Sacramento. At first, it was fun to be living together again."

Vi finished off her wine and poured more into her cup, in what Cami could only think was some sort of alcohol-fueled masochism.

"And then I kicked her out. Because of a man."

"Ah."

Vi gave a rough laugh. "Right. Ah. The last time we spoke after the holidays, we fought. I was angry at the way she was treating a friend of mine. A fellow teacher who instantly fell headlong in love with Lily. I told Lily she was playing with the emotions of a good man who deserved better. I said ugly things. Hurtful things."

She sniffed and wiped her arm on her hoodie. Cami wanted to comfort her, but she sensed this was something Violet had kept bottled up for a long time and she needed to talk about it, no matter how painful.

"We would have gotten through it. I could never stay mad at her for long. I was supposed to come up to the Cape that weekend and we were going to dinner so we could talk things out. I was looking forward to mending fences with Lily and hearing all about their plans for the glampground."

She folded her arms around her upraised knees and rested her chin on her shoulder, looking out at the moonlight dancing across the waves.

"Instead, I got a phone call from Mom, telling me Lily had died."

Cami frowned. "I hope you don't think for a minute that her death was somehow your fault."

Violet was quiet, the only sound the sea washing against the shore.

"If I hadn't kicked her out, she wouldn't have been living back in Cape Sanctuary."

"And two little girls might have been dead."

Violet let out a breath. "I wish I had kept my mouth shut. Why did I have to say those ugly things to her?"

Though the words came out in a rush, Cami was quite certain Violet had been thinking about them for a long time. Probably since that day she learned her twin had died.

"It wasn't even my place. Not really. Why did I feel like I had to call her out to protect a man who was perfectly capable of handling his own romantic relationships?"

"Because he was a friend and you didn't want to see him hurt."

"I hate so much that the last time we spoke, I was angry and hurtful. That's what she took to her grave with her, probably thinking I hated her or something."

She let out a sob. Chest aching, Cami wrapped an arm around her. Violet leaned into her and let out another sob, then went quiet, though Cami could still feel her trembling.

"She couldn't think you hated her," Cami said softly. "I'm sure of it. For every one hard word, she had a thousand other wonderful memories of the two of you together. A hundred thousand more."

Vi sniffled in answer.

"You were a team," Cami went on firmly. "One disagreement couldn't change that. Lily knew you loved her. I'm sure of it."

Violet wrapped her arms around Cami and they held each other, grieving for the third Porter sister and all the words they would never be able to say to her, while the strawberry moon played on the waves.

"I'm afraid of the water, suddenly," Violet said, as if she were confessing a grievous sin. "I never used to be, but now... I start to have panic attacks when I'm close to it. Going with Alex on his whale watching excursion was torture. I wanted to bail from the moment I walked onto the boat."

"But you didn't. You went and spent four hours on the water."

"Quietly freaking out the whole time."

"That's only natural."

"Lily was so brave. She jumped into the ocean to save those kids. Meanwhile, I have panic attacks even if my feet get a little wet."

"People show courage in different ways," Cami said quietly. "Anytime someone is afraid but plows forward anyway, that's the very definition of courage."

"It's hard to tell myself that in the midst of crippling self-doubt."

"That's when you should believe it most of all."

After a few more moments, Violet sat back on the blanket and picked up her wine cup again. Cami sipped at hers, too, and found that the more she had, the better it tasted.

"So," Violet said after a long moment. "What's the story with you and our sexy neighborhood archaeologist?"

Cami could feel her face flush and told herself it was the wine.

"No story. Not really. I like him."

"I do, too," Violet said. "I should probably be mad at him

about kicking the glampground off Rafferty land, but somehow I can't manage it."

"Jon isn't the villain of this situation. He's only trying to protect his vulnerable father."

"What are we going to do about Wild Hearts? Mom doesn't want to move it."

Cami sighed. She had given this a great deal of thought and wasn't really any closer to a solution. "I don't know. We can't keep the status quo, though. Mom can't run it by herself, especially if she has to move it somewhere farther away from Moongate Farm. You can't come home every summer to help. Cape Sanctuary is probably the last place you want to be right now."

"Not the last place." Violet's smile was watery. "This is actually pretty good, right now."

Cami couldn't disagree.

"Who knows? Maybe Jon will change his mind."

"Like I told Dad. Don't hold your breath. Why would he?"

Violet gave her a sideways look. "You could probably talk him into it."

She laughed. "I think you vastly overestimate my powers of persuasion."

"I think you vastly *under*estimate them," Violet said. "Not to mention that Jon Rafferty couldn't keep his eyes off of you at dinner."

Her snort came out terribly inelegant. Violet apparently thought the sound was hilarious. She laughed hard, which made Cami laugh, too, mostly with relief that her sister seemed to be feeling better.

They laughed and drank and talked until the wine was gone and the moon had slipped behind the clouds.

"We should probably go home. It's late. Tomorrow is going to be a rough day for me," Cami said.

Violet was quiet as she folded the blanket and shoved it into her backpack. "And me. I'm going with you to the ceremony."

Cami was suddenly so tired, she almost didn't have the energy required to lift an eyebrow.

"If I recall, you said you wouldn't go and that nothing Rosemary said could change your mind."

"I think we've established tonight that I have a bad habit of saying things I don't always mean."

"We all do."

"Lily gave her life to save two girls. The least I can do is be brave enough to honor that sacrifice along with the rest of Cape Sanctuary. She had her faults, yes. But overall, she was amazing, and I want to celebrate that."

Cami bumped her shoulder against her sister's. "You're pretty amazing, too."

Violet smiled at her and linked her arm through Cami's. "I might be amazing, but right now I'm drunk on bad wine and too many tears."

"Same."

"One of us better be sober enough to make it back to the bunkhouse or they might find us here, curled up in the sand of Rose Creek Beach in the morning, hungover and covered in seagull poop."

"We've got this," Cami said with an optimism she didn't completely feel. "The Porter sisters can handle anything, as long as we're together."

Violet hugged her arm, and together they walked side by side up the trail toward home.

28

VIOLET

RIGHT NOW, VI COULD CERTAINLY USE A LITTLE of that courage she and Cami had talked about the night before.

Her head was splitting, her stomach roiled and her smile felt like it had been stuck to her face with a wallpaper roller.

She didn't want to be here, despite what she had told Cami the night before.

If she had her way, she would be holed up back at Moongate Farm, lying in the hammocks with a good romance novel, instead of here, surrounded by noise and people and chaos.

All those sympathetic faces. That was the hardest thing to take.

She knew their friends and neighbors meant well. Everyone

was concerned about her emotional state. That didn't make those worried looks any easier.

Summer Sanctuary wasn't the largest festival in the area. That had been claimed by the Arts and Hearts on the Cape event that took place toward summer's end and drew in art- and music-loving crowds from around Northern California as well as headliner attractions like Cruz Romero.

This was a more low-key event, a place for locals and past residents to come together to celebrate their town, local businesses and the many craftspeople who made this area home.

The celebration used to be called Heritage Days. Since some of the history of the area wasn't really anything to celebrate, like the lasting environmental impact from the timber industry and the injustices perpetrated against some of the original inhabitants here, a few years ago the town voted to change the name to Summer Sanctuary and hold it on the Saturday closest to the summer solstice.

The ceremony to honor her sister would be later that evening, prior to a free outdoor concert featuring one of the favorite area bands.

As she walked through the various booths and displays at Driftwood Park, Violet reminded herself she only had to keep it together for another six hours and then she could make her escape.

Six hours. She wasn't sure she could handle even ten more minutes.

"How are you holding up?" Cami asked.

Her older sister didn't look any happier to be here than Violet was.

"Fine," she answered with a smile she knew must look like it was going to crack her face apart at any moment. "You?"

"Same," Cami answered. "I would much rather be down at The Sea Shanty having a drink."

"Please don't mention anything alcoholic to me," Violet

grumbled. "I don't know how you made it through last night without a killer hangover. We drank an entire bottle of terrible wine, on top of what we had at dinner."

"Maybe I was pouring mine out in the sand when you weren't looking," Cami said. "Right now there are probably some really drunk and confused crabs staggering around the beach."

Violet laughed, then regretted it when her head pounded. She pressed fingers to her temples.

Somehow Cami's look of sympathy didn't bother her as much as those from everyone else. "Okay, the truth is I do have a hangover. I'm just trying to pretend I don't."

Violet smiled, grateful beyond words suddenly for this chance she'd been given to reconnect with her older sister. Something had shifted between them the night before. She remembered how Cami had comforted her while she fell apart. On impulse, she stopped next to a display of felted stuffed animals and hugged her sister.

"Thanks for last night. I needed it," she said.

Cami smiled. "I did, too. I would say let's do it again, but next time I'm picking the wine."

As they continued walking through the booths, pointing out things they liked and talking to a few people she knew, Violet realized she was almost enjoying herself.

The thought was accompanied by a little niggle of guilt that she staunchly suppressed.

Lily had always loved a party. Summer Sanctuary was one of her favorite weekends of the year.

Her twin wouldn't have wanted her to spend the rest of her life miserable. She would have been furious with Violet for spending even a moment grieving her.

"I wouldn't mind doubling back to pick up one of those fresh-squeezed lemonades they were selling a few rows back," Cami said after a moment. "Do you want one?"

"No. You go ahead." She gestured to a booth a short distance away from them. "I'm going to check out my friend Stephanie's store. She and her husband have an alpaca ranch south of town and she spins their wool herself and makes the softest hats and scarves."

"I'll find you after I grab a drink."

"No hurry. I haven't seen Steph in a long time. It will be good to chat with her between customers, if we get the chance."

She had taken only a few steps toward Steph's booth when she heard someone calling her name.

"Violet! Hey, Violet!"

She whirled around to find Ariana Mendoza hurrying toward her, beaming with delight.

"I thought that was you. Hi!"

Her heartbeat accelerated. Where Ariana went, her father was probably close behind. She scanned the crowd but couldn't immediately see Alex.

"Hey, Ariana. How fun to see you here."

"Of course we're here, silly," Ariana said. "We're helping when they have the ceremony later for Lily."

She immediately looked guilty. "I don't know if I was supposed to tell you about the ceremony. I hope it wasn't a surprise."

Violet smiled down at her. As always, she was charmed by this sweet young girl. "It's not a surprise. That's the whole reason I'm here."

"Me too. Well, that and I'm going to buy some kettle corn if they have it. That's my favorite."

"It is delicious," Violet agreed. "I did see some over where they have all the food vendors."

"Oh yay. I'm definitely buying some. I have my own money and everything."

Before Violet could answer, a pretty dark-haired woman pushing a double stroller approached.

"Ari! There you are. You can't run away like that."

"Sorry," Ariana said. "But look who I found! Violet. I told you she looks exactly like Lily."

"Look at that. You were right."

She knew that voice, Violet realized. She looked closer at the woman and was stunned to realize this woman giving her a warm smile was none other than her nemesis.

Claudia abandoned the stroller and rushed toward her, arms out. She wrapped them around Violet and hugged her so tightly, Vi couldn't breathe.

"Oh, Violet. I was so hoping I would bump into you before the ceremony tonight."

She stood frozen in the other woman's embrace, not sure what to say or what alternate reality she had stumbled into where Regina George was being so nice to her.

"Here I am."

Claudia stepped away, dug into her pocket and pulled out a tissue. She wiped at her eyes, where tears spilled out and down her cheeks.

When Violet cried, she always looked like a big red splotchy disaster, but Claudia only managed to look even more ethereally lovely.

"Oh, I'm an emotional mess," Claudia exclaimed. "I have been for months. Being pregnant again doesn't help anything."

She pointed to her belly, which had a small baby bump.

"Congratulations." Violet forced a smile, trying to process this whole surreal encounter.

Why was Claudia being nice to her? She had even *hugged* her.

Claudia was The Enemy. Capital letters. From the moment Violet and Lily moved to Cape Sanctuary when they were twelve, Claudia had decided she despised them. Violet didn't know why.

For some reason, she hadn't really picked on *Lily* with her subtle gibes and the many micro- and macro-aggressions.

Only Violet.

By the time they were in high school, the animosity and dislike between them was obvious to even teachers. More than one teacher tried to keep them after school to ask how they could help clear the air. All to no avail.

And then her sophomore year, Alex Mendoza had asked Violet to go to the prom.

Alex, a football player and one of the most popular seniors, had gone out with Claudia a few times, though in Alex's mind, they were never seriously dating.

Claudia apparently disagreed. From then on, the gloves were off. Claudia accused her of cheating in class, swapped the shampoo Violet kept in her gym locker with mayonnaise, tripped her on the bleacher stairs during a school basketball game.

Worse, she started spreading vicious yet ridiculous rumors that Violet was sleeping her way through the entire football team.

It had all been ridiculous high school drama, over a long time ago. But then Alex and Violet decided to take a break from their relationship and Claudia had moved in immediately to offer sympathy and solace. And sex.

Now Claudia was acting as if they were old and dear friends, and Violet did not know how to process the change.

"I'm sorry. I swore to myself I wouldn't blubber all day, yet here I am." Claudia took a deep breath. "Do you want to grab a coffee?"

Not really. She wanted to slip through the crowd and make her way back to Moongate Farm, even if she had to hitchhike.

"Sure. I could use some caffeine."

"The local coffeehouse has a booth here. It's right next to the playground, which I don't think is a coincidence. Maybe we could have a latte and catch up while my kids work off some energy on the swings."

Violet instinctively wanted to say no. She didn't trust this nice version of Claudia whatsoever.

On the other hand, Claudia seemed sincere. Surely she couldn't fake those tears.

Violet didn't want to seem ungracious. Wishing Cami was still with her to provide moral support, she finally nodded. "That works."

As they made their way through the crowd toward the food trucks, she craned her neck looking for Cami or their parents, who had walked off as soon as they all arrived at the park to check out the folk singer performing at the small stage where the ceremony would be later.

She couldn't find anyone.

Oddly, her headache seemed to have completely disappeared.

"What would you like?" Violet asked. "I can order for us while you set up the kids at the playground."

To Violet's dismay, Claudia's lovely brown eyes filled up with more tears. "That is so sweet of you. Thank you. I shouldn't have any, because of the baby, but my doctor says a small decaf latte once in a while won't hurt."

"Got it."

Grateful for something to do, she stood in the line behind three other customers, then placed her order and stood to the side.

When the barista called her name, she grabbed the two beverages, then made her way back to the benches surrounding the playground. Claudia was holding the toddler on her lap while she said something to Ariana and the little boy.

She looked like any other pretty, slightly frazzled mother. More attentive than some, actually, who spent most of their time looking at their phones instead of parenting.

"Thank you," the other woman breathed when Violet handed over her latte. "I can't tell you how much I needed this. I only wish I could have the real stuff."

Not quite sure what to do, Violet sat down on the bench next to her, trying to ignore the eerie feeling that she was sidling up to a saber-toothed tiger.

"What are your other children's names?"

"My boy over there on the swings with Ari is Charlie. He's named after my husband's father. He's five and thinks he should be captain of his own spaceship right now, exploring the galaxy."

"Is he in kindergarten?"

"Next year. He missed the cutoff by about a month. And then my little girl is Maya. She's two and does her best to keep up with Ari and Charlie."

Maya had fallen asleep in her mother's arms, Violet realized. She was curled up against Claudia's chest with her thumb in her mouth.

"This one is another boy," Claudia said. "I've already told Rocco we're done after this. Two girls and two boys is the perfect mix, right?"

Violet did her best to ignore the twinge of envy. While four children under the age of ten would be about three too many for her to handle, she did want a family someday.

"That's great. Congratulations." She looked over at the children. Ariana was helping her little brother get down from the swings and run to the slide. "I've had a chance to spend a little time with Ariana over the past few weeks since I've come back to town. She's a great girl. Smart, compassionate, kind."

"She's amazing." Claudia sniffled again. With her arms full of sleeping toddler, she wiped the tears away into her shoulder. "I have been living in a constant state of gratitude for months. I still have my girl, because of one person."

Ah. This was no doubt the reason Claudia wanted to talk to Violet. It was also the reason Violet hadn't wanted to come at all today. She didn't know which was worse, the sympathy or the gratitude.

"If Lily hadn't been there that day," the other woman went on, "if she hadn't been willing to jump into that cold ocean, my bright, wonderful Ariana wouldn't be here. I don't have the words to tell you how grateful I am to Lily."

She sipped at her coffee. How was she supposed to answer that?

I'm glad your daughter survived but really wish my sister hadn't died in the rescue.

She finally nodded. "Thank you."

"I know how close you and Lily were. Her death must have hit you so hard. She was your best friend, wasn't she?"

Those last angry words between them seemed to echo through her head. If only she could take them all back.

"Yes," she murmured.

"I just... I wanted to say how sorry I am that she's not here."

Claudia paused, looking tortured suddenly. "And for everything else."

"Everything else?" Violet said, though of course she knew.

"I was so terrible to you. I can't look back on our school years without cringing. I have no excuse. Not really. I was jealous. That's what it comes down to. Everything seemed to come so easily to you."

Violet stared, stunned into silence.

"You seemed to have it all. Friends, good grades, cute clothes, while every day was a struggle for me."

"You had friends."

"Not really. Not true friends, the kind that bring out the best in you. Mine were the total opposite. We thrived on causing trouble."

She rose and expertly laid the sleeping toddler in the stroller without waking her.

"I didn't like myself when I was with them, but because I didn't like myself, I didn't try to make friends with others who might have brought out a better side to me."

She was quiet as she sat back on the bench beside Violet. "I was a mess, Violet. That's no excuse, but my life was shit when

I was a kid. My father left when I was in elementary school and my mother was…well, she wasn't a nice person. She died right after we graduated from high school, and while I mourned that we didn't have the kind of relationship I wanted, I wasn't sorry."

Violet was deeply grateful suddenly for Rosemary. Her mother could frustrate her sometimes, but Violet never doubted for a moment that she was loved.

She had been so busy trying to survive the attacks, she never thought much about why Claudia had lashed out at her.

"I'm sorry things were tough for you. I wish I'd known."

Would it have made a difference in how she responded to Claudia's vitriol? She wasn't sure. She had been a self-absorbed teenager herself.

"I have no idea why you became the focus of all my bitterness and jealousy. You were so smart and pretty and just seemed so happy and nice all the time. The opposite of how I felt about myself. And then you started dating Alex and I convinced myself you deliberately stole him from me. That just made everything worse."

Violet opened her mouth to answer, but Claudia shook her head.

"In my heart, I knew even then it wasn't true. Alex always had a thing for you. Always. He was just waiting for you to notice him. I was the one who asked him out, the few times we dated in high school. Did you know that?"

"No. He didn't tell me."

Claudia wrapped her hands around her paper coffee cup. "It's really painful to look back on your life and see all the places you wish you could have made other choices. He always loved you. I knew that. But I still wanted him, mostly because you had him, but also because he was a great guy."

She couldn't argue with that.

"After you two broke up, I saw my chance with him. He was hurt and sad, and I was only a rebound relationship. I knew that in my heart but I didn't care. Alex was a great guy," she repeated. "Maybe the best guy I ever dated back when I was too dumb to know what was really important. I didn't want him to slip away again, so I…did what I could to make it impossible for him."

Claudia began to cry again. This time she didn't try to hide her tears, just looked at Violet with a raw vulnerability that stunned her.

"You got pregnant on purpose." She had always suspected it. Having her suspicions confirmed gave her no comfort.

"I knew he could easily walk away from me." Claudia spoke in a low voice filled with self-disgust. "He was already heading in that direction. But he would never turn his back on his child."

Violet wanted to hate Claudia all over again for what she had done to Alex, but the honest regret and misery in her voice only made her sad for poor choices and lost chances.

"We tried to make it work. For nearly three years, we tried. Ariana was the best thing to happen to me and I would like to think to Alex, too. But we both knew our marriage wasn't working, as hard as we wished otherwise."

She paused. "And I knew exactly why."

"Why?" She had to ask.

To her further shock, Claudia, the woman she had always considered her nemesis, gave her a watery smile. "Because he never really got over you."

She wanted to argue but the words wouldn't come. Alex had basically told her the same thing. Hearing it confirmed by his ex-wife was painful and exhilarating at the same time.

"Why are you telling me this?"

Before the other woman could answer, her little boy came over. "Mama. Guess what? I did the big slide and I wasn't scared a *bit*."

"Good job, Charlie." She hugged him with a warmth and affection that seemed so discordant, coming from the woman who had made her high school years so hard.

"I'm going to go again. Watch, okay?"

"You got it."

The little boy ran off again to join Ariana, and Claudia turned back to her.

"Alex and I were divorced for a year when I met Rocco. I fell hard for him right away, but I felt so unworthy. He was such a good man and I was just a stressed-out single mom from a terrible background who had trapped my first husband into marrying me. What could he possibly see in me?"

She gave a soft, tender, radiant smile. "Somehow, he knows the worst about me but loves me anyway. It still feels like a miracle. Like a precious gift I didn't do anything to deserve."

"That's great."

"We've been together almost five years now, and each day, I feel luckier than the day before."

"I'm…happy it worked out for you."

To her shock, Claudia reached out and grabbed her hand. "Alex has never stopped loving you. If you have any kind of feeling for him, I would love for things to work out between you. It might help me let go of some of this huge guilt I feel for what I did to him."

Violet felt unmoored, as if everything she thought she knew had just been washed away.

"I've…I've moved on with my life. I'm over him," she lied.

Claudia seemed to buy her dishonesty. She withdrew her hand, looking disappointed. "Oh, sure. It's been a long time. Of course you have. It was worth a shot, right?"

"I appreciate your honesty. It couldn't have been easy for you to dredge it all up again. It's…admirable."

She couldn't believe she was saying this to Claudia or that she meant the words.

Claudia gave a small smile. "The best things in life don't come from taking the easy path, do they?"

"No. I suppose they don't."

"And aren't we lucky that the terrible choices we made when we were young don't have to define us for the rest of our lives?"

Violet didn't have an answer to that. She could only nod, sip at her coffee and be grateful for this small moment of grace.

29

CAMI

HER MOTHER SEEMED TO KNOW EVERYONE IN Cape Sanctuary.

Cami had met up with her parents shortly after she and Violet separated. She thought it might be fun to walk through the Summer Sanctuary fair with them, but she was learning that Rosemary couldn't make it more than ten feet before someone else would grab her to start up a conversation.

They had chatted with a man who carved whimsically beautiful sculptures from a certain type of driftwood that only washed up on a particular beach.

In the next booth, her mother knew the woman selling homemade chocolates, and they talked about some of the interesting things she had added to her offerings, like chili peppers and dried pineapple.

A man selling local raw honey that glowed a rich amber in the sunlight turned out to be a beekeeper who kept a few hives at Moongate Farm.

The vendors were one thing, but her mother also seemed to know all the other members of the browsing public.

Cami and her father were relegated to following along behind her and smiling politely when Rosemary would introduce them as "her oldest daughter" and "the girls' father."

"A little different from LA, isn't it?" Ted said as they made their slow way through the displays.

"You could say that," she answered. "That's not necessarily a bad thing."

"No. It's just different. It's easy to see why your mom loves it so much. This fits her, much better than being the wife of a busy law partner ever did."

"Yes. This is definitely her element."

Because of the past few weeks spent here in Cape Sanctuary with her mother, Cami felt like she had a new perspective of Rosemary.

"She seems much more free, living here by the sea where she can have her garden and her yoga and her friends."

"Yes. That's it exactly," her father said.

"When you two split up, I felt like she was turning her back on us. It hurt so much, being left behind. But that wasn't really the case, was it?"

Ted shook his head, his features a little sad as he threw an arm around her shoulders. "Sometimes we grown-ups make decisions we think are best for everyone, but in the end, they don't turn out that way. I'm sorry you ever felt that, pumpkin. I wish I could go back and fix it for you."

She rested her head on her father's shoulder for a moment,

grateful she had him during her teen years. She had always known her father loved her, even when he was in the middle of a stressful court case. He had also always made sure someone was there when she came home from school, even if that was their longtime housekeeper.

Rosemary turned around when her companion moved to speak with someone else. "What are you two talking about with such serious faces?"

Ted gave her a look filled with so much tenderness, Cami's throat felt tight. "Oh, you know. This and that. You. The past. How perfect this town is for you," he said.

Her mother's expression softened. "You're going to make me bawl before we even get close to Lily's award tonight."

"We can't have that," Ted said. "I say we grab something to eat."

He paused and looked over Cami's shoulder. "Aren't those your neighbors, Rosie?"

Cami turned quickly. Too quickly, she realized, when her father's gaze sharpened.

She spotted Jon and Franklin looking at a collection of carved figures on the other side of their row, and her heart rate seemed to accelerate.

Her breathing caught and her insides felt as if she'd just taken a ride on a dinghy through fifteen-foot swells.

This was ridiculous.

She *had* to get control of herself around him or any moment now she was going to be looking at Jon with the same kind of tenderness Ted gave Rosemary.

She wanted to slip through the crowd and move down another aisle, but Rosemary waved enthusiastically at them and moved in that direction.

"Hello, Franklin. Jon. Isn't this a lovely day?"

"Beautiful," Jon said. Cami felt breathless all over again when it seemed he was looking directly at her.

Her father smiled. “Great to see you both again.”

Franklin frowned. “I’m sorry. I know you’re Rosemary’s husband, but for the life of me, I can’t remember your name.”

“Ted Porter,” her father said kindly. Cami was touched and grateful that Ted didn’t bother to correct him about his true status as Rosemary’s *ex*-husband.

“Right. That’s it. And you’re Camellia, of course.”

Hardly anyone but Rosemary called her Camellia. She was shocked that Franklin even knew that was her full name. He must have heard her mother refer to her that way.

“Yes. Hi.”

He reached for her hand and she was charmed when he lifted it to his mouth like a French courtier, as he had done with Rosemary the night he gave the history lecture to their guests.

“Lovely as ever, my dear.”

“Um. Thanks.” She smiled at him, then shifted her gaze to Jon. For just an instant, she thought she saw something in his eyes, something hot and raw and hungry, but it was gone just as quickly and she told herself it was a trick of the sunlight.

Oh, that kiss. Why couldn’t she get it out of her head?

“It really is a lovely day,” Franklin said jovially. “We aren’t always so blessed by the weather gods in June. I remember plenty of past Founders Day celebrations where it was raining cats and dogs and others where the sea mist was so thick, you couldn’t see five feet in front of you.”

“Aren’t we lucky this year?” Rosemary said. “At least for now. A storm is coming later tonight, but it’s not supposed to hit until all the celebrating is over.”

“Have you two grabbed a bite to eat yet?” Ted asked. “We were about to head over to the food truck area to see what they have and would love you to join us.”

“We would be delighted.” Franklin answered before his son could squeeze in a word. Jon, Cami couldn’t help but notice, didn’t look as if he necessarily agreed.

"Excellent," her father said. "Let's grab a table and I'll text Violet and tell her where to find us."

"That sounds perfect."

Her mother slipped her arm through Franklin's, looking as if she had planned the whole thing. As her father was walking ahead of them in his usual no-nonsense stride and looking down at his phone as he texted, that left Cami to walk beside Jon.

She was intensely aware of him as they walked the short distance to where various food trucks were parked in an area shaded by large trees.

"There's a perfect table," Rosemary said. She and Franklin walked toward a picnic table with a lovely view of the water.

"What sounds good to you, Dad?" Jon asked. "Why don't you sit down and I'll grab something for you. Looks like there's a taco truck, fish and chips, crepes, Thai, ribs and Dutch oven."

"Ooh. I always like Dutch oven meals, especially if they're doing chicken and those cheesy potatoes."

"That sounds good to me, too," Ted said. "What about you, Rosie?"

"I'll take the potatoes and a salad, if they have one."

"You got it. What about you two? What sounds good to you two?" he asked her and Jon.

"Tacos," they both said in unison, as if they had rehearsed it, which made her father beam with delight.

"I guess that settles that. You go grab your tacos and I'll get the rest. When Violet shows up, I'll grab something for her."

Left with no choice, Cami moved toward the taco truck, decorated with painted palm trees and curling surf.

"Since your dad is paying for my dad, the least I can do is buy your dinner. What sounds good?"

"You don't have to do that."

He gave her a sideways look. "What if I want to?"

Arguing with him seemed ungracious, so she shrugged. "Then thank you. I'll have the fish street tacos and a horchata."

"Sounds good." At the window, he ordered the fish tacos and the popular drink for both of them.

"If you want to go back to the table, I can take our food over when it's ready."

"I don't mind waiting. It might be hard to juggle two plates and two drinks, especially with your bad arm."

He made a face. "My arm is fine. I keep forgetting all about it, if you want the truth."

"No more infection?"

"No. It's just about healed. I'm coming out of it with a nice scar and a good story."

She smiled. "You can tell your children and grandchildren about the time you were injured in a machete attack."

His laugh was low and seemed to sizzle along her nerve endings. "Yes. Kiddies, gather round while I tell you about the good old days."

Though he spoke the words in jest, she thought she saw a glimmer of wistfulness in his expression.

"You love it, don't you?" she said softly. "The fieldwork, I mean. Not the machete injury."

He took his time answering. "Being on a dig can be hot, sticky, frustrating work, with weeks at a time where you feel like any progress is measured in inches. Then you stumble onto something that changes everything you thought you knew about a culture. It's like no other feeling in the world."

The passion in his voice left her feeling vaguely discontented. She liked her chosen career and thought she was good at it, especially her specialty of intellectual property law. But she had never experienced even a sliver of that enthusiasm.

"When I'm on a dig, I can lose all track of time and place. I once spent thirty-six hours straight inside a cenote underground because monsoon season was on the way and we were trying to preserve a ceremonial site before the rains came. I could hardly see when I came back into the sunlight, but in the end, we made some significant discoveries about a historic drought in the area that led to widespread famine and disease."

He broke off, looking faintly embarrassed. "Sorry. That was probably more than you wanted to know."

"No. It's fascinating to me. It's obvious you love it." She paused. "I'm sorry you have to walk away from something you love so much."

"For now. Not forever," he said. "Yes, it's hard to leave, but I'm exactly where I need to be right now. I'm trying to focus on that."

That tenderness she had been fighting seemed to wash over her in gentle waves, like the baby breakers against Driftwood Beach at low tide.

How was she supposed to resist this man? Sexy adventurer, passionate explorer and devoted son, all wrapped up in one delicious package?

She was falling in love with him.

She stared, momentarily speechless as the stunning realization seemed to come out of nowhere.

She couldn't be. This was simply an attraction, right?

No. She couldn't avoid the truth. She was falling for Jon and she had no idea what she was supposed to do about it.

"By the way," he said, jerking her from the tumult of her thoughts, "you might be interested to know I had an email from my dad's former partner this morning. Our guardianship hearing apparently is scheduled for this week. Tuesday."

She had to take a moment to breathe through her shock before she trusted herself to answer. "That's good. I'm sure it will be a relief to have it all settled."

"Yes." He paused. "I know my dad would appreciate having you there to help represent him. He trusts you, unlike the ad litem. He says the guy took a phone call from his girlfriend during their consultation, which Dad considers highly unprofessional. He said the man can deal with his social life on his own time."

"I can't argue with that." She forced a smile, still reeling. "I'm sorry. Ordinarily, I would be happy to help your father, but I'm catching a flight back to LA early Monday morning."

"That soon?" Now he was the one who looked shocked.

She nodded. "I've been gone too long already."

His mouth tightened. He opened it as if to speak, but the worker at the taco truck called his name before he could.

With an expression that seemed a cross between frustration and something else she couldn't read, Jon's gaze met hers for only an instant before he looked away and headed toward the pickup window, leaving her to follow after him, all the while wondering what he had intended to say.

30

VIOLET

BY THE TIME THE ACTUAL CEREMONY ROLLED around where Lily would be recognized, Violet felt oddly numb.

That conversation with Claudia earlier in the day seemed to bounce through her head in strange, surreal fragments.

If someone had told her a few weeks ago that she could spend a half hour in the other woman's company without one of them emerging bloodied and broken, Violet would have thought they were high or delirious.

She wasn't physically battered. She couldn't say the same about her emotions.

She couldn't stop thinking of everything Claudia had told

her. About trapping Alex through her pregnancy. About the failure of their marriage. About the other woman's own difficult childhood.

Now, as she sat beside her sister in the front row of seats at the amphitheater at Driftwood Park, Violet didn't know what to think. She suspected it would take her a long time to process everything.

"How are you holding up?" Cami asked.

"Better than I feared."

"It will be over soon." Her sister gave her a reassuring smile. "You don't have to stay for the concert afterward if you don't want to. Nobody will think anything at all if you slip away after they give us Lily's award."

"I've always liked Pacific Dreamers. I'll have to see how I'm doing."

Cami squeezed her hand and Violet was suddenly intensely grateful for her sister.

How sad that Lily's death was the catalyst for bringing them closer, one tiny flicker of light to come from a dark, sad time.

The mayor of Cape Sanctuary, Lynda Ferguson, walked to the microphone and Violet drew in a deep breath. A few more moments and this would be over and they all could work on figuring out the rest of their lives.

"Thank you all for coming. We've had an amazing Summer Sanctuary. The town council would like to express our deep appreciation for all the volunteers and committee members who have helped everything run so smoothly."

Everyone, including Violet, broke into a round of applause. Small towns couldn't function without an army of volunteers, working together to make their communities prosper.

"I know you're all anxious to hear Pacific Dreamers, but we have one important matter of business first." She smiled down at the crowd, her gaze focused on Violet and her family in the front row.

"Each year, as you all know, the town council and administration choose one person to be the Citizen of the Year for Cape Sanctuary. This could be someone from our business community, from that hardworking volunteer corps I was talking about earlier, from our thriving art scene here. But sometimes we choose to name someone who has provided extraordinary heroism in a moment of need. This year, for the first time in my memory, our choice was completely unanimous. At this time, I would like to invite Lily Porter's family to come on stage."

Violet's face felt hot as the crowd exploded in a huge outburst of applause—not for them, but for Lily.

"Everyone in town knows about the events that happened in February of this year. For the rest of you who might not have heard, let me tell you about a moment of courage and strength. Lily Porter, a young woman I actually taught in middle school, was minding her own business, taking pictures of the coastline one afternoon, when she saw a rather ordinary scene in Cape Sanctuary, two young girls looking at the tide pools."

She gazed down at the crowd. "Lily was the only one who witnessed the wave surge that day, when the previously calm sea at low tide suddenly and unexpectedly rose up to grab the girls and pull them in.

"Lily could have chosen to call for help that day, to let others step in to rescue the girls. Instead, with extraordinary courage and without care for her own safety, Lily jumped into the cold waters of the Pacific. She was able to find not one of the girls underwater, but both of them."

The mayor paused and wiped at her eyes. "I would like to tell you the story had a happy ending. While it did for those girls, unfortunately, it didn't for Lily. Just as she got the second girl to safety, another in that set of unusual waves, possibly triggered by a small earthquake offshore, came and pulled Lily under."

Violet's chest ached. A few more moments. She could make it through a few more moments, for Lily's sake.

"Here to tell you in her own words what happened that day is one of the girls who was rescued. Ariana Mendoza."

Ari walked out, accompanied by both Claudia and Alex. She wore a sweet white dress with pink flowers and her hair was curled instead of being in its usual ponytail. She looked momentarily frightened of the crowd assembled for the concert, especially when they applauded for her, but she quickly seemed to regain her composure and walked to the microphone.

"The scariest day of my life was the day I almost died. My friend Ella and I were looking at the tide pools. We both want to be marine biologists and love to look at the sea urchins and sea stars. We were busy looking at a little octopus that day and didn't see the waves coming, but Lily did. I remember cold water grabbing me, pulling me under. I was so scared. One minute, I was drowning and was sure I was going to die. The next, someone grabbed me and pulled me to the shore. Lily told me to run for higher ground as fast as I could. Then she went back for Ella."

She drew in a breath, as if for courage. "She was our guardian angel that day. I will always be grateful to her. I know if Ella could be here, she would say the same thing. Because of Lily, I have a future. I can meet my new baby brother. I can maybe have a family of my own someday. Who knows? I might even grow up and save the ocean."

She met Violet's gaze. "Lily Porter was my guardian angel and I know she's still watching over me today. Maybe she's watching over you, too."

She gave a tentative smile, then walked back to stand by her parents while the crowd applauded loudly.

Mayor Ferguson walked to the microphone again. "Ella Nish couldn't be here, as her family is living in Japan right now. They have sent a letter, which they asked me to read tonight."

The Nish family had come to the funeral and had been effusive in their gratitude. Ella's words, read by the mayor, were similar in tone to Ariana's.

When she finished reading it, the mayor folded the letter and then picked up a large plaque. "It is my very great honor to award our Citizen of the Year to Lily Anne Porter. While we wish, more than anything, that she could be here in person to accept this well-deserved honor, we are grateful to have her family present to accept on her behalf."

The mayor handed the plaque to Ariana. While cameras flashed, the girl approached Violet's family and handed the award to Rosemary. Violet's mother took it and hugged the girl tightly.

As soon as Rosemary released her, Ariana ran to Violet and hugged her.

Something tight and hot and painful seemed to lift from her chest. She loved this little girl, and not only because she and Lily would forever be connected.

Because she was unique and sweet and wonderful.

She loved Ariana. And she loved Alex.

The truth of it seemed to ring through her like church bells on Easter Sunday.

She loved Alex Mendoza. Had never stopped.

She had fallen for him when she was too young to know what she wanted out of life. Now she was older, hopefully wiser, and she knew exactly what she wanted.

Alex.

She looked down at the plaque her mother still held and read the words engraved there.

To Lily Anne Porter, Cape Sanctuary citizen of the year. Your extraordinary heroism is an inspiration to us all.

Lily was willing to risk her life to do what was necessary.

All Violet had to do was risk her heart.

She looked at Alex, now shaking hands with the mayor.

She couldn't do it. She wasn't brave. Not like Lily. She never had been. Lily had been the better twin, Violet the pale imitation.

31

CAMI

ROSEMARY AND TED HELD HANDS ALL THROUGH the Pacific Dreamers concert. When the folk and soft rock band played a romantic ballad, she saw Rosemary lay her head on Ted's shoulder.

Cami wasn't quite certain how she felt about that. She wanted to point it out to Violet, but her younger sister hardly seemed to notice. All through the concert and even as they loaded into the car to drive back to Moongate Farm, Violet seemed lost in her own thoughts, her features rigid and closed.

"That was a really lovely evening, wasn't it?" Rosemary said.

"And I'm so glad the storm isn't here yet. I was so worried they would have to cancel the concert."

Cami looked out the window of the vehicle at the sky that seemed to turn darker with every passing moment.

"Everyone was so kind and respectful tonight and had such beautiful things to say about Lily," Rosemary went on. "It makes me proud to be her mother."

"You should be," Cami agreed.

She glanced over at her sister. Cami couldn't gauge Violet's emotional state in the dim light of the car, other than from the tension in her frame. Worry pressed in. She wanted to hug her but also didn't want to make things worse.

"The plaque is nice and it will be lovely to see the matching one at the town hall."

"How often do you go to the town hall?" Ted teased.

"Not often," Rosemary admitted. "But maybe I'll go more now that I have a good excuse."

Their father's laughter rang through the car, warm and genuine. Cami couldn't remember the last time she'd heard him laugh like that.

When Ted pulled up in front of the house a moment later, he turned off the engine but made no move to get out.

"Girls. Do you mind coming in for a minute?" Ted's voice, which could be so forceful and commanding in a courtroom, sounded hesitant. Nervous, even.

"Now?" This was the first word Violet had said.

"Yes. I know it's late and we're all tired, but…this shouldn't take long."

Puzzled and a little apprehensive, Cami followed them into the house. Violet trailed behind, apparently still lost in thought.

By the time Cami gathered Baxter from the kitchen, where he had a doggie door, a soft bed and plenty of food and water, Rosemary and Ted were sitting side by side on the sofa of the front room, not touching. Now both of them looked decidedly nervous.

Cami took a seat near Violet, with Baxter in her arms.

"What's up?" she finally asked, when her parents made no move to explain why they had called a family meeting.

Ted cleared his throat, as if he were about to make the opening arguments in a career-defining case.

"How would you girls feel if your mother and I…started dating again?"

Now Violet seemed to snap back into the conversation from wherever else her mind had wandered. "Dating?"

"For now." Ted gave them an uncertain smile. "We're starting there, anyway, and we'll, um, see where things go."

Rosemary reached out and took his hand with an expression Cami could only describe as besotted. "In the time since we lost your sister, your father and I have started to…reconnect. We started talking more than we have in a long time and we have both realized we still have feelings for each other."

Violet stared at them, eyes wide and shocked. "You what?"

Cami wasn't sure why her sister seemed so surprised. Had Violet completely missed all the signs? The different energy between them?

Maybe Violet hadn't noticed them holding hands or seen the yearning in Ted's expression when he looked at their mother.

"I have always loved Rosie," Ted said. "Since the moment I met her more than thirty years ago. The older I get, the more I realize what matters to me most."

He reached for Rosemary's hand. "We've both reached a stage in life where we've realized we're happier together than we ever were apart."

"How will this work? Long-distance relationships can be tough," Cami felt obliged to point out. "What's changed between you, really? You're still a senior partner at the firm. If anything, things are more complicated now that Mom has Wild Hearts to think about."

"It's time I start slowing down," her father said. "Handing off more responsibility to the younger generation. We have plenty of capable legal minds at the firm. If I cut back my caseload, I could spend more time here in Cape Sanctuary with Rosemary. Semiretirement by the seashore sounds pretty appealing right about now."

He lifted Rosemary's hand to his mouth. "Especially if I'm with the woman I've always loved."

Rosemary blushed and gave him another of those besotted smiles.

"What will you do here in Cape Sanctuary?" Violet asked. "Help Mom run the campground? Pick peas and strawberries every day instead of arguing cases and winning appeals? How long do you think you'll be happy doing that?"

Both Ted and Rosemary looked startled at her skeptical tone. It surprised Cami, too, and made her realize she didn't have the exclusive right to feel damaged by their parents' divorce. All this time, she had thought the twins had the better end of the deal. At least they had each other. That was a childish, immature perspective, she realized.

She suddenly remembered Violet telling her about the long string of go-nowhere relationships Lily had had. As for Violet, Cami couldn't remember the last time her sister dated anyone seriously, other than Alex Mendoza in high school.

"I can see me being happy here forever," Ted said. "As long as I have Rosie by my side, I'll have everything I need."

"Isn't that what you thought when you got married?" Violet pressed. "That it was forever? You made three kids together and then decided you could no longer live together, destroying all our lives in the process. Lily and I hardly knew Cami because you both decided you couldn't live together anymore."

Rosemary looked as if Violet had picked up the vase of cut flowers from the table beside her and tossed it in her face.

"It wasn't like that," she protested. "We always loved each other. That was never the issue. I tried to be happy in Los Angeles. But I was suffocating there."

Ted's features twisted with sadness and regret. "I didn't make it easy. I was never home and I constantly took your mother for granted. I had several death penalty cases going at the same time and they were consuming everything I had. I had nothing left to give to our marriage or our family."

"You were doing important work. I knew that," Rosemary said.

"Yes. But the well-being of this family should have taken precedence. You begged me to slow down and focus more on all of you. I should have seen how unhappy you were. It's easy to say that now, but at the time, all I could see were the lives that depended on me."

"They did depend on you," Rosemary said staunchly. "And you did a wonderful job of representing them. We both made mistakes, Teddy. Neither is wholly responsible for the breakdown of our marriage. I knew what I was signing up for when I fell in love with you, when we started a family. I loved your passion and your dedication to your clients and that brain of yours." She sighed. "I've never been good at bending. I should have tried harder to compromise—maybe spend summers at the Cape for my ocean fix and the rest of the year with you in LA."

"And I could have slowed down a little. I didn't have to save the entire world."

"Anyway, the past is past," Rosemary said. "Now that we're older, we've both learned from our mistakes and are in a better place to focus on what really matters."

"And we're just supposed to forget about the past sixteen years as if they didn't exist?" Violet asked.

"No," Ted said, a little sadly. "That's impossible for all of us.

But Lily's death was a stark reminder that life is fragile and infinitely precious. I don't want to spend any more of mine without the woman I love."

His words resounded with so much genuine emotion that Cami couldn't doubt he meant them.

What would it be like to have a man love her so much, he was willing to rearrange his whole life, his whole future, to be at her side?

For some wild reason, Jon Rafferty's face flashed through her mind. What would it be like to have *Jon* love her so much?

She wanted that. She wanted to be the kind of woman he couldn't live without.

"I think it's great," Cami said promptly, burying her own pointless yearning for now. "I love seeing you both so happy."

She rose and hugged her mother first and then her father.

Violet rose as well. She gave them a strained smile that didn't hide the turmoil in her eyes. "Yes. Congratulations. I hope it works out for you both this time. Lily would have been very happy for you, too."

"That's a lovely thing to say," Rosemary said with a soft smile.

"I still don't know what you're going to do about Wild Hearts, but I guess we don't have to figure everything out tonight," Violet said.

"It's been a long day for all of us."

Rosemary hugged the girls again and Cami thought of all the changes in her life since she had come to Cape Sanctuary only a few weeks earlier. She had a closer bond with both her mother and her sister and a deeper appreciation for this town beside the Pacific.

And she had fallen in love, for the first time in her life.

"Good night," Violet said. She ducked her head and hurried out of the house and toward the bunkhouse, but not before Cami saw tears trickling down her sister's cheeks.

"Good night," she said to their parents, who were so wrapped up in each other they hardly seemed to notice she was leaving. With Baxter racing ahead of her, Cami rushed after her sister and caught up with Violet before she could retreat into her bedroom.

"Hey. What's wrong?"

Violet didn't meet her gaze. "Nothing. Why do you think something is wrong?"

"Because I wasn't born yesterday," Cami retorted. "Either you have bad allergies tonight or you're crying."

"Allergies," Violet said, clearly lying.

After a moment, she must have realized Cami wasn't buying that, and she sighed. "I just don't want to see them make a mistake again, you know? They seem happy together tonight, but for how long?"

"I hope forever."

"Mom never really got over the divorce. She hardly ever dated. But Dad got married again. How can he say he always loved her? He must have stopped long enough to be with someone else!"

Ah. Cami suddenly understood.

"This isn't about Mom and Dad at all, is it? This is about you and Alex."

Violet hitched in a breath. "That's ridiculous. This has nothing to do with…with us."

"Doesn't it? Ever since Alex told you he wants to try again, you've been running scared. But now Mom and Dad are willing to start dating again and see where it goes, and some part of you is asking whether you should be willing to do the same."

Color rose high on Violet's cheeks. "I can't," she whispered.

"That's your choice, Vi. You know what's in your own heart better than anyone else. Just like Mom and Dad know what's in theirs."

Violet stared at her for a long moment, then turned away, picking up her purse and heading for the door.

"Where are you going?" Cami asked.

"I need to… I don't know. Think, I guess. I'm going for a drive."

"Now? A storm is on the way. They're saying it's supposed to be a big one. You should be hunkered down inside."

"Sometimes you have to be willing to step into the storm," Violet said.

She turned and hurried out of the bunkhouse without waiting for Cami to answer.

32

VIOLET

WELL, THAT COULD HAVE GONE BETTER.

As Violet climbed into her little SUV, she was torn between embarrassment and chagrin.

If her parents wanted to get back together, she should be happy for them. Rosemary was certainly capable of taking care of herself and making her own decisions. It wasn't Violet's place to watch out for her mother's emotional well-being.

As usual, her smarty-pants big sister was exactly right. The news had hit her hard because she couldn't help comparing their choices to her own.

Her parents were willing to try again, despite the mistakes of the past and the pain they had caused each other.

While she was terrified to do the same.

She left without any clear destination but had only driven a short distance into the night before she knew exactly where she needed to go.

The overlook.

The spot where she and Alex had spent so many joyous hours together.

When she reached it a short time later, she parked, grabbed the flashlight and blanket she always kept in her vehicle for emergencies and made her way to the bench Alex had put up.

She wrapped the blanket around her and watched the storm clouds move closer to the shore while the cool wind dried the tears on her face.

She had been there perhaps twenty minutes when she heard another vehicle pull up to the narrow parking area and an engine turn off.

Someone was coming.

For the first time, she realized it might have been foolhardy to come here by herself. Cape Sanctuary was generally a safe small town with good people who cared about each other, but it wasn't crime-free and she was alone after dark. Maybe not the smartest move on her part.

Violet's heartbeat kicked up and she reached for the pepper spray she always kept on her key chain. She was just about to spring up from the bench with the wild idea of sneaking back to her car when someone came through the trees.

She was too late. In a distant flash of lightning, she saw exactly who was moving toward her.

Alex.

It seemed inevitable, somehow. Had she come here hoping somehow she would see him?

No. That was ridiculous. How could she have known he would come to the overlook tonight, exactly when she was here?

He stopped a few feet away from her. "I just stopped at the bunkhouse and Cami told me you'd gone for a drive. I took a chance you might have come here."

"Good guess."

He moved closer to the bench and her heartbeat accelerated more.

"Do you want to be alone? If you don't want to talk to me, I can get lost again."

She paused for only a moment before shifting over and pointing to the empty space beside her.

After a frozen moment, Alex sat down, long legs extended. He was big, rangy, familiar.

Wonderful.

"To be honest," he said, his voice wry, "if you had said you wanted to be alone, I would have sat in my truck in the pullout back there all night, if I had to, so I could make sure you stayed safe out here by yourself."

She gave a small, strangled laugh. "I've been alone long enough," she answered.

She didn't only mean that evening. She had been so careful with her heart, never letting anybody inside.

The idea of him staying in his cold truck all night long just to make sure she was safe touched a small, bruised corner of her heart.

I never stopped loving you. Even with everything between us, some part of me always loved you.

His words the last time they were here seemed to float around her on the wind.

How could she find the courage to take a chance?

Courage. She closed her eyes, feeling each breath he took beside her.

She thought of Lily, risking her life to save two girls, and of

Rosemary and Ted, who didn't want to be parted through any of their precious years remaining. They were willing to try again, despite everything.

She was, too.

She drew in a breath, then another, feeling all the stress and uncertainty and fear seep away as if pulled out to sea by the tide, leaving only healing, blessed joy.

She loved Alex.

Their future glowed brightly, just on the other side of her fear. They could truly have the life they had talked about, dreamed about, all those years ago, but only if she dared reach out and snatch it.

She stretched out her hand and found his fingers with hers. He stiffened, and in another flash of lightning, she saw his eyes fill with shock and something else. A wary hope.

"I'm glad you found me," she murmured. "If you hadn't, I would have come looking for you."

His fingers flexed under hers, and he turned his hand around, lacing their fingers tightly together. She couldn't get away now, but then, she didn't want to.

"Why?"

She released a breath at the intensity of that single word. She smiled, feeling more at peace than she had in forever.

"Because I needed to tell you I love you. I never stopped."

The words were hardly out before he made a low sound and was kissing her with a fierce tenderness that made tears gather again, this time of happiness and a sweet, hard-won peace.

He kissed her there for a long time as the storm moved closer, rumbling and flashing offshore.

"I love you, Alex," she murmured against his mouth. "I'm sorry it took me so long to find the courage to tell you that."

His laughter had an uncertain note, as if he couldn't quite believe this was real. She wrapped her arms around his neck and kissed him again until both of them were trembling with long-buried hunger.

“What changed?” he asked. “I was so sure when we came here last week that you would never be able to see beyond the pain of the past.”

“The universe has been telling me in a hundred different ways that I would be foolish to throw away another chance with you.”

“The universe?”

“Or maybe it was Lily. Ariana says Lily is her guardian angel. I’d like to think maybe she’s helping guide me in the direction I need to take.”

She said a silent prayer for the sister who had been a part of her since they shared the womb. Her other half.

She would always miss Lily dearly, but it was time to let go of the guilt over the fracture in their relationship in the months prior to her death. Violet decided to give that to the ocean. If it could take her bright light of a sister, it could take everything else, including all her fears and doubts.

She and Alex still would have to figure out plenty of details.

His life and career were here by the sea with Mendoza Charters and his daughter, while in six weeks, she would have to go back to Sacramento to her students and her school and her job.

On the other hand, she was a special education teacher, a vocation always in demand. She could teach anywhere. She wouldn’t change anything right away, but eventually she could think about moving to a school district closer to Cape Sanctuary.

She didn’t have to solve all those problems right now. For this moment, she simply wanted to enjoy being in the arms of the man she loved.

He kissed her again as lightning arced across the sky, followed closely by thunder.

Another flash and clap sounded a moment later.

“That’s getting closer. We’re going to get drenched in a moment,” Alex warned.

She didn't care about getting wet, but wouldn't it be a tragedy if they were struck by lightning right now, when she was happier than she remembered being in a long, long time?

"I guess we should go."

She didn't want to leave his arms or this spot. They held hands as he tugged her toward his pickup. Inside the warm cab, she fell into his arms again.

"We should probably stop or I won't be able to," he said gruffly, sometime later. "I think I'm a little too old to make out in a pickup truck anymore. Plus, the windows are starting to fog up."

"Take me home. We can come back and get my car later."

She had always loved that hot, hungry look in his eyes. As he kissed her again, she laughed out loud against his mouth, joy and peace and love pushing away any lingering doubt.

She loved Alex with all her heart. This time, she planned to do everything possible to make sure they found the happy ending they had dreamed about for so long.

33

CAMI

I'm with A. Don't wait up.

CAMI LOOKED DOWN AT THE TEXT FROM HER sister, aware of a strange mix of emotions tangling through her.

On the one hand, she was cautiously optimistic for Violet.

On the other, here she was, alone. As usual.

Loneliness was a heavy ache in her chest as she sat in one of the rocking chairs on the porch of the bunkhouse, wrapped in a blanket while rain pounded on the metal roof and thunder growled nearby.

Her mother and her father had each other and now Violet was with Alex.

"At least I have you," she said to Baxter, asleep on her lap.

The dog snuffled but she drew him closer, wondering how she would be able to part with him when she returned to LA in a few days.

She was leaving so much behind.

And going back to what?

Discontent flickered through her. She enjoyed her work, but right now that was all she had. She worked long hours at the office, then went back to her condo so she could read law journals and take care of more work.

At this rate, she was in danger of becoming a workaholic like her father. Or was she already there?

The lights she had left on inside the bunkhouse suddenly flickered and then went out. Her mother usually left the porch lights on at the farmhouse, but those had gone dark as well.

The power must be out. Perfect. Cami sighed. Not only was she alone, but now she would be alone in the dark.

This certainly wasn't the first coastal storm to take out the power grid. It happened infrequently but with some regularity. Her mother usually kept emergency candles or light sources in various places at Moongate Farm.

Somewhere in the bunkhouse, Cami had seen a battery-powered lantern like the campers used in their tents. It took her a few moments to remember where, in one of the kitchen cabinets next to the range.

She had no idea if it was charged, but she would keep her fingers crossed. If not, the lantern could be charged by external battery backup, and she had one of those in her laptop.

Using her phone as a temporary flashlight, she rooted through the cabinets until she found what she was looking for. To her vast relief, when she hit the power button, the lantern came on with full battery charge.

She returned to the porch, Baxter at her heels. Yes, she might be alone, but there was definitely something comforting and warm about enjoying the storm tucked in a blanket where she was safe and dry.

She would wait until the power was restored, then would try to catch some sleep, she told herself.

A few moments later, her phone pinged with another text. She picked it up, assuming it would be Violet telling her she wouldn't be home that night.

Instead, it was from Jon, and the message was stark and terrifying.

Is my dad with you?

Another bolt of lightning hit somewhere nearby with a sizzling crack, but it was nothing compared to the panic suddenly slicing through her.

Franklin was missing? Out in this storm?

She started to text back an answer, but it would be faster to call, she decided, already hurrying inside to find her shoes and a raincoat.

"Hey." He picked up immediately, voice strained, and she could picture him, rain drenched and anxious. "Please tell me he's there."

"I haven't seen him. How long has he been gone?"

"I don't know for certain. It can't be long. He headed straight for his room when we came home. I thought he was already in bed. I was outside watching the storm roll in. When the power went out, the new safety locks must have disengaged long enough for him to slip out the back door."

"That wasn't long. It's only been out about fifteen minutes."

"I didn't go check on him until a few minutes ago, when I found his room empty."

"Maybe he's still at the house." She was grasping at straws, she knew. Jon wouldn't have reached out to her unless he had checked thoroughly.

"He's not." His voice was grim. "The back door was open and the shoes he was wearing earlier are gone. He's out here somewhere. I'm searching the grounds now."

"He can't have gone far."

"I hope you're right, but I don't have the first idea where to look. I can't see any sign of him close to the house. From where I was watching the storm, I had a clear view of the path leading to the beach. I'm certain he didn't go that way, but he could have taken the trail up to the bluff and maybe made his way down to the water from there."

"I'm on my way," Cami said, heading for the door with the lantern and her phone. "I'll check things out there and then meet you at Rose Creek."

"It's not safe for you to be out in this storm. Some of these lightning strikes have been too close for comfort."

"It's not safe for Franklin either," she said. "I can get to the glampground faster than you can, especially in one of the golf carts. I'll start there."

She could tell he wanted to argue, but he must have realized he couldn't do this alone. His father could have gone anywhere.

"I'll be in touch soon. We'll find him, Jon," she promised, praying she was right.

"Be careful."

"You, too. Don't run into any stray machetes."

"I'll do my best."

She ended the call and shoved the phone into the pocket of her raincoat, then rushed out into the cold rain.

When not in use, the office golf cart was parked in a small barn that used to hold cows and horses but was now mostly used for storage. Cami slid open the door and unplugged the cart, grateful to find another full battery charge.

She was also glad the cart had a roof of sorts, though the open sides did nothing to keep the rain out as she drove around the house toward the path leading up to Wild Hearts.

Before she could reach it, she saw a figure rushing toward her from the house, holding an umbrella.

Her mother looked out of breath. "Cami! I saw you heading for the golf cart. Where do you think you're going in this storm? It's not safe for anyone to be out."

She didn't want to take time to explain but thought it would be best to let as many people know as possible. "Franklin is missing again."

"Oh no! In this weather? That poor man! He'll catch pneumonia!"

Or worse. He could slip over treacherous terrain or be hit by lightning or be sucked out to sea. Cami didn't like thinking about the dire possibilities.

"I told Jon I would check up at the campground to see if he might have wandered up there."

"Here. Take the good flashlight. It's amazingly powerful."

"Thanks."

Cami took it and shoved it in the pocket of her raincoat. Her father joined them without an umbrella, his glasses coated in droplets. Rosemary sent him a worried look. "Franklin is missing. Cami's going to look for him up at the campground."

"What can we do?" Ted said immediately.

"If he's not up there, we'll have to organize a search. I'll text you."

Not wanting to waste any more time, she waved them off and bumped across the wet grass toward the gravel trail to the headland.

It was not the easiest drive, up the slick trail through the rain, with lightning flashing and thunder growling a warning.

She stopped periodically to sweep the area with the strong beam of the flashlight, hoping she would find him seeking shelter under some of the thick brush here, but she was disappointed each time.

As she crested the hill, the tents glowed against the storm, looking cozy and warm. They didn't have to worry about an electrical outage here, since the campground was off the grid anyway, using solar- and battery-powered lights and heaters. Until the external batteries needed to be recharged, anyway.

Was the thunderstorm passing? She hoped so. The rumblings seemed farther away, the lightning strikes fading. The rain continued steadily.

A couple was sitting on one of the porches watching the storm, and she recognized the Peterses, a couple who had been staying for ten days on a wine-tasting tour. They had attended the campfire lecture the previous week, she remembered, and had bombarded Franklin with questions, especially about the Russian fur trade.

"I'm looking for Mr. Rafferty. The older man who spoke to us last week about the history of the area. Any chance you've seen him?"

Terry Peters frowned. "No. Why would he be here, especially in this weather?"

She hesitated to reveal personal medical information about Franklin but didn't know how else to convey the urgency of the situation. "He can be…confused sometimes, and apparently he wandered off during the storm."

"Oh no! That's awful." Terry's wife, Jodi, looked distressed.

"I thought he might have come up here."

They both shook their heads. "We haven't seen him and we came out as soon as the storm started," Terry said.

"I mean, it's possible he slipped in from another direction when we weren't looking," his wife acknowledged. "Why do you think he might have come up here?"

"I have no idea," she admitted. "I'm just grasping at straws right now."

"If you want, we can help you check with the other campers to see if anybody else might have seen anything."

"That would be very helpful. Thank you."

"My mother had Alzheimer's for five years," Jodi said, her voice tinged with sorrow. "She died three months ago. It can be so tough."

So many people were caregivers or had loved ones with similar conditions. She hoped Jon had the chance to connect with support groups and talk to others who had been through some of the things he and Franklin faced.

She spoke with several of the other campers and was met with the same response. No one had seen or heard anyone coming through the campground.

"No luck." The Peterses met her near the covered social area a short time later, their faces grim. "We came up empty."

"Thank you for checking," Cami said. Her fear seemed to intensify, in contrast to the weather beginning to calm as the storm moved on.

What should they do now? She could think of a hundred other places he could have gone. The beach. The road. Into town.

She was going to have to call in reinforcements. She pulled out her phone and was about to text Jon when he appeared on the path coming from the house.

His features fell when he spotted her. "I was so hoping you found him."

She shook her head. "I'm sorry. Nobody has seen any sign of him."

Frustration was etched on his features. "Where the hell can he be?"

"We'll find him," she said, though the promise seemed empty when the search area was vast and rugged.

"We'll help you look for him," the Peterses both said at the same time. She was gratified to see several other guests leaving their warm, dry tents to join them at the small shelter.

"Thank you." Jon looked astonished but grateful for the support.

"You might want to have someone wait at the house, in case he shows up back there," Cami suggested.

He looked stricken. "Good idea. I should have thought of that."

"I'll call my parents. My father can run over there, if you want."

"Thank you."

"I think we need to call Search and Rescue to come out."

"He hasn't even been gone a half hour. Considering they're dealing with the power outage and other problems from the storm, I'm sure they'll tell us to check all his favorite places first before they come out. Only trouble is, I don't know all his favorite places."

A stray thought hit her, then was gone. She frowned and tried to reach for it, sensing it was important.

Something about a tree and his wife, she remembered, and suddenly gasped.

"The Fairy Tree! Maybe he went there."

34

JON

THE TREE!

Jon wanted to smack his forehead at Cami's suggestion. He should have thought of that. His father talked about it often enough, the gnarled, ancient old bristlecone pine that his mother in her whimsical moments had claimed was home to pixies and fairies.

His father had even mentioned it earlier that day, he suddenly remembered. He had wanted to visit it that morning.

"Your mother seems closer to me there than anywhere else," Franklin had said.

Jon had explained they were going to the Summer Sanctuary events instead and his father had agreeably given up the idea.

But maybe it was one of those things Franklin couldn't get out of his head, and for whatever reason, he had decided to strike out on his own.

Jon was failing at this.

His father wanted to stay at Rose Creek as long as possible. How the hell was Jon supposed to make that happen, when he couldn't seem to keep track of the man on any given day?

In a few days, he would have medical and legal power of attorney. Despite Franklin's wishes, Jon could find a facility for him, one where trained experts would be better capable of caring for him.

If he did that, he could return to the dig. Leave all this stress behind.

The temptation to do that shamed him.

He couldn't choose the easy way, as much as he wanted to right now.

"Dad?" he called as he made his way as fast as he dared up the rain-slick trail.

"I'm sure he's there. He has to be," Cami said from behind him.

He wanted to tell her to go back to the campground or to her mother's house, where she could be warm and safe, but he couldn't seem to say the words.

He needed her here.

How had she become so important to him in a few short weeks? He valued her friendship, relied on her emotional support, ached to taste her mouth again.

He thought of her first thing in the morning and right before falling asleep at night and a hundred times throughout the day.

When he realized Franklin wasn't in his bed, he had instinctively reached out to Cami.

He was in love with her.

He didn't need one of these ancient trees to fall on his head to show him that. But what the hell was he supposed to do about it?

Through the trees behind them, he could see other beams of light as campers from Wild Hearts joined in the search of the bluff.

Why would they do that? These were strangers who didn't know him and didn't know his father, yet were still willing to give up their own comfort to help them on a chilly rain-soaked night.

"Are you sure we're going the right way?" Cami asked.

"It's this general direction but not the exact spot," he admitted. "I haven't been there in years. I think my mom figured out pretty early that I wasn't much interested in fairies. If it had been an ancient settlement, that might have been another story."

"Someone's been here recently," Cami said. "Look."

She pointed down, and for the first time, he noticed muddy footprints leading into the woods.

"That way," she directed.

He veered off the path to an overgrown tangle of shrubs and grasses.

"Where's a machete when you need one?" he asked, fighting through the branches.

"Dad?" he called urgently. The wind snatched his voice and carried it again, but he thought he heard something in response, coming from his left. He pushed through the undergrowth until they stumbled through a gap in the bushes to a clearing.

There, he saw a figure huddled against the twisting trunk of the old bristlecone pine. His father's face was a pale blur in the beam of the flashlight and he was drenched through.

"Jon. Th-there you are." Franklin's teeth chattered. "I'm so g-glad. I can't find your mother anywhere. Have you seen her?"

He had to close his eyes against the wave of relief and sadness cresting over him. He had lost his mother far too early and now he was losing his father a little more every day.

He hurried forward, shrugging out of his own raincoat and wrapping it around his father's shoulders. "No. I haven't seen her. Why would you think she would be out here in the rain?"

His father didn't answer. He was looking at Cami, who appeared deeply relieved that they had found his father.

"Hello. I'm Franklin Rafferty."

"Hello, Mr. Rafferty. I'm Cami."

"Are you a sprite?"

She gave a ragged-sounding laugh. "I'll be whatever you want me to be. I'm so glad you're safe."

"Why wouldn't I be?"

"Let's go get you warmed up," Jon said. He grasped his father's arm firmly and guided him back toward the campground.

When they reached the tents, he found another golf cart pulled up beside Cami's and her parents standing under the shelter. Her mother had her face in her hands and her father had his arms around her shoulders.

Rosemary looked up when they approached, and he saw the same vast relief on her features that he had felt washing over him.

"You found him! Oh, thank heavens."

"Hi, Rosemary. Did you come to see the fairies?" Franklin asked.

She looked momentarily baffled, but Cami shook her head, as if warning her not to ask questions.

"I'm so glad you're safe. You can't go off in the rain like that, Frank. Are you all right? You're soaked through."

"I *am* cold."

"I brought a change of clothes for you, just in case." She held up a plastic bag.

"Thank you," Jon said, wishing he had thought to bring some of his father's own clothing.

"You can use our tent to change out of your wet things." The camper he had met earlier, the one who had instantly volunteered to help look for his father, made the offer.

"Thank you," Jon said. He took his father by the arm and went inside the tent.

It was blessedly warm from a small heater in the corner, and a battery-powered lantern provided plenty of light.

Franklin looked around. "Where are we?"

"The campground on top of the headland," Jon answered, helping his father out of his drenched robe and pajama top and pulling the hoodie over his head.

"This doesn't look like any campground I've ever seen."

Jon had to agree with that. "It's a glampground. A fancy version of tent camping."

"Up on the headland, you say?"

"Yes. Your neighbor, Rosemary, the nice lady who brought you extra clothes, runs it with her daughters."

"These tents are nice. And what a perfect spot. Your mother always wanted to build guest cabins up here."

"Did she?"

"Oh yes. She said the bluff held magic. A powerful place guarded by the ancient trees. People could heal here, she said, from the wounds of the world. She was looking into it and then something happened, but I…can't remember what."

His mother had died driving home from one of Jon's school events. And everything had changed.

He said nothing as he helped his father out of his pants and into the dry sweats.

"Tents," Franklin said slowly, a frown between his brows. "I remember now. Lily Porter wanted to put them here."

"Yes."

"It was my idea, actually," Franklin said. "When Lily told me she was thinking about buying a few luxury tents for guests at Moongate Farm, I told her she should put them here, on the headland."

Jon eased back, nonplussed. This was the first time Franklin had said anything about that to him.

He had fought hard against the campground, had assumed Lily Porter had taken advantage of Franklin's condition. He'd never expected it might have been Franklin's idea in the first place.

"Why here?"

"Why not?" Franklin shrugged. "We're not using it, are we? This place was meant for people to enjoy. It's the whole reason your mother wanted the conservation easement. So it would be protected for our grandchildren and their grandchildren to enjoy."

Franklin frowned suddenly. "Do I have grandchildren yet?"

"No," Jon said.

"Oh. Too bad."

Cami knocked on the door of the tent just then. Probably because of the recent conversation with his father, Jon suddenly, randomly, wondered if she wanted children.

None of his business. While he sensed she would be a lovely mother, kind and nurturing, he also knew that any children she had would be with someone else.

The thought held about as much appeal as spending the night in the rain under the gnarled branches of the Fairy Tree.

"The rain's stopped for now," she said. "When you're ready, I can take you back to the house in the golf cart."

"Just about. Dad, shoes. Let me help you."

He knelt down and slipped his father's wet socks back into his shoes, aware of Cami watching them with a strange expression that suddenly made him feel slightly breathless.

Outside, he found her mother and father as well as several of the campers still gathered under the covered shelter.

"Everything okay?" Rosemary asked. "Do you think he should go to the hospital to be checked out?"

"I think he's okay. His color came back quickly and I couldn't see any scrapes or bruises," Jon answered. "I'll keep an eye on him and take him to the emergency room later if I see anything concerning."

"Probably a good idea."

All of these people had come out in the rain to help look for his father. Not out of obligation. Only because they wanted to help.

He didn't need to carry this burden by himself.

The realization almost made Jon stumble. Throughout that day, he had seen how well-liked his father was. Everywhere they went, people had stopped to talk to Franklin.

His father was part of a tight-knit community here in Cape Sanctuary. A village of people who cared about his father, respected him, wanted the best for him.

He would be wrong to take his father away from this community he loved.

His father almost fell asleep on the jostling ride back to the house.

When Cami pulled up to Rose Creek, Jon saw the power was back on. The windows of the house glowed a welcome against the wet night.

Franklin climbed out slowly. "I'm so tired," he said on a yawn.

"You've had an exciting day. Let's get you to bed."

Franklin stumbled a little as they walked toward the house. In seconds, Cami was at his father's other side, offering her quiet support.

"A nice hot shower would be just the thing, but I'm afraid I'll fall asleep," his father said with a note of apology in his voice.

"I'll make sure you don't."

"Do you need help?" Cami asked.

He didn't want her to slip back into the night until he had a chance to talk to her, at least to thank her for her help and support.

"I'll get him to bed. Would you mind staying a little longer? I can grab something dry for you to change into."

She blinked in surprise. "I… Sure."

He quickly grabbed an old hoodie out of his bedroom and a pair of sweats that would certainly swamp her.

"There's a bathroom down the hall where you can change. Thank you. I'll hurry. I know you've had a long day, too."

"I'm fine. Do what you need to for Franklin," she said.

He nodded and hurried toward his father's room, wondering how he could watch her walk away in only a few days.

35

CAMI

WHY WAS SHE HERE?

After Jon retreated with his father to Franklin's room at the back of the house, Cami felt frozen with indecision. Should she slip away and return to the bunkhouse or stay to spend a little more time with Jon before she left town?

He had asked her to stay. She had no idea why. If she took the coward's way and left now, she would never find out.

She shivered, chilled and wet. She could at least change into dry clothes, since he had gone to the trouble of finding something for her.

A few moments later, she emerged from the bathroom feeling like a child playing dress-up in the roomy clothes he had left her. The hoodie was about three sizes too big and the sweats bagged around her waist.

She probably looked ridiculous, but she was at least warmer. In the family room off the kitchen, she found a gas-powered fireplace and hit the switch to turn it on.

The heat felt glorious and she closed her eyes, soaking it in. She had been so focused on her panic and the search for Franklin, she hadn't realized how cold she was until she changed out of her wet things.

After a moment, she settled onto a sofa in front of the fire and pulled a chunky knit throw she found there over her. A strange lassitude crept over her as the heat from the fireplace and the adrenaline crash after the search seemed to sap her muscles of strength.

She closed her eyes, for only a moment, but she must have fallen asleep. The room blurred a little, and the next thing she knew, she awakened with the strange sensation of someone standing near her.

Jon.

She opened her eyes to find him watching her sleep with a strange expression. Almost…tender.

She sat up. "Sorry. I didn't mean to fall asleep. It's been a… weird day."

"It's late. Nearly one."

"Did your father get settled?"

"Yes. He fell asleep immediately. I think I'm going to take him to the doctor in the morning anyway, just to be safe."

"Good idea."

He also had changed into dry clothes, she saw, a khaki shirt and jeans. His hair was still messy and he had a shadow of whiskers that made him look every inch the dangerous adventurer.

She swallowed as he moved closer and sat on the end of the sofa.

"I have to thank you first for your help. When I realized my father was missing, I immediately wanted to reach out to you."

She wasn't sure what to say to that. "I'm glad you felt like you could."

He reached out and picked up her hand, and the strange, intense light in his eyes made her suddenly breathless.

"I haven't let myself need anyone in a long time. Maybe not since my mother died. But I needed you and you immediately came to help."

"There are plenty of people who want to help you and your father, Jon. You only have to ask."

"I realized that tonight after we found him, when I saw all those strangers out in the rain, looking for him with us."

"Everyone wanted to help as soon as they learned he was missing."

"I realized something else. My father needs more than I can give him by myself. I can't do this on my own."

That couldn't have been easy for him to admit. She wanted to pull him against her and assure him he wouldn't have to, but she didn't have that right. She was leaving in only a few days.

"My mother will certainly help where she can."

He nodded. "I'm going to look into hiring round-the-clock care for him. Tonight showed me it's the only way to keep him safe."

"Probably a good idea."

"I promised him I would help him stay here at Rose Creek as long as possible. I have to do whatever it takes."

Oh. How could she possibly resist this man?

And why was she trying so hard?

"Your father is lucky to have you," she said, her voice ragged.

He gazed at her for only a moment and then reached for her almost blindly, burying his face in her neck and holding on tight.

He needed her.

He held her for a long time, his breath warm against her skin.

She brushed her fingers through his still-damp hair, wishing she could ease this burden for him.

"Thank you," he murmured. "I don't think I would have made it through these past few weeks without you."

"I didn't do anything," she protested.

"You had faith in me," he said simply. "That was the best gift you could have given me."

Before she could answer, he leaned forward and brushed his mouth against hers with a soft tenderness that made her want to weep.

She didn't want this moment to end. Ever. She wanted to stay here, safe and warm, wrapped in his arms while a coastal rain clicked against the window and the fireplace glowed against the cold.

He eased away, taking her hand in his. "I have to tell you something."

No. Let's just stay here, tangled together in this moment, Cami thought.

"What is it?"

"I'm calling Robert Layton tomorrow to have him write up a lease extension for Wild Hearts. The campground can stay on the bluff as long as your mother wants to run it."

She stared. "You're…what?"

"My dad told me tonight that my mother always wanted to put guest cabins on the headland. With absolutely no confusion in his voice, he told me he was the one who suggested the glampground idea to your sister. He said my mother would have wanted it there."

"You said your father didn't need strangers traipsing across your land in his condition."

He gave her a rueful smile. "I've said a lot of stupid things. Tonight those strangers were willing to go out into the wind and rain to find my father. Your mother is doing a good thing with the campground. She is bringing people together, teaching them to appreciate each other as well as nature's sacred places. The world certainly needs more of that."

"I don't know what to say. My mother will be thrilled."

She frowned suddenly. In all the chaos of looking for Franklin, she had forgotten about her parents' renewed relationship. How would that impact Rosemary's commitment to the glampground? She had no idea.

"At least I *think* she'll be thrilled," she amended.

"That doesn't sound very convincing."

"She and my father are dating again. They told us tonight. Neither has been happy since the divorce. They said Lily's death reminded them of what really mattered."

He studied her. "You don't sound completely convinced it's a good idea."

"I want it to work, for their sakes. They obviously love each other. I just don't know what that means for Wild Hearts. Maybe nothing. My father plans to go into semiretirement and spend part of his time here in Cape Sanctuary."

He gazed at her, that intense light in his eyes. "Would you ever be willing to do the same?"

His words seemed to hover between them.

Cami stared at him, wishing she could read his expression more clearly. What was he asking?

"Would I…what?"

"Would you consider spending more time here in Cape Sanctuary?"

She was afraid to hope. "My mother lives next door and it sounds like my father will be moving there at least part-time. My sister isn't that far away in Sacramento, though something tells me she's going to be splitting her time between there and the Cape for a while. My family will be here. So, yes. I *would* consider spending more time in Cape Sanctuary."

He reached for her hand. "Let me rephrase the question,

counselor. Would you consider spending more time in Cape Sanctuary with *me*?"

She swallowed, as joy fluttered through her like butterflies in her mother's garden.

"I would consider it. We might have to discuss terms."

He laughed and kissed her with a fierce emotion that stunned her. This wild, dangerous adventurer wanted *her.* Boring, nerdy Camellia Porter.

She had no idea why, but she wasn't about to argue with him.

"Anything you want, it's yours," he murmured against her mouth sometime later.

She shook her head. "Wow, I have my work cut out for me. You should never say that kind of thing at the beginning of a negotiation."

"But what if I know I have everything to lose?"

She swallowed, all trace of levity gone at the raw vulnerability in his eyes.

"I know it's only been a few weeks," he said, "but I'm falling for you, Cami."

This couldn't be happening. She still had to wonder if she had somehow stumbled and fallen out on the bluff and cracked her head open on the roots of the Fairy Tree.

"You hardly know me," she protested.

"Wrong. I know you're one of the most kind people I've ever met. I know you're fierce when it comes to your family. I know I haven't been able to get you out of my head since you helped me change a flat tire. And I know I don't want you to walk out of my life."

Cami closed her eyes. She didn't care if this was some concussed hallucination. If it was, she had a much better imagination than she'd ever guessed.

This was the single best moment of her life and she was going to savor every second of it.

She kissed him, her emotions simmering to the surface.

She'd never dreamed when she came to Cape Sanctuary to help her mother that she would end up discovering what she truly needed.

Her family. Community. This beautiful place by the sea.

And Jon, who filled her world with joy and laughter and the promise of so much more to come.

Epilogue

CAMI

THIS WAS HER DEFINITION OF THE PERFECT day.

On the twins' birthday four years later, Cami sat on a blanket on Rose Creek Beach watching the people she loved most in the world play a heated game of beach volleyball.

Rosemary and Ted, with Violet's stepdaughter, Ariana, now a teenager, were clearly outgunned. They were losing hard to a team made up of only Jon and Alex.

The two men had become close friends over the years, a bond forged solid when Alex offered to take him and Franklin out fishing once a week. They never caught much, but that hadn't been the point. Franklin had loved his time on the water.

Those fishing trips were only one of many things Jon had done to keep his father active and engaged.

She still didn't know what Franklin had enjoyed more, going out on the water with his son, his regular history lectures to the guests at Wild Hearts, the weekly yoga sessions Rosemary led them in or the archaeological digs he and Jon volunteered with through the California state parks system.

She felt a pang, missing her father-in-law dearly. In the end, his progressive Lewy body dementia hadn't taken him. Instead, he had died of pneumonia after catching a bad virus over the winter. She consoled herself that his last years had been as rich and fulfilling as they could manage.

Her parents cheered as the volleyball served by Rosemary landed in the sand between their two sons-in-law, earning them a point. Ariana didn't look nearly as happy.

"You missed that one on purpose," she accused her father. "A win isn't a win if you just hand it to us. We have to earn it."

Alex shrugged and only grinned at her. "I guess you're just that good."

On the blanket next to her, Violet shook her head. "That girl is so competitive. I have no idea where she gets it."

"Must be Regina's side of the family," Cami said. She rarely teased her sister about Alex's ex-wife anymore, mostly because Violet and Claudia, to the surprise of everyone, had become friends over the past few years of co-parenting Ari.

Violet shifted her three-month-old daughter, Lily Belle, to nurse on the other side, and Cami felt that weird combination of fear and anticipation in the pit of her stomach.

A few more weeks and that would be her, nursing her own baby. Hers and Jon's.

She touched her belly, which felt about three times as big as that volleyball her family was tossing around.

They had started having this celebration of life, a remembrance of Lily as well as to celebrate Violet's birthday, the summer when everything changed. It was a tradition she hoped would continue forever.

"How are you holding up?" Violet asked her.

Cami smoothed her hand over her belly, loving the feel of the baby kicking back at her. "Ready to pop any minute now."

"I'm sorry. It will all be over soon. The last few weeks were the worst with Belle. I couldn't sleep, my back hurt all the time and the heartburn! It felt like a forest fire in there."

Cami had to smile, though she loved being pregnant. She had been only a few months along when Franklin died, but she knew the anticipation of new life had helped ease that pain for Jon.

Their lives had shifted and settled into a beautiful mosaic in the years since that first summer in Cape Sanctuary.

Her father was almost completely retired, only taking the occasional pro bono case. He spent most of his days here at Cape Sanctuary. To everyone's astonishment, especially his, Ted had become a master gardener, currently obsessed with the size of his heirloom tomatoes.

He and Rosemary had been delighted to become stepgrandparents to Ariana and loved to spoil both her and Lily Belle. Cami knew they would spoil her baby, too.

The glampground kept Rosemary busy, though she had sold half the tents and furnishings to another resort farther down the coast. The smaller operation was easier for her to handle and had less environmental impact on the headland. Because reservations were so hard to come by now, Wild Hearts had become an exclusive destination, booked out at least a year in advance.

Violet tucked a wind-blown strand of hair behind her ear, laughing when Alex trash-talked Rosemary. As she watched her, Cami felt a wave of contentment wash over her.

Her sister and mother had become her best friends, closer

than she'd ever dreamed they would be. They all still grieved for Lily but had chosen to embrace life.

The game ended a few moments later and Jon came to stretch out beside her. Her gorgeous adventurer, who still made her toes curl with just a look.

"Good game," she said. He smiled, though she saw a hint of sadness in his eyes.

He gazed out to sea and she knew exactly what he was thinking.

"I miss him, too," she murmured.

He reached for her hand and held it tightly.

He was such a good son, just as she knew he would be a wonderful father to *their* son.

"I guess you won't be here next summer," Rosemary said to him as she plopped onto a nearby blanket and reached into the hamper she had brought along for some grapes from her garden.

"He's not leaving until next year and it will only be for two months," Cami said. "He'll be back before you know it."

Jon was making plans to take some of his students to Tikal, the vast buried Mayan city that still held so many secrets.

She knew he ached to be out in the field and she completely supported him. She would miss him desperately. She missed him already, even though he wasn't leaving for ten months.

Maybe in a few years, when their son was a little older, they would go with him when he did fieldwork. In the meantime, they would just have to have more of those sexy phone calls that had sustained her for the year they'd dated, when she had split her time between Cape Sanctuary and LA.

She didn't regret leaving Porter, Garcia & Sheen. Yes, the pace was slower here, working with Robert Layton in Franklin's old office. She didn't have many multimillion-dollar negotiations anymore, mostly real-estate contracts, estate planning and corporate law, but she found she enjoyed the work more when she actually felt like she was making a difference in her neighbors' lives.

She shifted again as the baby kicked harder, so hard Jon could see that one through the fabric of her shirt.

He grinned, placing a hand there to feel it.

Cami curled her fingers through his, and together they watched the sunlight dance on the water.

★★★★★